MW00461857

60 SONGS THAT EXPLAIN THE '90s

60 SONGS THAT EXPLAIN THE '90s

Rob Harvilla

TWELVE

THE RINGER

NEW YORK BOSTON

Copyright © 2023 by Robert Harvilla

Cover design and illustration by Tara Jacoby
Cover copyright © 2023 by Hachette Book Group, Inc.

Hachette Book Group supports the right to free expression and the value of copyright. The purpose of copyright is to encourage writers and artists to produce the creative works that enrich our culture.

The scanning, uploading, and distribution of this book without permission is a theft of the author's intellectual property. If you would like permission to use material from the book (other than for review purposes), please contact permissions@hbgusa.com. Thank you for your support of the author's rights.

Twelve
Hachette Book Group
1290 Avenue of the Americas, New York, NY 10104
twelvebooks.com
twitter.com/twelvebooks

First Edition: November 2023

Twelve is an imprint of Grand Central Publishing. The Twelve name and logo are trademarks of Hachette Book Group, Inc.

The publisher is not responsible for websites (or their content) that are not owned by the publisher.

Twelve books may be purchased in bulk for business, educational, or promotional use. For information, please contact your local bookseller or the Hachette Book Group Special Markets Department at special.markets@hbgusa.com.

Illustrations by Tara Jacoby

Library of Congress Cataloging-in-Publication Data

Names: Harvilla, Rob, author.
Title: 60 Songs that explain the '90s / by Rob Harvilla.
Other titles: Sixty songs that explain the '90s
Description: First edition. | New York : Twelve, 2023.
Identifiers: LCCN 2023026358 | ISBN 9781538759462 (hardcover) |
    ISBN 9781538764947 (ebook)
Subjects: LCSH: Popular music—1991-2000—History and criticism. |
    Popular music—1991-2000—Miscellanea.
Classification: LCC ML3470 .H378 2023 | DDC 782.421640973/09049—
    dc23/eng/20230601
LC record available at https://lccn.loc.gov/2023026358

ISBN: 9781538759462 (hardcover), 9781538764947 (ebook)

Printed in the United States of America

LSC-C

Printing 3, 2023

For Nicole.

CONTENTS

INTRODUCTION

ALRIGHT. It is my personal tendency—and also *my job*—to overthink everything, but let's not overthink this. What we got here is a book celebrating popular songs from the 1990s that combines, in theory,* shrewd musical analysis, vital cultural and historical context, and whimsical personal digressions. I tried to make it an even three-way split, but the whimsical digressions tend to dominate. For example:

TOP 20 WORST RED HOT CHILI PEPPERS SONG TITLES, IN ASCENDING ORDER OF BADNESS
 20. "Funky Crime"
 19. "Even You, Brutus?"
 18. "Get on Top"
 17. "Shallow Be Thy Game"

---

* Performative modesty, if not outright self-deprecation, is another of my personal tendencies. I usually blame this on my sturdy Midwestern Catholic upbringing, though I'm guessing that most Midwesterners (and/or Catholics) would prefer that I keep them out of it.

16. "Lovin' and Touchin'"
15. "Sir Psycho Sexy"
14. "Ethiopia"
13. "Suck My Kiss" (That song kicks ass, though.)
12. "No Chump Love Sucker"
11. "She's Only 18"
10. "Grand Pappy Du Plenty"
9. "Funky Monks"
8. "Skinny Sweaty Man"

(It gets much gnarlier from here, just FYI.)

7. "Catholic School Girls Rule"
6. "Party on Your Pussy"
5. "Sex Rap"
4. "Stone Cold Bush"
3. "Sexy Mexican Maid"
2. "Fela's Cock"
1. "Hump de Bump"

That sort of thing. More specifically, what we got here is a book-length companion to the podcast I started for *The Ringer* in October 2020 called *60 Songs That Explain the '90s*. One song per week. First I monologue about that song at incredible length.* Then I interview someone about it—a musician, say, or a fellow journalist or podcaster. Let me answer the first question you have right now.

---

* *Monologue* is a terribly pretentious verb to my sensitive Midwestern ears, but, like, one time I typed out 10,000 words about Pantera and then read them out loud into a microphone. Is there any other word for that? (Don't answer that.)

INTRODUCTION

Why 60 songs? Because I'd never done a podcast before and I worried that calling it *90 Songs That Explain the '90s*—a more pleasing and logical title—was super presumptuous, and I didn't want to be the humiliated guy with *90* right there in his podcast name who got shitcanned after five episodes.

Then why not 30 or 20 or 10? Isn't 60 songs still a potentially humiliating number of songs? Because that wasn't enough songs.

Anyway, then I extended the show and did 90 songs anyway, and then extended it again to 120, but kept the *60 Songs* name, because I thought it was a fantastic comedic bit, right, to have a podcast with an increasingly inaccurate title, and also as it turns out, *there are an awful lot of dope '90s songs to write ~10,000 words about.* But after I asked my rad and eternally patient superiors at *The Ringer* if I could jump up to 120, they said, in essence, *Fine, but after that, knock it off.* So that's gonna do it, show-wise. There are 100-plus songs in this book but it felt weird to put an exact number in the title so we didn't. Great bit. Hilarious. (I don't want this book to get too list-heavy, so my goal is to get them all out of my system in the intro.)

SONG AND ALBUM TITLES ETC. THAT I'VE BEEN MOST EMBARRASSED TO SAY OUT LOUD

- "Givin' Up the Nappy Dug Out"
- *Oooooooohhh… On the TLC Tip*
- The *Q* magazine headline "Hips. Lips. Tits. Power."
- *Coolin' at the Playground Ya Know?*

- The Liam Gallagher *Rolling Stone* quote that included the phrase "But I've just come in their gob..."
- "Lick the Balls"
- Various lyrical excerpts from "Sir Psycho Sexy" (nobody made me do this, or really makes me do anything, which is why it's so embarrassing)
- The early Liz Phair cassette *Yo Yo Buddy Yup Yup Word to Ya Muthuh*
- *Take Off Your Pants and Jacket*
- The Tori Amos quote where she said the C-word
- A dramatic reading of the isolated Vanilla Ice Posse backup vocals/ad-libs on "Ice Ice Baby," so like "WILL IT EVER STOP?" + "DAMMMMMMMN" + "BEACHFRONT AVE-NUE!" etc.
- The cursed Hootie and the Blowfish EP *Kootchypop*
- "Fela's Cock" (That's not the Tori C-word.)

I am loath to lay on you, even now, some ultra-pretentious Grand Unified Theory of the 1990s, which I've always glibly described as "Far enough away to feel like the past, but close enough to still be hounding the present." As an era the '90s does feel distinct and tangible and whole, with its own semi-unified fashion sense and sound and cultural ethos; those specifics radically differ, of course, from person to person, but I'm guessing the 2000s or 2010s don't conjure up quite as vivid a mental picture for you. But that's just a guess, and I'm suspicious of any attempt to retroactively frame the '90s as some frictionless halcyon era, because while the decade's got a few concrete elements in its favor—fewer wars, more journalism jobs, no Twitter—all that talk about how good we used to have it immediately raises thorny questions of the *how good for whom, and why?* variety. Generalizing makes me nervous. Even more nervous than usual.

And so, cards on the table, here's what really fascinates me about the '90s: It's when I grew up. That's it. The decade encompasses high school and college for me. That's enough. That's plenty. Did you ever notice that new music, now, is nowhere near as great as the music you loved as a teenager? And you know what? *You're right.* Whether you were a teenager in the '60s, the '90s, or the 2010s, you're right. The music you loved as a teenager is the sweetest music you'll ever hear; that music will be, in all likelihood, the greatest, wildest, purest love affair of your whole life. That's how music works; that's how being a teenager works. I did not start the podcast—deep into the first year of COVID, I might add, when the endorphin rush of unabashed nostalgia became that much more attractive—as some grand socio-political gesture. I just wanted to relive the glorious jams of my youth. Yes, even "Achy Breaky Heart."

DUMBEST MISTAKES I'VE MADE ON THE SHOW SO FAR (** IF CAUGHT IN TIME)

- Called them "drum rolls" and not "drum fills"
- Mispronounced Mutt Lange's name repeatedly
- Forgot to say that Flea and Dave Navarro played on Alanis Morissette's "You Oughta Know"
- Referred to the National Organization for Women as the "N.W.O." **
- Mixed up the Verve and the Verve Pipe

- Repeatedly stumbled while quoting DMX saying, "Fuck you, suck my dick" **
- Mispronounced OB-GYN as *ahhb-jin* repeatedly (my wife and I have three children)
- Described Alice in Chains guitarist Jerry Cantrell as "The David Banner to [AIC frontman] Layne Staley's Incredible Hulk"
- Referred to Montell Jordan as "Montell Williams" (just once) **
- Said that Mick Jagger sang the Rolling Stones song "Happy" (it's Keith)
- Implied that the lady in the "Confused Math Lady" gif was Julia Roberts
- Mispronounced Tanya Tucker's name repeatedly
- Described Cincinnati chili as "bean-forward"

The idea here, with all these whimsical personal digressions—and this is semi-pretentious, but I'm owning it—is that I talk about both spectacular and spectacularly mundane events from my own youth (and the dope songs that soundtracked it all) as a means of triggering, in you, your own memories of spectacularly mundane events in your own youth. It's the old The More Specific the Song, the More Universal the Sentiment philosophy, now applied to some guy talking about Pantera or Lauryn Hill or Nirvana or Biggie or Tupac or Britney Spears or the Mighty Mighty Bosstones or Coolio or Selena or the Dave Matthews Band or Shania Twain at incredible length. What I can tell you is that I regularly get drunk Instagram DMs about the philosophical implications of the Crash Test Dummies' "Mmm Mmm Mmm Mmm," and furious Twitter DMs about the time my guest for the R.E.M. episode shit all over "Nightswimming," and extraordinarily sweet emails about the songs people love and hate and are listening to right now or can never listen to again, and why.

Part of this I put down to the parasocial nature of podcasting, the still quite foreign-to-me-sensation of being informed by a stranger that she and her husband listened to my voice for the entirety of an eight-hour road trip. (This sort of thing is so bonkers to me; even my wife doesn't want to hear me talk for eight hours straight, or maybe I should say *especially* my wife.) Regardless of what's fueling what is easily the most feedback I've ever gotten for doing anything, this podcast has in fact been the professional thrill of my life, and ain't nobody asked me to write a book previously. Make of that what you will.

SONGS I COVERED ON ACOUSTIC GUITAR DURING MY UNFORTUNATE COLLEGE-OPEN-MIC-NIGHT PHASE, IN ASCENDING ORDER OF BADNESS

- The Cars, "Drive" (Capo on the fourth fret, nicely understated, once afterward a guy asked me if I wrote it)
- They Might Be Giants, "Don't Let's Start" (Arguably the coolest I have ever been)
- Talking Heads, "Heaven" (*Stop Making Sense* live version, got too yelp-y near the end but still pretty cool)
- Smashing Pumpkins, "Tonight, Tonight" ("Hello, I'm Rob, and I'm here to crucify the insincere")
- The Smiths, "Asleep" (Too mopey, even for me)
- John Cougar Mellencamp, "Jack & Diane" (Line delivery of "Suckin' on a chili dog" kinda sucked)

- Sebadoh, "Willing to Wait" (Even mopier)
- Beck, "Jack-Ass" (No idea what to do during outro)
- U2, "With or Without You" (Everyone could live without this)
- Radiohead, "Street Spirit (Fade Out)" (Way too many notes; did not immerse myself in love)
- R.E.M., "Everybody Hurts" (Played the whole song out of tune once and almost got arrested)
- Jeff Buckley's version of "Hallelujah" (Oh my God)
- The Police, "Every Breath You Take" (Incredibly hard to play, let alone play and sing, especially if you're on a date at the time, holy shit, Rob, what the fuck)

As of this writing I have done 91 episodes of the podcast, with those scripts totaling exactly 562,465 words. (In the monologues, at least, everything I say is scripted down to the word, which is, let's say, charming in its mild neurosis.) This book is shorter, and the songs are grouped into, let's say, charmingly whimsical categories of my own arbitrary devising. Let's not overthink this; I feel like the more I talk, intro-wise, the more overthought the intro gets. Let me answer the other question you have right now.

Who is this guy? In college I interned at a Cleveland, Ohio, alt-weekly that gave me my first professional bylines, which is to say they sent me to review shows by the esteemed likes of Ween, Sevendust, Big Bad Voodoo Daddy (this'll come up later), and the New Radicals (this too). Also, regrettably, one time I wrote a semi-bitchy preview of an upcoming U2 concert, which inspired the following Letter to the Editor.

INTRODUCTION

I have to question your criteria for hiring music writers. It seems that you have one too many young punks whose heads are still stuck in the Seattle grunge phase and who apparently don't know squat about good rock music. As a longtime U2 fan, I have to take issue with Rob Harvilla's short-sighted preview of the Elevation tour. I was at the concert. It was one of several U2 concerts I've attended, and I can assure you that the band is better than ever, and Bono is still a rock and roll god.

I suppose we can't expect much from a writer whose favorite bands while growing up included Hall & Oates, MC Hammer, and yes, even Vanilla Ice. But it's particularly disturbing to me, since I bought Rob's very first concert ticket. At the age of 14, he went to see U2 and thought they were "The Bomb." As parents, we do the best we can, but we can't control the direction our kids take when they grow up.

This too shall pass. We'll still set a place for Rob at Thanksgiving dinner.

Barb Harvilla (Rob's mom)

That's who I am, and that's what this is. Here we are now.

CHAOS AGENTS

SONGS DISCUSSED:

Céline Dion, "My Heart Will Go On"

Hole, "Doll Parts"

Madonna, "Vogue"

Spice Girls, "Wannabe"

Backstreet Boys, "I Want It That Way"

Eminem, "My Name Is"

Beck, "Loser"

Master P, "Make 'Em Say Uhh!"

Prodigy, "Firestarter"

The Chicks, "Goodbye Earl"

Erykah Badu, "Tyrone"

CÉLINE DION sings her songs like they owe her money. She sings her songs like she's a street-walkin' cheetah with a heart full of napalm. She sings as though the song were Sisyphus and she were the boulder. She came here to kick ass and sing songs, and she's about out of ass. She sings the songs that make the whole world cower in the storm cellar. She sings as though she intends to fell the mighty oak and drink every drop of the sea. PUT CÉLINE DION IN *SUPER SMASH BROS.* She sings like the floor, the ceiling, and also the very air she breathes is lava. She sings these songs like she has a very particular set of skills. Skills she has acquired over a very long career. Skills that make her a nightmare for songs like these.

She sings *hard*, man. Do you get what I'm saying? I don't want to belabor this. She sings hard even at her softest; she sings incomprehensibly loud even at her quietest. She is everything louder than everything else. She is the too much that will never be enough. She is the Final Boss of Popular Song. I picture her towering over the 1990s like a benevolent colossus, like a Quebec-born Godzilla with a sparkly microphone, like a volcano that can serenade itself.

Céline Dion helped define the decade but did not let the decade define her, and this is a pop star's greatest challenge, the eternal conundrum, the nigh-impossible mission: How to achieve true domination without getting trapped in the bejeweled amber of your prime. How to sow ecstatic chaos without succumbing to it. Her strategy? Sing harder. Sing louder. Sow even more chaos, ever more ecstatically. Baffle the masses even as you entrance them; get weirder as you get huger. That's how your songs go on, as does your legacy, as does your heart.

All of which explains why listening to this person sing is like drinking rosé from a fire hose. I have a visceral memory of sitting in my high school lobby and watching a friend of mine, a girl named Rachel, holding a small boombox quietly playing "The Power of Love," from Céline's 1993 album *The Colour of My Love*. (The letter *U* in *Colour* was *audible*.) My friend's eyes closed in rapture as she swayed along to the howitzer ferocity of that song's chorus—"'Cause I'm your *laaaady*"—while my own eyes bulged in respectful terror.

That's the whole memory. No context. One time I watched a teenage girl vibe extremely hard to "The Power of Love." I was overwhelmed by both Céline's voice and the profound effect her voice could have on someone. To plenty of snooty '90s critics, that sense of overwhelmedness is disqualifying, and almost inhuman: She sings love songs so overwrought that they couldn't possibly depict normal people being in love. If you wanna get super crabby about it, maybe the reason some of her biggest hits are on movie soundtracks—"Beauty and the Beast," or "When I Fall in Love" from *Sleepless in Seattle*, or "Because You Loved Me" from *Up Close and Personal*—is because those movies provide you with the tangible, flesh-and-blood love affairs, with the *humanity*. Which in turn frees up her songs to concentrate entirely on incomprehensible volume and intensity and grandiosity.

And then there's "My Heart Will Go On" from the zillion-grossing 1997 James Cameron colossus *Titanic*, which I saw in the theater on a double date and then tried to make myself cry on the drive home to appear more sensitive. Recall Céline Dion onstage at the 1998 Oscars, with a two-story, vaguely boat-like structure loaded up with a full orchestra looming behind her as she sings the bejesus out of this song. Is there chest-pounding, as part of her performance? I think you know there is. Does Céline win the Oscar in question? I think you know she does.

Now recall her fellow Best Original Song nominee Elliott Smith, already enshrined as a beloved, fragile, genius singer-songwriter before he takes the stage, alone, in a rumpled white suit, strumming his acoustic guitar, vibrating with cred-enhancing unease. He clearly doesn't want to be there, so he sings his beautiful and fragile song—"Miss Misery" from *Good Will Hunting*, a/k/a the *Titanic* of Boston—and then gets the fuck out of there. And here is a massive cultural and philosophical divide made tangible by the ginned-up conflict between these two songs sung by these two humans. Céline hugged Elliott backstage; Elliott said she was incredibly nice. But still: two opposing religions here. The sad quiet guy with the acoustic guitar and the bombastic pop diva with the full orchestra. Don't ever ask a rock critic to pontificate on this moment and the philosophical divide it represents. Just trust me. Feel free to slap me, if you ever catch me pontificating myself.

The knock against Céline, historically, is that she's cheesy, schmaltzy, pancake-handed, shameless. The idea is that she's such an absurdly powerful singer that it frays her genuine human connection to the song, to the people listening to the song, to the subject of the song. She sings about fundamental human emotions with inhuman force and precision. It's disconcerting. She's so real that she almost sounds fake.* But the new level of mastery that

---

* This sort of wonky rock-critic blather withers in the face of Céline's moments of entirely human and very public tragedy, including her husband René Angélil's death in 2016 and her 2022 announcement that she'd been diagnosed with a rare neurological disease called Stiff Person Syndrome, which triggered a fan-driven outpouring of love and support that's as overwhelmingly real as any song she's ever sung.

Céline brings to "My Heart Will Go On" is that she's figured out how to be super loud *quietly*. There is nuance. There is drama. There is precisely calibrated rising action. This song is a bear attack in a library. Which only makes that final, bellowed, gale-force chorus ("*You'rrrrrre herrrrrrre*") even more overpowering and exhilarating. Because the final chorus, historically, is where Céline Dion sings the hardest and makes most of her money and kicks most of her ass. She is a self-serenading volcano impersonating a mortal human woman. And she is convincing even as she erupts.

In about 30 seconds I could walk you from my high school lobby to the sepulchral office of our student newspaper, where one day a girl named Jessica rhapsodized to me about her favorite line from the Hole song "Doll Parts": "My pain is so real I am beyond pain." That's still my favorite line in the song; that line is not actually in the song. With any piece of music, though—any artist, any circumstance, any version of this decade or any other—your personal memory matters more than the reality. Remember that now. "Doll Parts" really does, however, include the line "I fake it so real, I am beyond fake." That's my second-favorite line, and, I like to imagine, one of Céline's favorites, too.

By certain objective measures—tabloid column inches, seething diss tracks from rival rock stars, the mountains of ground dust from all those gnashed teeth—Hole singer, guitarist, and ringleader Courtney Love has sown more chaos than any other rock star of her era or anybody else's. "Doll Parts," the frail and shattering semi-power ballad from the band's second album, 1994's *Live Through This*, was written and recorded long before Love's husband, Nirvana frontman and embattled generational totem Kurt Cobain, died by suicide on April 5, 1994. But that record came out a week later, and Courtney's searing pain on "Doll Parts" will forever be synonymous with an entire generation's pain, and grief, and anger, much of it directed at her.

The single line I will never forget from Kurt's suicide note is not actually in his note—it is, let's say, an editorial aside offered by Courtney as she tearfully read it aloud in a recording played at a candlelight vigil in Seattle a few days after he'd passed. She read the line like this: "'So remember'—*and don't remember this, because it's a fucking lie*—'it's better to burn out than fade away.'" It's the *fucking lie* that sticks with me, the heartbroken snarl in her voice as she ground her own teeth to dust.

I try not to think about it.

"It's better to burn out than fade away." Christ. For all his hallowed rejection of the rock-star myth, in this awful moment, as his final public gesture, Kurt Cobain quotes Neil Young. He extends the rock-star lineage. He aspires, on some level, to that lineage, however much of his public life he devoted to insisting that he didn't want it. Don't believe the hype of his rejection of the hype: Kurt wanted to be a rock star, no matter how furiously he insisted otherwise. But one reason people are still throwing stones at the cardboard cutout of his wife 30-plus years later is that she's way better at being a rock star than he ever was.

I try to think about my happier memories of '90s Courtney Love, and all the ways her own Godzilla-sized shadow loomed over me. She infuriated with every glance, antagonized with every word. She wore chaos like an elegant Oscar gown. She first convened Hole in L.A. via a Musicians Wanted newspaper ad that included the line "My influences are Big Black, Sonic Youth, and Fleetwood Mac"; the band's debut album, 1991's hilariously scabrous *Pretty on the*

Inside, was co-produced by Sonic Youth's Kim Gordon and did not sound like Fleetwood Mac at all. But *Live Through This* kinda did, and this, too, pissed people off. My personal favorite Courtney Love insult, flung at booing fans at an Atlanta show who found these new songs too tuneful and accomplished and radio-friendly: "I've grown, you haven't, the sex really isn't good anymore, and you know what? There's always gonna be a shitty band with girls in it that can't play."

But by the time the world heard *Live Through This*, Courtney had been recast as our most famous and most polarizing widow, and the split-second of silence between the first chorus and the second verse of "Doll Parts" was the scariest music I'd ever heard. You simply cannot imagine how terrifying that silence sounded to me, a doofus 15-year-old in 1994, holding up my ache to her ache. You can't conceive of how much grief, how much fury, how much subversion, how much chaos, how much misinterpretation you could pack into that tiny little space. *My pain is so real I am beyond pain.* Look her in the eyes and tell her that line isn't in this song.

But her heart went on. Her talents for provocation only intensified, diversified. The best Hole song appears on the band's third album, 1998's power-pop delight *Celebrity Skin*, which *very much* sounds like Fleetwood Mac and peaks with "Boys on the Radio," a monster power ballad about loving and hating and mourning and challenging and, yes, ultimately vanquishing them all—yes, even *the* boy on the radio. She outlasted all of it; she will outlast us all. When the apocalypse comes, it will come in the form of an Instagram post from God—God posts on the grid, and God's post will appear on your feed even if you don't follow God, if you catch my meaning—and the very last comment, on that post, will be from

Courtney Love. I leave it up to you, which emoji Courtney is most likely to use, to commemorate this solemn occasion. Not the grimace emoji. I know that much.* That's why I'm the one shivering in her shadow and she's the one casting it.

I use the phrase "I don't mean to be glib" a lot, usually right before saying some glib bullshit like *Courtney Love was the Madonna of the '90s*. See? Glib. But Madonna raises the same hackles for me, conjures up the same provocateur euphoria. I think of the scene from the 1992 no-crying-in-baseball classic *A League of Their Own*, when lovably loutish manager Tom Hanks busts into his all-female team's locker room and staggers to a urinal and pees for like 45 seconds. Great scene. I'm not being glib. And at first all the ladies recoil in disgust—except, of course, for Madonna's character, who inches closer in sheer wonderment and grabs a watch and starts timing him. That's Madonna to me. Except usually she's the one standing at the urinal.

With apologies to my loving and supportive parents, I was raised by MTV, and with apologies to Jesus (and my mom again), I worshiped the gods of '80s MTV: Michael Jackson, Janet Jackson, Prince, and, well, *her*. Quick '80s Madonna highlight reel for you. Best album: *Like a Prayer*. Best song: "Like a Prayer." Best ballad: "Crazy for You." Second-best ballad: "Live to Tell." Best video: "Material Girl." Second-best video: "Open Your Heart." Best live performance: "Like a Virgin" at the 1984 MTV Video Music Awards, rolling around in her wedding dress. Best fashion

---

* Recently on Instagram, Courtney Love called me a "stentorian voiced dudely bro," confirmed that she would never use the grimace emoji, and instead stated her preference for the wave emoji adapted from *The Great Wave Off Kanagawa*, the famous 1831 woodblock print from the Japanese artist Hokusai. Make of that what you will.

accessory: in a huge upset, the floppy hat with the giant bow on it in the "Borderline" video. Best movie: *Shanghai Surprise*. (Just kidding.) Best controversy: the "Papa Don't Preach" discourse, which impressively angered both conservatives (unwed pregnancy) and Planned Parenthood (vaguely anti-abortion). Best one-liner: "Crucifixes are sexy because there's a naked man on them." That's Madonna to me, to everyone. In the year 1990 she turned 32. The future's so bright she's gotta wear shades.

This format's really doing it for me, so, quick '90s Madonna highlight reel for you. Best album: *Ray of Light*, from 1998, a marvel of vaguely spiritual dance-floor ecstasy. Best song on *Ray of Light*: "The Power of Goodbye." Best controversy: the gleefully porny "Justify My Love" video. (My mom hated it.) Best movie: You pick between *A League of Their Own* and her bonkers 1991 documentary *Truth or Dare*, in which she fellates a glass bottle and it's like the 10th most bonkers thing that happens.* Best book: uh, her *Sex* book. Weirdest album: *I'm Breathless*, her chaotic jazz-moll companion to *Dick Tracy*, the 1990 comic-strip flick in which she starred opposite her grouchy then-boyfriend Warren Beatty. Second-best song on *I'm Breathless*, in a huge upset: "Hanky Panky." Best song on *I'm Breathless*: fucking "Vogue."

"Vogue"! As glamorous, as sensual, as immaculate, as *timeless* as she ever got, in the absurdly luscious David Fincher video especially. Why is this perfect song on the fucking *Dick Tracy* soundtrack? Why not? Does Madonna reel off the names of so many timeless, glamorous stars—Greta Garbo, Marilyn Monroe,

---

* *Truth or Dare* is often cited as a huge influence on reality TV, but the scene where Madonna's grouchy then-boyfriend Warren Beatty sasses her for always wanting to be on camera basically invented the fine art of *performatively hating reality TV.*

Grace Kelly, Ginger Rogers—because she wants you to worship them, or because she's trying to convince you she's one of them? Why not both? Is Madonna crudely appropriating the hallowed art of voguing, as depicted in the heartening and heartbreaking 1991 Jennie Livingston documentary *Paris Is Burning*, or is she celebrating it, honoring it, casting a warming mainstream light upon it? Why not all of the above?

When I hear "Vogue," I do think of Venus Xtravaganza, a transgender performer in *Paris Is Burning*, a film that lovingly depicts the New York City ballroom scene, its lexicon (*realness, reading, shade*) long ago absorbed into corny mainstream culture, its wildly talented performers divided into "houses" because they're often estranged from their biological families, due to who they are or who they want to be. Venus Xtravaganza talks about how she started dressing as a woman when she was 13, 14 years old, and soon thereafter ran away from her biological family so she wouldn't embarrass them. She talks about hustling in New York to make her money, enduring the slurs and the physical threats. She talks about wanting to be a model. About wanting to be a complete woman. Late in the movie there's a beautiful shot of Venus at the edge of a New York City pier at sunset, leaning on a railing next to a giant '80s boombox as somebody lights her cigarette. That's when someone else starts talking about having to tell Venus's biological family that Venus was murdered.

I think about Venus, in the film, saying, "I would like to be a spoiled rich white girl. They get what they want, whenever they want it. And they don't have to really struggle with finances and nice things, nice clothes, and they don't have to have that as a problem." I think about how she's basically describing Madonna, in the

"Material Girl" video in particular, but really Madonna in general, Madonna in perpetuity. It is audacious of her, to say the least, that Madonna put out "Vogue" at all, evoked this embattled and defiantly nurturing culture at all. Not everybody loved it, to say the least. But it wouldn't be Madonna if everybody did.

I don't mean to be glib, but who was the '80s Madonna of the '90s? Were there, perhaps, *five* '80s Madonnas of the '90s? Were their names, perhaps, Sporty Spice, Ginger Spice, Baby Spice, Posh Spice, and Scary Spice? The Spice Girls—a galactically giddy English quintet convened by a father-and-son management team aiming to capitalize on the U.K. boy band boom that gave us Take That, East 17, Boyzone, A1, Let Loose, MN8, and other fine groups that pretty much nobody in America ever gave a shit about—dropped like a bomb on 1996. "Wannabe" is a riotous combination of "Material Girl," "Ray of Light," and "Hanky Panky"; the "Wannabe" video, as indelible in its way as the "Vogue" clip, finds the Spice Girls playfully wreaking pillow-fight-type havoc in a fancy nightclub restaurant speakeasy situation. Sporty Spice does a handspring on a candle-strewn table; a stuffy gentleman's monocle falls out in scandalized surprise; Scary Spice scrambles up a staircase to join her bandmates in that cute and fierce dance during the first chorus that you are definitely picturing, move for move, right now.

Next time you rewatch the "Wannabe" video for the 50,000th time, focus on Ginger Spice, who is clomp-clomp-clomping around in extra-giant high-heel boots and acting spontaneous while also trying super-visibly hard to be where she's supposed to be, blocking-wise. All fun and all business, all at once. This, to me, is the very essence of Girl Power, the group's notorious catch phrase/rallying cry/marketing slogan, which, depending on your age and disposition at the time, was either empowering or infantilizing, calculating or achingly sincere. But why not all of the above? In 2019, reporting on yet another Spice Girls reunion—this one minus Posh, alas—the *New York Times* writer Caity Weaver summarized the group's vibe as "sleepover antics turned career," which she meant, of course, as a huge compliment. "Their skill," she added, "was in depicting a young girl's idea of adulthood."

And that skill extends to the group's extra-silly 1997 feature film *Spice World*. "I LOVED *Spice World* when I was 12," a friend of mine once told me, before adding that she'll never rewatch it because "I have no intention of ever finding out how wrong I was." This is the right attitude. I was a Radiohead-loving college freshman when the Spice Girls blew up, and there I sat in a midwestern college dining hall, polishing off yet another chocolate-and-vanilla-twist ice cream cone and coolly regarding the "Wannabe" video from a snooty-college-radio-DJ remove as it graced the dining hall's video screens for the 50,000th time. Exuberance! Silliness! Wholesome chaos! Friends forever! Yes: Girl Power! I was fascinated but knew enough to pretend my fascination was ironic, contemptuous. But I wasn't fooling anybody.

Nor did I fool anybody a few years later, in my new guise as a snooty college-newspaper columnist, when I described the Backstreet Boys in print as "walking sex furniture." I got no idea who I stole that phrase from, and no idea what idea I was even trying to convey with it. All I knew is that by 1999, those fellas—and fellow ascendent boy band colossi *NSYNC—had joined the ranks of our new pop overlords. Which made MTV's mighty *Total Request Live* the foundation of our new religion, and Swedish songwriter/superproducer Max Martin our mysterious new Wizard of Oz, and the Backstreet Boys' own "I Want It That Way" our new international anthem.

"Tell me why," what? To what does the why refer, in that chorus? Who is the *I* in "I Want It That Way"? Is it me or is it you? What is the nature of *that way*? To what way does *that way* refer? How does a song that starts off by rhyming *fire* and *desire* descend so quickly into semantic chaos? And why do we find that chaos so purifying, so edifying, so satisfying? What makes "I Want It That Way" math, and pop, and art, and scripture, and inarguably the single greatest boy-band song ever born?

The answer—with apologies to Nick, AJ, Brian, Kevin, and Howie—is the jolly and hirsute man behind the curtain, Max Martin, who both co-wrote (with Andreas Carlsson) and co-produced (with Kristian Lundin) "I Want It That Way," an early exemplar of his soon-to-be-famous songwriting philosophy of Melodic Math. Every mildly garbled phrase in this song from "Tell me why" forward is a triumph of syllables over words, melody over coherence, math over language. Martin, a glam-rock survivor who learned at the feet of beloved Swedish guru Denniz Pop, carried on that grand tradition after Pop died, of stomach cancer, at only 35, in 1998. And soon Swedish pop—as exemplified by early Max Martin collaborators Ace of Base, whose supernova hits (including "The Sign" and "All That She Wants") are as mathematically thrilling and lyrically vague as anybody's—was just *pop*, period. A gleaming, dominant, international hit factory with no focal point, no overexposed ringleader. Just a mountain of gleaming cogs in the most wondrous and baffling pop-music machine ever built.

A Max Martin joint is never a Max Martin *solo* joint—often

there's a half-dozen other writers and producers in the mix, and the sheer number of people involved gives you some idea of how difficult it is to generate such simple pleasures. The resulting block-buster songs are less songs than *equations*, albeit luxurious equations that entail one pop star or another purring sexy-adjacent nonsense directly into your ears. At first this might feel antiseptic, or inau-thentic, or just robbed of the intimacy of a single human writing and then singing a perfect song to another single human. But you gotta know the math to fully appreciate the art. Think of it as "I fake it so real, I am beyond fake" on an industrial scale, but gen-erating bombastic and frighteningly *immediate* stadium anthems, redolent with fire and desire, that enthrall millions, billions. This was pop music's atom-bomb-bright future, and it threatened to blind us all whether we were wearing shades or not.

NOT EVERYBODY WAS INTO it; not everybody was polite about not being into it. The teen-pop backlash—as helmed by such (occasionally) charming nü-metal goons as Korn and Limp Bizkit*—stretched from the late '90s into the early 2000s, but nobody straddled the 20th and 21st centuries with more contemptuous gusto than Eminem. *The Slim Shady LP*—which introduced the wider world to the feral Detroit rapper otherwise known as Marshall Mathers, with a then-crucial cosign from rap god Dr. Dre himself—blew up in 1999 and ensured that we'd be

---

* Both of whom appeared at the notorious hellscape that was Woodstock '99 along with Orange County punks the Offspring, whose frontman, Dexter Holland, regaled the crowd by whacking five Backstreet Boys mannequins with a giant red bat to rapturous bro-cheers.

dealing with this guy for the whole next millennium, as indeed we did, we have, we are, we will.

Within 40 seconds of his breakout hit "My Name Is," Eminem is musing about which Spice Girl he'd like to impregnate. Then he's musing about Pamela Lee's breasts. Then he's stapling his English teacher's nuts to a piece of paper. Then he's announcing that his mom does more dope than he does. Then he's badgered for an autograph at White Castle, and so he signs it, "Dear Dave, thanks for the support, *asshole*," which makes me laugh every time. Then he's musing about *his mom's* breasts. The song's lethally whimsical video played out like a gritty, hard-R-rated reboot of *Pee-wee's Playhouse*; in 1999, starstruck kids watched it all summer (on *TRL!*) and probably wondered how anybody would even make it to winter 2000 alive. Eminem was a one-man Y2K scare, except that Y2K turned out to be bullshit, whereas within a year our newest and weirdest Best Rapper Alive candidate would be sowing more chaos than every '90s chaos agent combined.

Eminem was a white rapper, see, who could rap dazzling circles around the likes of early-'90s crossover knuckleheads like Vanilla Ice and Snow. Matter of fact, Jim Carrey, who viciously parodied both those knuckleheads during his pre-superstardom *In Living Color* years, was the second-best white rapper of the decade. Is that glib? Maybe that's glib. Is it glib to call *Beck* the second-best white rapper of the decade? Is it possible to replicate one's first exposure to "Loser," the mainstream's introduction to the wily, breakdancing, blues-honking, folk-singing, rapper-approximating L.A. troubadour Beck Hansen? You only get to hear this dude rap about being a monkey in a time of chimpanzees for the first time once.

And then, if you were alive in 1994, you got to hear "Loser"

50,000 more times, with its radiantly scuzzy slide-guitar riff, its barrage of non-sequiturs ("Drive-by body-pierce!"), and its expert shoddiness, as though you spent the whole song trying to snap it out of a drug-induced stupor. That vibe extends to the MTV-ubiquitous video, from the blood-squeegeeing Grim Reaper to the graveyard calisthenics that replay the "Smells Like Teen Spirit" goth cheerleaders as farce to the affable dissonance of Beck himself, who wanders around like a time-traveler from either 1972 or 3072.

My buddy Mike saw Beck live in the mid-'90s and reports that Beck kept yelling, "WHO GOT THE SPICE?" to total audience confusion, until he clarified, "ALL Y'ALL GOT THE SPICE." And this is how I picture him (Beck, not Mike) going forward, demanding to know WHO GOT THE SPICE in various splendid and confounding guises, from the vaguely earnest folk surrealist of 1998's *Mutations* to the soft-R-rated Prince-adjacent gonzo lover-man of 1999's *Midnite Vultures* (his best album) to the *severely* earnest and heartbroken troubadour of 2002's *Sea Change*. Who's got the spice? What is the spice? Is he a rock star, a pop star, a rapper, a folkie, a youthful disruptor, or a creaking establishment totem who will one day rob Beyoncé of an Album of the Year Grammy? Why not all of them, on a long enough timeline? Is a white guy break-dancing in a flannel shirt cultural appropriation? How many times is too many times to laugh at "Get crazy with the Cheez Whiz"? Is *every time* too many times?

The truth is that MTV was *still* raising me in the '90s, but the cultural landscape it depicted had atomized; whereas in 1987 I was sufficiently awestruck by just one astronaut planting a colorful flag on the moon, now each new video gave birth to a new galaxy, a new religion, a new type of pop star, a new radiant persona to build your whole life around. There is a scene from the video for Master P's triumphantly gratuitous 1997 hit "Make 'Em Say Uhh!"—in which a guy in a monkey suit, wearing a jersey with HUSTLERS emblazoned across the front, executes a phenomenal free-throw-line-length trampoline dunk amid several cannon bursts of confetti—that strikes me as being in conversation with the total glorious absurdity of Beck's "Loser," even if that conversation is, *Keep that weird breakdancing white guy away from me.* That moment, it's less that you see God than you see Master P seeing God; same deal with *the gold-plated tank* that rumbles onto the basketball court as the song begins and eventually fires a missile at one of the backboards. Shaquille O'Neal—this is primo, early-Lakers-era Shaq—is among the "Make 'Em Say Uhh!" video's special guests, which include more dudes in basketball jerseys in one place than you've ever seen in your life, including at an actual basketball game.

Nobody was more disruptive, more garish, more prolific, more polarizing, more conspicuous in his consumption, nor arguably more *successful* in 1997 and 1998 than Master P, New Orleans rapper and legit-genius businessman. In '98 alone, his label, No Limit Records, put out *23 albums*—from the likes of Snoop Dogg, Silkk the Shocker, Mia X, Mystikal, and (personal favorite) Fiend—most of which anecdotally last between 75 and 79 minutes. We're talking nearly *romcom-length* listening experiences. And these were *rewarding* experiences, clearly, because *16* of those albums went either Gold (500,000 copies sold) or Platinum (a million). No Limit peaked just as the music industry, the CD era, had begun to peak. And thanks to one of the most famous business deals in rap history—a distribution deal with Priority Records that is arguably more famous and more artful than any one song he ever put out—Master P got a huge cut of all that money, compared to your average flat-footed major-label artist. In 1998 he told the *New York Times*, "I guess I want to be the ghetto Bill Gates." A few paragraphs later in that story, Ice Cube called P "one of the best businessmen I've ever run across."[*]

As a mere mortal *rapper*, Master P's true innovation, as his most famous song implies, is the word *UHH*: its boundless utility, its emotional versatility. Depending on the song, *UHH* can be an expression of grief, of menace, of wistfulness, of revelry, of virility, of dissatisfaction, of profound self-made-multi-millionaire-type satisfaction. "Make 'Em Say Uhh!" definitely leans toward revelry if not outright virility, a breakneck procession of verses from P, then Fiend, then Silkk, then Mia X, then Mystikal, all this energy combining into an infectious Fun Night Out With Friends, a gilded pillow-fight with a tank round concealed in each pillowcase, a festival of gaudy giddiness every bit as endearing as the Spice Girls' "Wannabe" video. The party didn't last for No Limit, but the best parties don't, and Master P got to shatter quite a few monocles in his day, many of which he ground up beneath the treads of his gold-plated tank.

THE PEOPLE WHO HATE a hot new band can define that band's identity every bit as much as the people who love it; you learn as much from who runs from the chaos as you

---

[*] It would be glib of me to compare Master P, as a shrewd and uncompromising independent label owner, to Fugazi/Minor Threat luminary Ian MacKaye, or by extension to compare No Limit to Ian's righteously ascetic Washington D.C. punk oracle Discord Records, so I'm not going to do that, but I want you to know that I really wanted to do that, and basically, I just did.

do from who runs toward it. This always sounded like mythologizing music-industry bullshit to me, but the rumor is that when the video for the Prodigy's "Firestarter" aired for the first time in the U.K. in 1996 on *Top of the Pops*, the BBC got a record number of viewer complaints. Not because the "Firestarter" video is terrifically offensive—it's basically just black-and-white footage of singer/rapper/disconcerting focal point Keith Flint stomp-stomp-stomping around in an old London Underground tunnel—but just because Keith, what with the myriad piercings and spiky rainbow hair and devilish mien, is a delightfully alarming-looking human. So stuffy, scandalized, monocle-wearing English people were basically just calling the BBC and going, *Please get that scary-looking arsonist man off my television.* Which is fantastic, even if it is mythologizing music-industry bullshit.

By 1997, when "Firestarter" propelled the group's breakout third album, *The Fat of the Land*—released in America on Madonna's own label, Maverick Records, because she knows where the action is—to inexplicable chart-topping infamy, rock 'n' roll was dead and had been replaced forevermore by *electronica*, according to many reputable music magazines I devoured at the time. The Prodigy—founded in 1990 by misanthropic producer/songwriter/mastermind Liam Howlett, but synonymous in the public imagination with Keith Flint's leering visage from the moment the "Firestarter" video hit the air—were no strangers to infamy by then. The first big Prodigy single, 1991's disturbingly childlike "Charly," proved so upsetting (and influential) that Howlett appeared on the cover of the dance-music publication *Mixmag* with a gun to his head above the headline "Did 'Charly' Kill Rave?" The old journalism rule *If the headline is a question, the answer is NO* applies here, but nonetheless, it's fair to say these guys immediately drove everyone nuts.

I was not cool enough (or old enough, or English enough) to be devouring *Mixmag* in 1991, but rest assured I was a devoted *Rolling Stone* man by the time a leering Keith Flint graced the cover in the summer of 1997, next to the far less aggro headline "Hot Phenom: Prodigy Catch Fire." I can tell you it was summer '97 because I read all about the death of rock 'n' roll and the implacable rise of electronica while on a relaxing Myrtle Beach vacation with my buddy Mike's family, lulled by the crashing waves, digging my feet in the sand, and plotting to go home and throw out all my Nirvana CDs. "It's quite deep," Flint told *Rolling Stone* reporter Chris Heath, flagging the "Firestarter" lines "I'm the self-inflicted mind detonator" and "I'm the bitch you hated." "I don't know if I want to say. I could explain it to you, but I wouldn't for the magazine." *Dammit.*

Were these disruptive fellas quite deep, in a low-key, off-the-record sort of way? Fuck no. But "Firestarter" sounded far more turbulent and unruly and *dangerous* than most actual rock music in 1997, and also the song sampled a quite random-feeling surf-ish guitar riff from a 1993 tune called "S.O.S." by the stupendous Dayton alt-rock band the Breeders, a personal favorite of mine then and now, and so it's always been awfully fulfilling to picture nicer furniture just materializing in Breeders singer-songwriter Kim Deal's house any time "Firestarter" starts playing somewhere.

But the Prodigy's time as internationally known bitches we hated was mercifully brief. The BBC controversy over "Firestarter" paled in comparison to the enmity that greeted another big *The Fat of the Land* single, "Smack My Bitch Up," which first of all is *called that*, and also featured a long, dumb, lurid, violent, semi-pornographic video that aired on MTV for like a week, preceded by a sweaty Kurt Loder disclaimer and climaxing with the revelation that the POV character committing all this lurid, semi-pornographic violence *is a lady*. This was disturbing, provocative, truly mind-blowing shit in 1997, trust me. But a couple years later, the Chicks' "Goodbye Earl" would burn it to a crisp.

When's the last time you watched *that* video? Holy shit. "Goodbye Earl" is a gleeful domestic-violence revenge fantasy and mass sing-along from the Dallas country trio's 1999 album *Fly*, their second straight album (after 1997's *Wide Open Spaces*) to go Diamond, which means it's sold more than 10 million copies in the U.S. alone. The artists then known as the Dixie Chicks—with lead belter Natalie Maines joining founding members Martie Maguire and her sister Emily Strayer—were incomprehensibly huge in the late '90s, Nashville disruptors and triumphant standard-bearers all at once, a living, fire-breathing rejoinder to the stuffy, venal, unimaginative, chauvinist, artistically and emotionally bankrupt, timid, soulless, cheese-dicked nincompoops of Music Row.

But yeah, the "Goodbye Earl" video is a dance party. Blinding sunlight. Garish primary colors. The Chicks flashing bright smiles as a cavorting pack of delighted civilians, eventually including kids, bops around behind them in a hospital room. The plot: Earl assaults his wife, who then conspires, with her friend Mary Anne, to kill him with poisoned black-eyed peas, to the delight of everyone. I am not a horror person—surprise!—so ain't no way I'm watching that movie *Midsommar*, but this is the cruel-sunshine vibe I'm picturing when I read about that movie on Wikipedia. Jane Krakowski plays Wanda, the abused woman, and I would venture to say that her eye-injury makeup in the "Goodbye Earl" video is, by design, the single most upsetting image ever broadcast on CMT, or for that matter VH1 or MTV, in part because she's *smiling*. Lauren Holly plays her friend/co-conspirator Mary Anne, and Dennis Franz plays the titular husband-turned-abuser Earl as a zombie corpse for part of the time, and he's dialed into the kooky black humor of it all, comporting himself like a sketch-comedy stooge who also, briefly, grabs the camera and violently shakes it as though the camera is his wife.

My eyes welled up when I revisited the "Goodbye Earl" video recently, not because it's crying-emoji funny, and not because it's trying to be jump-scare upsetting or maudlin or melodramatic. It was just my baffled reaction to a piece of mass-market pop art so tonally dense and horrifying, but also goofy, but also deadly serious. It's as close to truly shocking as I think a nationally distributed music video is ever gonna get, and shit, then I'm skimming the YouTube comments and someone argues that the most crushing line in the song is "Right away Mary Anne flew in from Atlanta on a red-eye midnight flight," because it depicts a friend dropping everything to come to an abused woman's aid, and now my eyes are welling up again. "Goodbye Earl" was of course never about Earl, but it's not just about Earl's long-suffering wife, either: It's also about the friend who comes to her aid. The point of the song is that *somebody helps her.*

It is tempting now to view "Goodbye Earl" as the prelude to a music-industry tragedy, as the capstone to a late-'90s country-music era that at least in imperfect retrospect is held up now as a glorious and bountiful Garden of Eden-type paradise for female country superstars: Shania, Faith, LeAnn, Lee Ann, Trisha, Martina,

Reba, *et al.* The tragedy is that this era *ended*, definitively, in the early 2000s, as America reverted to wartime footing and country radio pushed its women to the margins with such blatant ferocity that it's common knowledge now that many DJs *aren't supposed to play two female artists back to back.* So think Adam and Eve back before Adam got a backwards baseball cap and a deck of "Iraqi Most Wanted" playing cards and hooked up with Nelly and bought a comically oversized pickup truck he couldn't see over the hood of and started singing exclusively about his barefoot ripped-blue-jean beauty queen, while Eve got kicked off the radio and banished to the Much Tinier Garden of Americana.

But let's not do that. Let's not reduce the Chicks to mere victimhood. *Earl* is the ultimate victim of "Goodbye Earl," and the twirling, jubilant, shining-faced crowd that surrounds the band in the video as they not-so-metaphorically bury him is proof of this song's, and this moment's, everlasting power. It's like they made the whole plane out of the black box of Johnny Cash singing, "I shot a man in Reno just to watch him die." They just came up with a way better motive.

It was Johnny Cash's late-'60s double shot *At Folsom Prison* and *At San Quentin*, in fact, that first transformed me into a Live Album Person. I was enraptured by the boisterous and menacing unruliness of those crowds, hooting along to Johnny's tales of murder and misanthropy with what I hyperbolically imagine anyway is *bloodlust*. On *At Folsom Prison* Johnny even laughs out loud when he pulls out "Long Black Veil" and sings about lying in the arms of his best friend's wife and *someone in the crowd applauds*. I love that sort of electric ambiance, that volatile and immersive interplay between performer and audience. I love doofy stage banter, too: "This next one is the first song on our new album," goes the semi-breathless line from 1978's *Cheap Trick at Budokan*, as affectionately sampled to kick off the Beastie Boys' *Check Your Head* 13 years later.

But nothing beats a Random Crowd Outburst, an unexpected disruption that makes the whole song, the whole album. We've got the ecstatic woman who *screams* midway through "Lost Someone" on James Brown's *Live at the Apollo* from 1963. We've got the whole captive audience *booing the sheriff* to kick off B.B. King's *Live in Cook County Jail* from 1971. We've got the presumably soused fellas quite emphatically requesting "Gary's Got a Boner" on the Replacements' *The Shit Hits the Fans* from 1985. We've got the nervous laughter after Kurt Cobain jokes, "What are they tuning, a harp?" that briefly punctuates the reverent eeriness of Nirvana's *MTV Unplugged in New York* from 1994. And best of all, we've got the rapturously misanthropic screams of several women in the crowd when neo-soul giant Erykah Badu opens a new song, "Tyrone," with the line, "I'm gettin' tired of your shit / You don't ever buy me nothin'." They scream like they've loved this song for years, and they *know* Tyrone, they've *dealt with* Tyrone, they *loathe* Tyrone, and they are ecstatic now for this opportunity to share that loathing with the whole wide world.

Erykah Badu is my vote for the best live performer of her generation. The wittiest, the wiliest, the coolest, the fieriest. I've seen her half a dozen times or so, and consequently I've spent more time waiting for her to take the stage than anyone in history, with the sole exception of Lauryn Hill. Erykah processes time differently. I'm not proud of this, but apparently I complained on Twitter about how long it was taking her show to start in *two separate incidents* in the year 2010 alone. Two shows like six months apart. And both times—every time—all that waiting was *worth* it. You stand around for an hour or two, you get irritated, you fiddle with your phone, your feet hurt, you consider walking out, you don't walk out, you wait some more, and like 90 minutes later Erykah finally deigns to take the stage, and the second she does you forget about *all of it*, because she's the best live performer of her generation.

Baduizm, the Dallas singer's smoky and luminous 1997 debut album, was early proof of concept for the neo-soul movement, a somewhat sweaty genre-as-marketing-scheme that sought to elevate enigmatic young stars like D'Angelo and Maxwell* while also spiritually linking them to all the '60s and '70s giants: your Marvins, your Stevies, your Arethas. Indeed, there's always been something pleasingly unstuck-in-time about Erykah: the mystical silkiness, the swaggering vibrato, the lithe jazz scatting that inspired her to take the stage name *Badu* in the first place, the regal goofiness. (Her first job was waitressing at Steve Harvey's Comedy House in Dallas, but she quickly talked her way onstage.) You can talk yourself into praising *Baduizm* as a hip-hop-conversant recreation of an idealized past, but it's an awful shame, on the other hand, to compare her to anyone, or anything, from any other era. And Erykah's radiant singularity is best captured on the album she simply called *Live*, also released in 1997, less than six months after her hugely successful debut, because everyone needed to know how captivating she was onstage as soon as possible.

Erykah explains, before "Tyrone" starts, that "Tyrone" is her next single, she just recorded it, and she'd originally improvised it

---

* Kedar Massenburg, who managed both Erykah and D'Angelo, coined and trademarked the term *neo-soul*, which frankly in name alone seemed a little rude to, y'know, regular soul, but marketing new artists is hard, man.

onstage with her band during a sound check in London. It is fair to assume that most people present for this live version are not familiar with this song; I sound naïve as I say that, but it is terribly important to me to maintain my belief that the women here in the crowd screaming with malevolent joy at every line Erykah Badu sings are having a genuine instinctive reaction to how hilariously indignant and mean this song is. These are malevolently joyful screams of recognition, of commiseration. Erykah and all these women are sharing a moment here, as she sings what is, in essence, a fairly simple and clearly quickly improvised song about a crap boyfriend she is about to kick out of her house because he's broke and all his crap-dude friends are always hanging around. (The titular Tyrone is not the crap boyfriend, but one of the crap boyfriend's crap friends; the main thing to know about Tyrone is that his name rhymes with "but you can't use my phone.")

The dialogue between performer and rapt audience here, the mass catharsis shared between a newly minted star and her instantly devout fans, is some of the sweetest music I've ever heard. And every time I return to the version of "Tyrone" on *Live*, I am reminded of my first Erykah Badu concert, in the early 2000s, and specifically of the moment when she punctuated one song—I forget which one, and the vagueness kinda bums me out, though it's a lovely idea that I'd all but blacked out from pure joy at this point—by ripping off her giant Afro wig and *bouncing it on the stage like a giant basketball.* Just, *BOOOOOING.* I was *shocked.* I was *flabbergasted.* And she was the Queen of the World.

SELLOUTS (OR NOT) (OR MAYBE)

SONGS DISCUSSED:

Metallica, "Enter Sandman"

Pantera, "Walk"

Temple of the Dog, "Hunger Strike"

Coolio, "Gangsta's Paradise"

Ice Cube, "It Was a Good Day"

Reel Big Fish, "Sell Out"

The Mighty Mighty Bosstones, "The Impression
   That I Get"

No Doubt, "Just a Girl"

Fugazi, "Merchandise"

Green Day, "Longview"

L ARS ULRICH is the Derek Jeter of drummers. I take no joy in reporting this; I say this with great affection. No, wait, sorry, that's not true: I take great joy in reporting this. Sorry. Let's establish up front that making fun of Metallica is *fun*. It's fun if you hate them, or if you are indifferent to them. But it's extra fun if you *love* them, if you worship them, if they constitute your whole lifestyle. That way, you can take the greatest possible joy in making fun of them with the greatest possible affection.

And so, Lars Ulrich = Derek Jeter. Lars is a god, an all-timer, a Hall of Famer, whatever. But he's also a *crazy overrated* drummer. He's flash over competence. He's ostentatious. He's booting easy ground balls, and diving all over the field unnecessarily, and diving into *the stands* unnecessarily. The Lars Ulrich experience, particularly in the band's early thrash years, is one giant drum fill: *BRUMBUDDABRUMBUMBUMBUM*. Listening to an '80s Metallica album is like falling down the stairs for an hour. And yet Lars struggles, as many have observed, to keep time. *His own bandmates* have observed this. "To this day, he is not Drummer of the Year," Metallica frontman James Hetfield conceded to *Playboy* in 2001. "We all know that."

And we all do! But the larger truth—given that making fun of this band gets more fun the more you love them—is that Lars is the all-time Drummer of the Year *precisely because* we know he's not, he's a Hall of Famer *because* he's crazy overrated, he's a god *because* he's such a profoundly flawed mortal. While in the studio recording Metallica's massively popular 1991 self-titled record— better known as the Black Album, and righteously kicking off with the immortal "Enter Sandman"—Lars talked to the journalist/ biographer Mick Wall about how he used to idolize the flashiest drummers imaginable, like Neil Peart from Rush or Ian Paice from Deep Purple. But now Lars had learned to love the unflashy, laid-back, rocksteady guys like Phil Rudd from AC/DC or Charlie Watts from the Stones. "I used to think that stuff was easy," he conceded. "But it's not."

"Enter Sandman," then, is the moment when Lars finally committed to making the routine plays.

"Enter Sandman" is also the moment when Metallica sold out. Maybe. I say that with great affection. This notion of selling out—compromising your art for money, for fame, for mainstream validation—absolutely dominated the decade; the great author/ critic/pop philosopher Chuck Klosterman, in his 2022 book *The Nineties*, described the sellout question as "the single most nineties aspect of the nineties." Here in the 2020s, it is just as dominantly fashionable to marvel at how antiquated,* how *irrelevant* the sellout question seems now that even the coolest artists in any medium are encouraged to get as rich as possible by appealing to as many people as possible. But at the time, mainstream popularity was a colossal embarrassment, and even modest ambition a mortal sin. That's an oversimplification, but what isn't, what wasn't? And who can blame Metallica, then or now, for chasing true pop stardom with "Enter Sandman," and succeeding beyond anyone's wildest imaginations?

Metallica fans, that's who. The Los Angeles-born band's first

---

* As Chuck notes, even a fizzy romantic comedy like 1994's *Reality Bites* registers as science fiction now, in that it argues with a straight face that getting paid for doing what you love is uncool, and really *having any sort of job at all* is uncool. Also, Winona Ryder totally ended up with the wrong dude.

three albums—1983's *Kill 'Em All*, 1984's *Ride the Lightning*, and 1986's deified *Master of Puppets*—are a holy trinity of thrash metal,* hellaciously fast and heavy and punishing and uncompromising. Those are also the three Metallica albums to feature beloved original bassist Cliff Burton, whose shocking death in a 1986 tour-bus accident in Sweden—he was only 24—is the band's defining tragedy, in part because he's haunted his bandmates ever since. Everything Metallica does, every record the band has released from that moment forward is suspect, is sacrilege. *What Would Cliff Have Done? Would Cliff Have Done That?*

What makes it worse is that Cliff was Metallica's avatar of integrity, of staying true to their roots. But he was also the most open-minded guy in the band, musically and visually. You read about Metallica now and you're constantly reminded that Cliff wore bell bottoms, and looked like a hippie, and was obsessed with Bach, and listened to Yes and Lynyrd Skynyrd and Kate Bush and R.E.M. So post-Cliff Metallica is screwed now if they stay the same, because Cliff wouldn't have done that, but they're extra-screwed if they radically evolve and get more commercial, because Cliff wouldn't have done that either.

Post-Cliff Metallica certainly gets off to a rollicking start with 1989's scabrous and labyrinthine…*And Justice for All*, which, in a hilarious act of hazing perpetrated against new bassist Jason Newsted, features *no audible bass whatsoever*. But the harrowing and

---

* In the original "Enter Sandman" episode I scrapped this super-hilarious bit where I compared the Big 4 thrash-metal bands to *Sex and the City* characters, but for the record, Metallica = Carrie, Slayer = Samantha, Megadeth = Miranda (redheads), and Biohazard = Charlotte (which doesn't work at all, hence why I scrapped it).

intense anti-war dirge "One" scores the band some honest-to-God radio play, and a ton of MTV play. The universe is bending to the band's will, and at first it really is the mainstream embracing Metallica, not the inverse. "One" is not the sound of a band compromising to get famous; it's the sound of a band getting famous for refusing to compromise.

"Enter Sandman" is...different. Brighter. Shinier. Catchier. Huger. "The idea," Lars himself once explained of the Black Album as a whole, "was to cram Metallica down everybody's fucking throat all over the fucking world." Very well. As helmed by the band's new hotshot producer, a guy literally named *Bob Rock*, the Black Album is conceived, from the onset, as a Heavy Band Goes Supernova record. Think AC/DC's *Back in Black*. Think Def Leppard's *Hysteria*, my favorite album of all time when I was 9. Think 16 million-plus copies sold in America alone. Think lead guitarist Kirk Hammett's indelible, indestructible opening riff to "Enter Sandman," as butchered daily by millions of teenagers in every Guitar Center or Sam Ashe that ever existed. Think James Hetfield's comically gruff but still somehow *vulnerable* lyrics about childhood nightmares, about unconquerable demons, about Never Never Land.

The Black Album defines heavy music in the '90s just as surely as Nirvana's *Nevermind* did, but Metallica spends the rest of the decade letting the '90s define *them*. Nirvana, and the grunge and alternative-rock explosion more broadly, rattles our heroes quite a bit. Metallica's reinventions, the makeovers, the zeitgeist schemes of really the next 25 years or so, starting with 1996's even slicker haircut-and-piercings provocation *Load*...it's all baffling. Just incredibly strange behavior. Not terrible, even, necessarily. Some of Metallica's work in the last quarter-century is truly great: Their 2004 film *Some Kind of Monster*, for example, is the greatest music documentary ever made. But all of it is just so *strange*. The Lou Reed record! The folding-chair-snare-drum record! The song literally called "The Unforgiven III"! If only every rock band courted mainstream acclaim with such outrageous success; if only every artist sold out with this much *zest*.

For, uh, another perspective on Metallica's Black Album, let us turn now to Pantera bassist Rex Brown, writing in his 2013 memoir *Official Truth, 101 Proof: The Inside Story of Pantera*. "We thought it sucked, of course—I mean we thought it was just terrible—we didn't get the commercial sound of it at all, and this made us even more determined to make our new record even heavier than anything we'd attempted before."

Alright! Born in Pantego, Texas, in 1981, Pantera—whose first stable lineup featured generational guitar god Dimebag Darrell, wailing horndog Terry Glaze on lead vocals, future memoirist Rex Brown on bass, and Dimebag's older brother Vinnie Paul on drums—spent most of their first decade as armadillo-trousered Spandex-clad knuckleheads who at various times can sound like KISS, Iron Maiden, Motörhead, Slayer, Ozzy Osbourne, Journey (!!), and, yes, early Metallica.* But with 1990's almighty *Cowboys From Hell*, the band's second album to feature super-growly new

---

* Pantera have more or less disavowed their first four records—they're not officially streaming, and they're not really even canon—but I can report that their 1983 debut *Metal Magic* has an all-time hilarious album cover, and I had a profoundly spiritual moment in a Home Depot once with a 1984 tune called "Heavy Metal Rules."

frontman Phil Anselmo, Pantera reinvented themselves as "groove-metal" mercenaries who favored colossal, concussive, uncompromising riffs in an ongoing effort to, as Anselmo himself once put it, "Trim off all that other bullshit, man."

Now, let me tell you a secret. A lot of rock bands, even *decent* rock bands, when they super-ostentatiously announce that they're gonna trim all the bullshit and rebrand as a *no-bullshit rock 'n' roll band*, quickly discover that their sound was entirely bullshit, and if they ever truly cut out all the bullshit, they'd be left with *literal silence*. Rock 'n' roll, broadly defined, depending on the era and the subgenre and the specific band, is anywhere between 85 and 99.7 percent bullshit. That's the point. The bullshit is the point. The bullshit is the vast majority of the point. Whether they're trying to sell out or not, very few rock bands in world history could even conceivably cut out all the bullshit, and basically none of those bands *should*.

But Pantera could. Pantera did. And '90s Pantera quickly emerges as an invaluable counterpoint to '90s Metallica: no compromise, no pandering, no mercy, and, sure, no bullshit. No *sale*. I don't know if I agree with these guys that Metallica's Black Album sucks, but the highest compliment I can pay Pantera's exhilaratingly brutal 1992 album *Vulgar Display of Power* is that it sounds like a bunch of guys who think that Metallica's Black Album sucks. And that brutality peaks with "Walk," driven by a deceptively simple blunt-force-trauma Dimebag Darrell riff that almost any amateur guitarist can learn to play poorly, but no other guitarist on earth can play *correctly*. Not with Dimebag's swing, his semi-pornographic feel, his swagger, his *soul*. That's why Dimebag appeared on roughly 10,000 guitar-magazine covers in his lifetime; that's why *Guitar World* magazine loved him the way *People* magazine loved Princess Diana.

I'll put it like this: If you ever need to teleport to a strip club, just put on a '90s Pantera record and crouch. (I would try it right now, but I'm wearing pajamas.) Moreover, as the decade progressed, the boys somehow got bigger as they got gnarlier: *Far Beyond Driven*, from 1994, is by universal consensus the hardest and heaviest and least accommodating No. 1 album in *Billboard* chart history. In 1996, Metallica cut their hair, got a few exotic piercings, and put out *Load*, a disconcertingly "alternative"-feeling power play that further alienated their core thrash fanbase; Pantera, meanwhile, served up the bombastic shriekfest *The Great Southern Trendkill*, which sounds like a bunch of guys who think that *Load* is the worst fuckin' album ever made.

The Pantera story ends in acrimony, dissolution, and unimaginable tragedy: In 2004, Dimebag Darrell was shot and killed in Columbus, Ohio, while onstage with Damageplan, a new band he'd started with his brother Vinnie, who died of a heart condition in 2018. But their legacy is unimpeachable: Nobody sold more records while pushing harder toward seemingly uncommercial extremes. Pantera cut out all the bullshit, and everybody wanted a piece.

What prompted Metallica's edgy, cringe-y makeover between '91 and '96, anyway? Why, "alternative rock," of course, with its new breed of Seattle-based rock stars ambivalent toward if not outright hostile to the very idea of rock stardom: its compromises, its moral depravities, its commercial demands. Consider "Hunger Strike," the 1991 karaoke classic from Seattle supergroup Temple of the Dog, in which Soundgarden frontman Chris Cornell and recently anointed Pearl Jam frontman Eddie Vedder, whose respective bands are about to sell millions of records, tenderly duet on a song about their reticence to sell millions of records.

"We were living our dream, but there was also this mistrust over what that meant," Cornell explained to *Rolling Stone*, describing his existential crisis when Soundgarden first triggered a major-label bidding war. "Does this make us a commercial rock band? Does it change our motivation when we're writing a song and making a record? 'Hunger Strike' is a statement that I'm staying true to what I'm doing regardless of what comes of it, but I will never change what I'm doing for the purposes of success or money."

And so, when Eddie and Chris sing about stealing bread from the mouths of decadents, they're talking about cashing checks from major labels. As an added moral wrinkle, Temple of the Dog's sole self-titled 1991 album was a full-length tribute to Andrew Wood, frontman for ascendent Seattle glam-rock band Mother Love Bone, whose own major-label debut album, 1990's *Apple*, was set for release mere days before Wood died, at 24, of a heroin overdose.* Wood, by all accounts, was *very* into the idea of rock stardom: the swagger, the grandiosity, the devotion, the scarves. Think '80s Pantera, not '90s Pantera; think Guns N' Roses, not Metallica. Andrew Wood clearly wouldn't have minded selling millions of records; with "Hunger Strike," Cornell paid tribute to his dear

---

* Temple of the Dog also featured two dudes from Mother Love Bone (bassist Jeff Ament and guitarist Stone Gossard), Soundgarden drummer Matt Cameron, and newish lead guitarist Mike McCready, all of whom of course are now in Pearl Jam, enjoying the stratospheric rock-stardom Wood found so alluring and Vedder finds so alienating.

friend* while further emerging as a generational rock star himself, but one who'd rather go hungry than do it for the wrong reasons.

W HAT ARE THE RIGHT reasons to be a rock star, though? Such a dilemma can't help but feel a tiny bit frivolous in the face of the existential crisis facing young hip-hop superstars at the same time. By 1991, the Compton-raised rapper Artis Leon Ivey Jr., a/k/a Coolio, was in his late twenties, and had survived poverty and incarceration and addiction, and could describe the several lifetimes he'd already lived with a youthful ferocity and vivacity. He was so charming that it almost scared him. "Should I dance on it for a couple of dollars?" he rapped in 1991 as a member of the L.A. group WC and the Maad Circle. "Or sell away my soul to put a rope on my collar?" Coolio has a grim awareness of how rap music is sold—how the rappers themselves are sold—to those rap fans not raised in South Central Los Angeles. And he is aware of the national cultural biases he is expected, by those eager outsiders, to confirm.

Here's where I tell you that as an early-'90s junior high doofus, I adored Tone Loc's "Wild Thing," and Young MC's "Bust a Move," and Vanilla Ice's "Ice Ice Baby," and MC Hammer's "U Can't Touch This," all massive, cheerful, turn-of-the-decade crossover rap smashes you could (very awkwardly) dance to. Here's where I tell you that I still wince a tiny bit on MC Hammer's behalf when I listen to "Check the Rhime" by deified Queens rap group A

---

* Cornell took his own life in 2017, which makes the warm but funereal *Temple of the Dog* record a tough listen now, the magnificent power ballad "Say Hello to Heaven" especially.

Tribe Called Quest, when Tribe leader Q-Tip disses Hammer and announces, "Rap is not pop / If you call it that, then stop."

Is a rap song less credible if it crosses over to the pop charts, to the suburbs? Do you take a hit rap song less seriously if it makes you want to dance, if it's funny, if even the white kids are dancing, if the white kids are *laughing*? Who gets to laugh, and at what, at whom? This conflict did not originate with Coolio, but few chart-topping, fun-loving rappers of the '90s did a better job of unifying America, and pretty much nobody found that experience more alienating. Both his success and his discomfort peaked, in 1995, with "Gangsta's Paradise."

Coolio's debut album, 1994's *It Takes a Thief*, kicks off with an ecstatic and unifying little tune called "Fantastic Voyage"; that song's hit MTV video made him a huge and hugely uncomfortable star. The charisma. The whimsy. The beach-BBQ geniality. The spidery braids of his hair. The guy is quite a striking human being, and musically, his lane appears to be revelry and goofball humor and breezy escapism, even if there is quite a chasm, physical and metaphysical, between what many of his newly minted MTV-bred fans might be escaping and what Coolio, himself, is escaping.*

"Gangsta's Paradise" is his attempt to bridge that divide, or maybe his attempt to burn the bridge between that divide. The galactic flip of Stevie Wonder's 1976 classic "Pastime Paradise" is unforgettable, and the same goes for Coolio's thunderous opening

---

* In 1995, Coolio told *Rolling Stone* that after "Fantastic Voyage" blew up, he worried that he'd alienated his core audience, so for his first album's next, and last, single, he picked the much grittier and funkier "Mama, I'm in Love Wit a Gangsta." He also said, "I don't think you can classify rap as pop. The only time people classify rap as pop is when they start playing it on white stations."

line about walking in the valley of the shadow of death. It's the shockingly Tupac-caliber intensity of his voice, the genuine despair, the preacher's grandiosity. This is Coolio reveling in all his charisma, and ferocity, and even swagger, but he ain't laughing, and this time nobody else is, either.

Nobody's laughing, right? The song first blew up on the soundtrack to the 1995 Michelle Pfeiffer drama *Dangerous Minds*, which Butt-Head, he of the distinguished MTV duo *Beavis and Butt-Head*, once astutely described as "that movie where, like, you know, that white chick goes into the hood and teaches everybody how to get good grades." And indeed, the "Gangsta's Paradise" video mostly consists of Michelle Pfeiffer sitting in a chair in a smoky room and listening to Coolio rap, and I was always struck by how *hard* Michelle Pfeiffer listens. It's just a very intense physical display of listening. It's like someone told her there was a Pulitzer Prize, or at least an MTV Video Music Award, for Hardest Listening.

Did anyone *hear* him though? The pain? The devastation? The isolation? Are we *sure* nobody was laughing? Enter "Weird Al" Yankovic, whom I love with all my heart and soul, and who is rocking Coolio's spidery braids on the cover of Al's 1996 album *Bad Hair Day*, which does indeed include a transcendent "Gangsta's Paradise" parody called "Amish Paradise."* Coolio hated it. "I ain't with that," he told reporters backstage at the 1996 Grammys, after "Gangsta's Paradise" beat out both Biggie and Tupac for Best Rap Solo Performance. "No. I didn't give it any sanction. I think that

---

* Top 5 all-time "Weird Al" moment: The scene in the "Amish Paradise" video when he's churning butter, and the foxy Amish lady walks past him, and he starts churning butter faster. It's the subtleties.

my song was too serious. It ain't like it was 'Beat It.' 'Beat It' was a party song. But I think 'Gangsta's Paradise' represented something more than that. And I really, honestly and truly, don't appreciate him desecrating the song like that."

Now, Weird Al always asks an artist's permission before doing a song parody, and most artists take it as a profound honor—Kurt Cobain was thrilled, for example. But in this case Al's label had talked to Coolio's label, but Coolio himself was unaware, and Al was unaware that Coolio was unaware, and Al was very upset and apologetic about all this, and Coolio, eventually, would soften his stance on "Amish Paradise," telling *Rolling Stone* in 2015 that his initial opposition to the parody was "probably one of the least smart things I've done over the years." Weird Al vs. Coolio is now safe, defanged, nostalgic trivia. But Coolio, at the Grammys, using the word *desecrated*, still knocks me sideways. "Gangsta's Paradise" is, at heart, a very serious song. An anguished song. A tragic song. And a pop song whether Coolio wanted it to be one or not. And the least generous read of "Amish Paradise" that I can offer you is that for some large percentage of Weird Al's target audience (and Coolio's less-targeted audience), the Amish lifestyle and the gangsta lifestyle are equally remote, equally exotic, equally unimaginable.

Ice Cube knew that, too. "I do records for Black kids," he once told the revered feminist author bell hooks,* "and white kids are basically eavesdropping on my records." Many of those songs—including 1988's almighty "Fuck tha Police," from his brief but

---

* That quote comes up early in Eric Harvey's great 2021 book *Who Got the Camera? A History of Rap and Reality*, which shrewdly traces the intertwined universes of *America's Most Wanted* (the indefensibly trashy true-crime TV show) and *AmeriKKKa's Most Wanted* (the electrifyingly vicious Ice Cube album).

genre-defining stint with instant Compton supergroup and eventual Rock and Roll Hall of Fame inductees N.W.A.—already constituted some of the rawest, most vividly confrontational rap music ever made by 1992, when Cube released his third solo album, *The Predator*. But on that record, he unveiled his most seductive rap-as-pop provocation yet, and what he deftly sold all those eager eavesdroppers isn't quite what many of them thought they were buying.

"It Was a Good Day" is the Ice Cube song seemingly everyone knows, everyone loves, everyone can recite by heart. The galactic flip of the Isley Brothers' 1977 classic "Footsteps in the Dark" is *astoundingly* beautiful, and indeed, nearly every word out of Cube's mouth is absurdly quotable: the breakfast with no hog, the triple-double, the Lakers beating the Supersonics, the Fatburger, the AK he doesn't even need to use. It's all great fun. Have fun. Ice Cube's having fun and he wants you to have fun. But it's a Good Day when he doesn't have to use the AK because *usually he does*. It's a Good Day because it includes no police cars, no police *helicopters*. It's a Good Day because "nobody I know got killed in South Central L.A." It's a Good Day because he'd started it "Thinkin', will I live another 24?" He *can't believe* it was a Good Day.

A lot of people who listen to, and love, and rap along to "It Was a Good Day" are eavesdropping. Let's put it that way. I was. I am. For all Ice Cube's anger (delightfully sprayed all over his solo catalog) about other rappers who sell out, who go pop, who can New Jack Swing on his nuts, this song, on his terms, is immaculate, revered, enduring pop music. It's fun. Have fun. Rap along to it. Or rap along to most of it. But depending on who you are and where you come from and what experience you have with where Ice Cube comes from, just respect the fact that your favorite lines might feel a little different in your mouth. The next song on *The Predator* is called "We Had to Tear This Muthafucka Up." It's about the L.A. riots in the aftermath of the 1992 acquittal of the four LAPD officers who beat motorist Rodney King half to death, on camera, not that it mattered in court. "It Was a Good Day" is a song about one day. The rest of Cube's catalog is about every other day.

A H GEEZ, SELLING OUT is supposed to be easy; it's supposed to be *fun*. And what's more fun than ska? Let's do three ska songs real quick. Well, 2.5 ska songs. Maybe 2.0005 ska songs. You get the idea. "The record company's gonna give me lots of money," chant Orange County rapscallions Reel Big Fish, "And everything's gonna be alright." Then the horns kick in. The year: 1996. The song: Oh, hell yes, it's called "Sell Out." The album: Reel Big Fish's sophomore effort and major-label debut, skardonically* titled *Turn the Radio Off*, which is, in fact, the first ska CD I ever bought. You're welcome, fellas.

"Sell Out" is a boisterous, self-deprecating, giddily infectious, and defiantly whole-ass ska song; Reel Big Fish frontman Aaron Barrett wrote it in defense of his friends in the Northern California ska-punk band Dance Hall Crashers, who'd weathered vehement sellout accusations for the double sacrilege of (a) signing to a major label, and (b) dropping their horn section and emphasizing the *punk* element of their abruptly white-hot genre. "It's ridiculous to me, watching what happened to the Dance Hall Crashers," Barrett told Aaron Carnes, author of the rad 2021 book *In Defense of Ska*. "I

---

* I just made up this word.

dreamt about getting my band to play in front of as many people as we can. That's all anybody's trying to do."

And it worked for Barrett and kept working even if "Sell Out" was his band's biggest song by orders of magnitude, and even if 10 years later, his former label would release a Reel Big Fish greatest-hits album with the title *Greatest Hit...And More*. Rude. But nonetheless: ska! A huge mainstream deal in 1996 and '97, perhaps just because we wanted to hear something upbeat for a change! Ska making people money! Which prompted an existential crisis in *several* ska bands!* Wow! Sometimes selling out means *changing your sound to get popular*, and sometimes it just means *getting popular because ska is suddenly popular*. Boston lifers the Mighty Mighty Bosstones already boasted a well-deserved rep as a fantastic live band and were already on their fifth album in seven years when their infectious pep talk "The Impression That I Get," a surprise hit from 1997's *Let's Face It*, blew up on the radio and landed the boys on *Saturday Night Live*. (The footage of Chris Farley bellowing, "Ladies and gentlemen, the MIGHTY MIGHTY BOSSTONES" is really something.)

As an abruptly discerning 19-year-old ska fan myself, my feelings on the matter, in no particular order, were (a) the dude in the Mighty Mighty Bosstones whose only role was dancing onstage had the best job in America, (b) the best Bosstones song was either "Simmer Down" or "Someday I Suppose," and nonetheless (c) it's

---

* I will never tire of telling everyone that in 1997 I played bass in a midwestern college ska band called Skantily Plaid (a fantastic name that was not my idea), which broke up in less than a year and reformed without me as an emo band (obviously not my idea either).

extremely rad that cuddly-growly frontman Dicky Barrett begins
the chorus to "The Impression That I Get" like so:

"No!"

"Well..."

""IIIIIIIIII"

Great song; also a whole-ass ska song, obviously. As fluke radio
hits go, sometimes you're in the right place at the right time, and
sometimes you find your place early and stay there for so long that
it's bound to be the right place sometime.

Which brings us to the sellout-adjacent song that is only .0005
ska, if that, if anything. So. "Just a Girl," the extra-fun and extra-
super-breakout 1995 single from Orange County ska-ish band No
Doubt, is a great many things. An agitated feminist anthem.* A
zippy New Wave monolith worthy of Cyndi Lauper or the Go-Gos
or the B-52s. A delivery system for lead singer Gwen Stefani, the
blindingly sunny pop star and wildly out-of-pocket cultural appro-
priator who combined the appeal of Jessica Rabbit, Olive Oyl, Cher
from *Clueless*, and Jem from *Jem and the Holograms*. But it's also the
lead single off an album (1995's *Tragic Kingdom*, their third) that
sold *16 million copies worldwide*. You can buy *so many* porkpie hats†
and trombones and Skankin' Pickle records with that money.

Tragic Kingdom, the '90s record I'd most underestimated as a
commercial behemoth when I returned to this decade as a nostalgic podcasting adult, documents the world's most cheerful hostile

---

* For the No Doubt episode I was gonna do this whole extra-super-hilarious bit
comparing third-wave ska to third-wave feminism, which is like 20 times stupider
than even the Thrash-Metal Bands as *Sex and the City* Characters fiasco.

† I'm sorry, but I'm still tripping out over the word *skardonically*. I just came up with
that off the dome. Incredible. That's a full day's work where I come from.

takeover, with Gwen's bandmates (including her brother, outgoing co-founder Eric Stefani) all but physically knocked offstage by the fearsome power of her spotlight. It's not that the band entirely abandons its ska roots on this record (see the first and last 10 seconds of the anti-phone-harassment anthem "Spiderwebs"), but those roots are no longer a focal point (see the whole rest of the song, a zippy New Wave jam in its own right). But maybe with "Just a Girl" it's best to imagine No Doubt as a space shuttle where the rocket boosters burn out and detach once it achieves true superstar orbit, and in this case, those abandoned rocket boosters just happen to be labeled "SKA" and "EVERYBODY IN THE BAND OTHER THAN GWEN." That's not really selling out; that's a little something called *personal growth.*

There is an abstract quality to all these accusations of selling out, a know-it-when-you-see-it vagueness, an impossible ideal. What— or better yet, *who*—is the precise opposite of selling out? To whom are all these money-grubbing apostates being unfavorably compared? Fugazi. The answer is Fugazi. Fugazi the Sainted. Fugazi the Untouchable. Fugazi the post-hardcore deities who are every bit as towering and breathtaking a Washington D.C. monolith as the Washington Monument itself. Fugazi who wouldn't sign to a major label if you paid them 10 million bucks, which was reportedly *the actual offer.* Fugazi who capped concert prices at $5 a ticket, all-ages shows, with various booths and onstage speakers espousing the band's various righteous political causes. Fugazi who broke up after putting out their best record, 2001's *The Argument,* and have thus far refused to do a cash-grab reunion tour even though that *really pisses me off.* Fugazi who *wouldn't even sell T-shirts.* Fugazi who wrote a song about how they wouldn't sell T-shirts and called it "Merchandise."

SELLOUTS (OR NOT) (OR MAYBE)

As a clueless high school kid, I first encountered Fugazi through the unlikely medium of those bootleg THIS IS NOT A FUGAZI T-SHIRT shirts, which I found awfully confusing, as they sure as hell seemed to be Fugazi T-shirts. Were these guys just really sarcastic? Awesome! I love sarcasm! I don't think I ever even noticed the "Merchandise" quote on the back of the shirt: "You are not what you own." It was years before I heard the song itself, on Fugazi's second-best album, 1990's *Repeater*, whose very track list struck me as a declaration of monastic integrity that doubled as a cruel taunt. First you listen to the utterly stupendous "Repeater" (track 2), with one of the greatest bass-and-drum grooves ever born, and you think, *I love this, and I am going to make this band my whole lifestyle, and I am therefore going to buy SO MANY T-shirts.* And then you hit "Merchandise" (track 4), in which Punk Pope Ian MacKaye informs you that he won't sell you any fuckin' T-shirts because he's got way too much integrity. You can't sell out if you won't sell anything besides records and $5 concert tickets.

I am genuinely relieved that I didn't get super heavy into Fugazi until adulthood, because I would've been absolutely insufferable as a Fugazi Teen. If I'd truly *heard* "Merchandise" as a 16-year-old, I'd have strutted around sanctimoniously accusing anybody with the gall to sell me anything—from random ska bands to the merch guys at rock concerts to Wendy's employees—of selling out. It's not that the term has zero merit, as a far sharper and cooler-sounding way to say *Be true to yourself and don't pander to idiots.* But Fugazi, both as a band and an ethos, work best for me as, yes, truly, an impossible ideal. You will never make anything as great as "Merchandise," the song; you will never achieve the purity of "Merchandise," the ethos. There is a genuine comfort in that, in keeping your feet on the ground while weighing the philosophical pitfalls of reaching for the stars.

WHICH LEADS US, AS all roads eventually lead us, to Green Day. Let me tell you a story about a melodramatic fool. It is Saturday, September 10, 1994. Green Day—the East Bay punk-rock trio who recently released their major-label debut, *Dookie*, which will eventually sell *20 million copies* worldwide—are playing the Blossom Music Center, a stately Cleveland-area amphitheater with terrible parking. Five bucks a ticket. (Fugazi!) Bonkers sold-out show. Legendary show. Green Day are the biggest and coolest band in America. And now we got roughly 23,000 teenagers frolicking on the Blossom Music Center lawn, myself included.

Welcome to paradise.

This is a Saturday in early September, so we got major over-amped back-to-school vibes, and a truly fearsome physical quantity of explosive nervous teenage energy to dispel. I know a guy, he's also a rock critic now, who took a limousine to this Green Day show, somehow, and there was a mosh pit, in the limo, after the show. Legendary show. And it ended with a grass fight. An amphitheater-wide grass fight. It had rained recently, I believe, and now you've got 23,000 teenagers ripping out clumps of wet grass and chucking them at each other. I picture myself now standing on a hill with a panoramic view of the Blossom lawn, Green Day onstage, grass flying in all directions, this feral and jovial warzone, like it's a scene from *Apocalypse Now* or *Braveheart*. I am almost certainly embellishing this memory now, in a self-serving, panoramic, melodramatic sorta way, but that's what teenagers do, man.

And so I buy a T-shirt, at the merch booth, at the big Green

Day concert. Dark green T-shirt. *Green Day* in red bubble letters, floating over a big brown pile of, uh, poop. (The album's called *Dookie*; what're you gonna do.) I also buy a Green Day bumper sticker, and I proudly slap it on the back of my 1987 Chrysler LeBaron, which I drive to school Monday morning whilst wearing my dark-green Green Day T-shirt. And I'm thinking, *I'm the coolest dude in America right now. Look at this T-shirt. This is my identity now. This is the expression of my individuality. Nobody else thinks like me or listens to the cool music I listen to. All the chicks in school are gonna go crazy for me in my Green Day T-shirt. It's gonna set me apart from all those other chumps.* And so on. And then I walk into school and *literally everyone* is wearing the same Green Day T-shirt.

Yeah. A veritable roiling dark-green ocean of Green Day T-shirts. THIS IS FOR SURE A GREEN DAY T-SHIRT. You think I'm exaggerating? Fine: *At least one-third of the student body* is wearing the same Green Day T-shirt. Hundreds of dark-green T-shirts with brown piles of poop on 'em, roaming the halls. We are all iconoclasts. We are all rugged punk-rockin' avatars of individuality. I'd thought this band was still kinda sorta my little secret, but I was *mistaken*.

And Green Day sold out to do it. Famously. Infamously. The Green Day chapter in Dan Ozzi's fantastic 2021 book *Sellout: The Major-Label Feeding Frenzy That Swept Punk, Emo, and Hardcore (1994–2007)* is truly agonizing and will make you feel truly bad for these dudes, or as bad as you can feel for dudes who sold 20 million copies of one album. Green Day played their first show under that name in Berkeley, California, on May 28, 1989, opening up for the legendary ska-punk band Operation Ivy at 924 Gilman Street, otherwise known as the Alternative Music Foundation, otherwise known, simply, as Gilman, one of the most austere and morally upright and eternally revered punk-rock venues in the country, if not the world. Gilman is like if Fugazi were a building, and its core tenants are spray-painted right on the wall: NO RACISM, NO SEXISM, NO HOMOPHOBIA, NO ALCOHOL, NO DRUGS, NO FIGHTING, NO STAGE-DIVING. And also, added later but just as important: no major-label bands.

And Green Day loved it, and in a visceral sense *lived it.* "That place and that culture saved my life," declared frontman Billie Joe Armstrong in his band's first of five *Rolling Stone* cover stories, long after jumping from Berkeley's tiny Lookout! Records to a major label, and therefore theoretically getting banned from Gilman forever, and earning the righteous enmity of much of the core audience they'd cultivated up to that point. "They were very young and felt they were being rejected by the scene that had been so vital and important to them," their former label boss, Lookout co-founder Larry Livermore, explains in Dan Ozzi's *Sellout* book. "It's got to hurt a lot. On one hand, you've got everybody, sometimes even famous people you've looked up to your whole life, telling you, 'Oh, you guys are geniuses, you're wonderful, you're amazing!' And on the other hand, you're thinking, *Yeah, but all my old friends hate me.* I think it came very close to destroying them."

Nobody sold out more effectively than Green Day—20 million copies sold, plus apparently 10 million T-shirts, too!—but nobody paid more to do it. It's hard to describe *Dookie*'s global impact without sounding dippy and hyperbolic; the album landed in February 1994, two months before Kurt Cobain took his own life, and its massive barrage of hit songs, from "Longview" to "Basket Case" to (personal favorite) "Welcome to Paradise," offered a hooky, playful, candy-colored alternative to the dourness and snarliness and "Hunger Strike"-type self-loathing of grunge. I still remember watching the "Basket Case" video on MTV for the very first time: the hyper-saturated colors. Billie Joe Armstrong's teal guitar. The mental institution setting, very *One Flew Over the Cuckoo's Nest*, even if I didn't get the reference at 16. Drummer Tré Cool's wheelchair. And just the wonder of it, the energy, the unfamiliar *enthusiasm*. Maybe Green Day's old friends hate them now. You know who *loves* Green Day, now, though? *Me*.

In the mid-2000s, I moved from Ohio to Oakland to take a job as music editor for an alt-weekly called the *East Bay Express*, which gave me the opportunity to check out Gilman for myself.* And I have this vibe I exude, at famous music venues: When I'd go to CBGBs or Preservation Hall or whatever, I'd think, *Yes. Yes. So historic. This place is cool. Lookit how cool this place is. Lookit how cool I am, being here, in this cool historic place*. But standing in Gilman, listening to whatever band I was listening to, I had the tangible thought, *This isn't mine. This was never mine, and I can never make it mine*. It wasn't a hostile, antagonistic *I don't belong here* feeling, but just this sense that I don't belong to this place, and it doesn't belong to me, and I can never have what this place gave to the people who belonged here. And I found that beautiful; I respected that immensely. I'd pay a lot of money to get what Gilman gave to so many people, Green Day included. But it's not the sort of thing you can buy.

---

* I used to edit the paper's weekly concert listings, which is why I can tell you that my favorite band that ever played Gilman was named Ye Olde Buttfuck. I didn't actually see that show and I've never heard a single song of theirs, but I will remember that name for the rest of my life.

WOMEN VS. "WOMEN IN ROCK"

SONGS DISCUSSED:

The Sundays, "I Kicked a Boy"
The Cranberries, "Zombie"
Garbage, "Only Happy When It Rains"
PJ Harvey, "Man-Size"
Alanis Morissette, "You Oughta Know"
Tori Amos, "Cornflake Girl"
The Breeders, "Cannonball"
TLC, "No Scrubs"
Sinéad O'Connor, "Nothing Compares 2 U"
Fiona Apple, "Criminal"
Sheryl Crow, "If It Makes You Happy"

M Y HUMBLE PLEDGE TO YOU, dear reader, is that I will never again call a lady a *badass*. Don't do this. I have done this. I will stop now. Sorry.

I do understand my impulse to do this; I respect it. (Not really.) So take this band the Sundays, for example. From Bristol, England. Jangling indie-pop melancholia. Dismal splendor. As the '90s dawned, they hit the spot if you loved the Smiths— forever the kings of dismally jangling English melancholia, even if mononymous frontman Morrissey revealed himself, in the fullness of time, to be a huge knucklehead—and especially hit the spot if you loved the Smiths so much you hadn't left the house since the Smiths broke up in '87. Perhaps you recall the Sundays' sumptuously dismal breakout hit "Here's Where the Story Ends," from their 1990 debut album *Reading, Writing and Arithmetic*; perhaps you recall their achingly gentle 1992 cover of the Rolling Stones' "Wild Horses," which is playing in that trashy '96 stalker-bro flick *Fear* in the scene where Mark Wahlberg and Reese Witherspoon (ahem) ride a roller coaster.

But let me direct your attention to a lesser-known *Reading, Writing and Arithmetic* jam called "I Kicked a Boy," a viciously gentle song in which Sundays lead singer Harriet Wheeler recalls a (presumably) childhood incident in which she "kicked a boy till he cried." Yes, I was drawn to this song by its title. Yes, I fully flipped out when Wheeler sang the line, "Oh I could've been wrong / But I don't think I was." Yes, my initial reaction to that line was, *Wow, she's such a badass.*

No. Stop it. *Wow, that's badass. What a badass. So many badass*

54

female singers. You see this phrasing a lot; you see a righteous backlash to this phrasing a lot. I think that if you grew up in the 1990s
and early 2000s, in the golden age of the Women in Rock magazine cover package, there's an ingrained sweaty clumsiness you
have to unlearn where you feel compelled to praise female artists by
clumsily asserting that they're tougher than the men. This impulse
gets real weird and condescending real fast, yeah? *Harriet Wheeler*
could kick Morrissey's ass up and down the street. No. Don't do that.
I'll stop doing that.

Now, Harriet singing the line, "Oh I could've been wrong / But
I don't think I was" in a strikingly radiant bouncing-beach-ball
voice on a song called "I Kicked a Boy": That's objectively rad, and
the dissonance between the caustic nature of the song title and
the much-less-caustic nature of that line delivery is a huge part
of the radness. It's a deliciously mean line sung with a deliriously
genuine sweetness. Let's just relax, though. We (the royal we) can
acknowledge the radness without slipping into overwrought try-
hard Girl Power silliness, I think. I hope. (Everything I said about
Céline Dion still stands, though.) I'm trying to do better. Let's
try right now. Keep an eye on me here and let's see if I can lavish
praise on the Cranberries' "Zombie" without burying it in bumbling dudeliness.

A less embarrassing phrase I overuse is *grunge counterprogram-*
ming, which I have heroically deployed to describe anything on the
radio from 1991 to 1995 that was milder, sweeter, less caustic and
self-loathing, and more melodious than Nirvana or Soundgarden
or what have you. Think Counting Crows, or Hootie and the
Blowfish, or the Gin Blossoms, or even a sweet-but-caustic power
pop bro like Matthew Sweet. And then you've got the Cranberries,

straight outta Limerick, Ireland, led by singer/songwriter/guitarist Dolores O'Riordan and improbably setting the world aflame with their extra-melodious 1993 debut album, *Everybody Else Is Doing It, So Why Can't We?* That album's almighty shimmering jams "Linger" and "Dreams"* dominate alt-rock radio in 1993, despite the fact that alt-rock radio in '93 is generally dominated by robust and blustery and self-loathing dudes advertising, to varying degrees of effectiveness, their badassness.

Whereas Dolores O'Riordan does not need to sing a super-heavy, mega-distortion rock song to thrive amid the many thousands of super-heavy, mega-distortion rock songs extant in this moment. The first Cranberries album (produced, BTW, by frequent Smiths cohort Stephen Street) will eventually sell 5 million copies in America alone, making them easily the biggest Irish rock band since that other big blustery Irish rock band. But the next Cranberries album, released just a year later in 1994 and called *No Need to Argue*, is even bigger, and eventually sells 7 million copies, and boasts a legitimately shocking hit single that kicks quite a few boys.

The terrifying burst of pure, righteous, gnarly, more-grunge-than-grunge distortion that kicks off "Zombie" is not expected by 16-year-old me in 1994, based on my prior knowledge of and affinity for the Cranberries. This jump-scare intro is designed, quite skillfully, as a Holy Shit moment. The Cranberries are through fuckin' around. The Cranberries don't give a shit if you get what

---

* The Hong Kong actress and pop phenomenon Faye Wong, who co-stars in Wong Kar-wai's woozy 1994 romance *Chungking Express*, also sings a phenomenal cover of "Dreams" in Cantonese on the soundtrack. She also sings along to "California Dreamin'" for like 45 percent of the movie.

you want no matter how many times you say *please*. The Cranberries would just as soon kill you as—ah, shit, I'm doing the *badass* thing again, aren't I? Sorry.

But here's what I remember so vividly about "Zombie": I remember Dolores O'Riordan's giant guitar. Dolores is five-foot-two. (Shorter than Bono!) This is not always obvious, given the tremendous vitality of her voice and her natural towering rock-star charisma, but the electric guitar she uses when the Cranberries do "Zombie" on *Saturday Night Live* and *Late Show with David Letterman*—she plays a Gibson ES-335, I think, and if not, I don't want to hear about it—looks huge on her, and looks *heavy*, and exponentially multiplies the song's heaviness. "Zombie" is one of roughly 12 billion songs released in the 1990s that alternate between Deceptively Quiet Verses and Incredibly Loud Choruses, but the bonus sneak-attack aspect here—the whiplash abandonment of the sweetness and light that made "Dreams" and "Linger" so indelible—just knocks me on my ass. Sorry, sorry. There's just got to be a better way to put that, but I haven't found it yet.

"Zombie" is inspired by, and dedicated to, the memories of Johnathan Ball and Tim Parry, the two children killed by an Irish Republican Army bomb planted in a trash bin on a busy street in Warrington, in Northwest England, on March 20, 1993. Tim was 12 years old; Johnathan was 3. Dolores read all about it in the paper. As a 16-year-old ignorant of the historical context here—and ignorant of everything else, really—I do recall my puzzlement when Dolores sings, "With their tanks / And their bombs / And their bombs / And their guns." With even the simplest, most direct pop songs and pop songwriters, there's a natural instinct to avoid the clunky-to-my-young-ear repetition of *bombs* there, to find another rhyme, to find a clever-er way to put it. But now the *bombs* double-shot strikes me as shocked, indignant, almost childlike emphasis, and only further underscores the plain fact that "Zombie" is the hardest, toughest, brashest, scariest, and most thrilling rock song released by anybody in 1994. And maybe the trick to avoiding tumbling down Badass Condescension Mountain is to just say that and move on.

When Dolores O'Riordan died, in 2018, at 46 years old, in a bathtub in a London hotel room, after what was officially ruled an accidental drowning after heavy drinking, I found myself unexpectedly shattered by the reaction of Shirley Manson, lead singer of the great alt-rock band Garbage. "I think what hit me the most when I heard the news about her passing," Shirley told *The Huffington Post*, "was that it really shook me because I thought, *Oh, they're coming for my generation now. This is it.*" David Bowie's death, for example, had devastated Shirley, but Bowie was, well, *older*. Dolores was different. She was a peer. A contemporary.

What somehow really upset me, though, was that Shirley and Dolores never got to be friends. "I didn't know her, and I never had the pleasure of meeting her," Shirley continued. "But we were always like ships passing in the night: We were often on the same bills or at the same festival but on different nights. I know we shared a lot of our fans who loved both bands. When 'Linger' was at the height of its popularity, we were making our first record, so I have very strong memories of her, and I loved her voice."

That stupendous first Garbage record, the viciously catchy self-titled jam from 1995 with the eerie pink cover, is the one with "Only Happy When It Rains," the ecstatic chorus barely louder and snarlier than the riotously glum verses, Shirley's inner torment barely distinguishable from her ferocious triumph. And reading her ode to Dolores now, I suddenly had a photorealistic vision of these two women barreling through that song's chorus together on some towering stage, screaming, "Pour your misery down on me" into one another's faces with pure feral communal joy, likewise laughing in the faces of any chump with the temerity to call them *badasses*. I would've been humiliated; I would've been honored.

A MEMORY: I AM A 15-year-old, MTV-obsessed doofus, and I am abruptly petrified by the sight of Polly Jean Harvey, native of Dorset, England, in the video for "Man-Sized," from her eponymous band PJ Harvey's second album, 1993's goth-blues-punk behemoth *Rid of Me*. "I'm coming up man-sized / Skinned alive," she playfully half-lip-syncs, but her vocals are mixed so low amid the quietly seething electric guitar and concussive snare drum that I have to lean in closer to my TV to hear her, and indeed, this is yet another of the billions of '90s songs with Deceptively Quiet Verses that lead into Incredibly Loud Choruses, but this one is, for some reason, petrifying. She's the reason. PJ is sitting in a chair, pulling menacingly goofy faces, playing with her hair, headbanging, winking, waving her hands about, somehow projecting both oceanic calm and severe agitation. "Douse hair with gasoline," she concludes, the light in the room darkening around her. "Set it light and set it free." Holy shit.

A headline: "HIPS. LIPS. TITS. POWER." From the cover of *Q* magazine in May 1994, above a photo of PJ Harvey, Björk, and Tori Amos, who apparently "have rogered the charts with their special brew of spooky, left-field weirdness and estrogen-marinated musings," as the venerable U.K. publication helpfully explains. Yo:

That's not how estrogen works. Estrogen is not a marinade, you weirdos.
GET IT TOGETHER.

Let me be clear that music magazines—*Rolling Stone* and *SPIN* primarily, though also the likes of *Q* and *The Source* and *Mojo* and *XXL* and *Vibe* once I got a little cooler and broader-minded—made me, or at least made me the professional music obsessive who slouches before you today. I don't mean to dredge up 30-year-old semi-cringey headlines now as a pompous way to assert my present-day moral superiority, because that's ridiculous (and pompous). Let's not get all self-congratulatory here; I'm not clowning that headline now, or clowning those sorts of headlines in general, but clowning my stumbling attempts, back then, to process those headlines, and reconcile them with the vitality of the music they're attempting to describe.

And so, a memory: I am a 17-year-old, MTV-obsessed knucklehead with, miraculously, a girlfriend, and she's obsessed with Alanis Morissette, the Canadian pop prodigy who has blown up to overnight megastardom thanks to her monster 1995 hit "You Oughta Know." It is a song of heartbreak, it is a song of romantic betrayal, it is a song about a crap dude (heavily rumored to be *Full House* star Dave Coulier), and in essence serves as the public execution of a crap dude, in the guise of a series of questions posed to the crap dude about the girl he spurned Alanis for, the bluntest and most profane of these questions being, "And are you thinkin' of me when youuuuuuu fuck her?" I, personally, did not want to think about Dave Coulier thinking about fucking someone while fucking someone else, but in the '90s, back when the internet was a mere twinkle in the eye of the nerdiest kid you knew, you often did not get to choose what you were listening to or thinking about.

WOMEN VS. "WOMEN IN ROCK"

So there's me and (miraculously) my girlfriend, hanging around her living room after school with (unfortunately) her mother, and my girlfriend is blasting Alanis' ludicrous blockbuster 1995 album *Jagged Little Pill*, and every time "You Oughta Know" comes up she has to cough, strategically, to keep her mother from hearing the F-bomb. "And are ya thinkin' of me when you [*COUGH*] her?" There is just no way that actually worked, but her mom never made us turn the record off.

A headline: "ANGRY WHITE FEMALE." From the cover of *Rolling Stone* in November 1995, next to a photo of Alanis Morissette. That's a reference to the 1992 stalker-lady flick *Single White Female*, FYI. Now, there is no denying the galvanizing anger of "You Oughta Know," but what is harder to capture in three words is how *funny* Alanis can be, and how much funnier she gets the angrier she gets, which is bad news for the crap dude but great news for us, such that the best moment in the whole song is the vehemence with which she spits out the words, "I hate to bug you in the middle of *dinner.*"

It's hilarious. Truly. "I don't mind being one-dimensionalized violently and reduced to one emotion, as complex as humans may be," Alanis explains to Andy Cohen on his Bravo talk show *Watch What Happens Live* in 2020. "I think anger is one that I'll take." She flashes a thumbs-up, she smiles, she laughs, she's funny even when she's not joking. Andy asks her if the "ANGRY WHITE FEMALE" headline pissed her off especially, and she says, "Yeah, I'm pissed about a lot of things, but I also have 750,000 other emotions." She's smiling as she says it; Andy's smiling as he hears it.

A memory: the Tori Amos concert I never saw. I can recreate this show so faithfully, despite never having been there. The

collective hush, the religious veneration, the electric crackle of sacrilege. Of all the '90s alt-rock stars I did *not* see live in the 1990s,
I regret never seeing Tori Amos the most. (Other candidates here
include Morphine and Fugazi.) Oh, I've heard stories, and I've seen
videos: I'm aware that Tori live is a Not Safe for Work situation.
The way I would describe her typical onstage posture is *manspreading*. She is staring down her silent/reverent audience; her whole
vibe is *proudly indecorous*. Major Prince vibes, somehow, from Tori
Amos live. She is the Little Red Corvette. Most of the time she is
playing the piano as if attempting to impregnate it.

I'm following her lead here, imagery-wise. "A lot of women have
said I offended them," Tori tells *US* magazine in 1994. "And I'm
like, 'When you get up onstage, I'm not going to bust your ass. If
you want to stand there and not move your hips and think that's
feminist, fine.' But I'm not doing this for any movement. It's about
awakening my being. And part of my being is a sexual being. You
know when they talk about 'The Goddess'? This is not a dry entity!
This is fertilizing the cornfields! This is making things grow! This
is a very juicy concept!"

I'm so pissed at myself for never sitting in that cornfield. I spent
so much of the '90s as a moody teenager driving around suburban
Cleveland, Ohio, moping beneath the industrial-strength gloom
of a gunmetal-grey midwestern sunset, entranced by whichever
Tori Amos song happened to be on the radio. The extra-hushed
and pulverizing hyperballad "Winter" as my sputtering car heater
proved no match for the February chill. The sacrilege-as-veneration
of "God," with his 9-iron in the backseat and Tori's sardonic purr
as she sings, "Do you need a woman to look after you?" The string
of one-liners that likewise animates "Crucify," especially "Just what

God needs / One more victim." The "Boy, you better hope I bleed real soon" line on "Silent All These Years," her funniest and chilliest provocation of all. And "Past the Mission," wherein she lovingly reduces the voice of Trent Reznor—Trent Reznor! the most barbaric and furious and untamable human being I could imagine at the time!—to an ominous, obedient murmur.

All those songs hail from 1992's *Little Earthquakes* (her debut album if you don't count 1988's glam-metal-band oddity *Y Kant Tori Read*, which she doesn't) or 1994's *Under the Pink* (which is the one with "Cornflake Girl"). Talk about grunge counterprogramming: It's hard to convey now how *bizarre* "Cornflake Girl" sounded on the radio in '94, sandwiched between, say, "Heart-Shaped Box" and "Interstate Love Song." This is for the best. What made this particular Tori song* pop on the radio was the sheer intangible improbable *oddness* of it, the uneasy rhythm, the eerie whistle melody before she's even sung anything (Tori had to really fight for that), the mandolin, the super-improbable but quite welcome presence of Meters bassist Greg Porter Jr., and above all the sheer ferocity of Tori's piano solo near the end, a display every bit as cathartic and virtuosic as, say, Pearl Jam guitarist Mike McCready's barrage of radness on "Alive." We could say *Tori kicks Mike's ass up and down the street*, but let's not and say we could've.

A headline: "Ginger Nut." A further description: "She's a Grade A, Class One, turbo-driven fruitcake, but Southern belle TORI

---

*This is not a pleasant topic of conversation, but Tori's never had any problem telling anybody that "Cornflake Girl" is inspired by the 1992 Alice Walker novel *Possessing the Secret of Joy*, and specifically its description of female genital mutilation, and by extension the terrible things women sometimes do to other women—other girls—because it's allegedly for their own good. Teenage Me had no idea; I assure you that whatever Teenage Me thought this song was about was extremely stupid.

AMOS might just be the antidote to all those cloying bottle-blonde bimbettes currently hogging the spotlight." From the *NME*, that even more venerated U.K. publication, in January 1992. *Jesus.* Now, a huge part of Tori's charm is her willingness to inform, say, *US* magazine that "I've been a Viking in loads of other lives. I know what stealing the babes from the Irish coast is all about." But this media tendency to reduce her audacity and eccentricity down to the phrase *turbo-driven fruitcake* is especially unpleasant when you get down to the matter of the *Little Earthquakes* track "Me and a Gun," in which she describes, a cappella, in unflinching and unbearable detail, her experience with sexual assault.

A headline: "Tori Amos has been a classical pianist, a cheesy lounge act, a metalhead in thigh-high plastic jack-boots, and a victim of rape. She's a woman on a mission." (That's *SPIN.*) A headline: "This brave new voice sings about rape and rage. The twist is, she makes us feel sexual, powerful and alive." (*Glamour.*) A headline: "Tori Amos has gone from singing about rape to worshipping the goddess of fertility" (Yep, *US.*) None of those headlines are outright disrespectful, of course, but there's something so jarring about that word deployed in a large font size as a data point, as a *topic of conversation*, as fodder for that classic magazine construction: "Tori Amos Talks to Us About X, Y, and Z."

Not that any of that matters, really. What matters is that in 1994, Tori Amos became the first official spokesperson for the Rape, Abuse & Incest National Network, a/k/a RAINN. What matters is that for the rest of her life, you can find Tori backstage, talking to her fans, having the only conversations about "Me and a Gun" that matter. A *Rolling Stone* interviewer once brought up a friend of his who said, "Tori Amos is one of the reasons I'm still here." Tori's reply: "When people say this to me, I say to them: You saved your own life."

A NOTHER HEADLINE: "WOMEN OF Rock." *Rolling Stone*, September 1997. Tina Turner, Madonna, and Courtney Love on the cover. Another headline: "Women in Rock." *Rolling Stone*, October 2002. Britney Spears, Mary J. Blige, and Shakira on the cover, with Alanis, Avril Lavigne, and Ashanti in the foldout. A headline: "Women Who Rock." *Rolling Stone*, October 2003. Missy Elliott, Alicia Keys, and Eve on the cover. That's not as many "Women [Preposition or Pronoun] Rock" *Rolling Stone* headlines as I thought, to be honest, or in any event *that's enough.*

You ever seen the video for the Breeders' "Shocker in Gloomtown," their cover of the Guided by Voices song? The fact that these two bands are from Dayton is roughly 85 percent of the reason I'm proud to be from Ohio. GBV, led by ultra-prolific gentleman bro Bob Pollard, are scruffy, hard-drinking, dudes-rock gods who've put out approximately one million basement-as-arena-rock albums with 13 billion songs on 'em; the Breeders, led by twin sisters Kim and Kelley Deal, have a complementary basement-as-arena energy and are one of my favorite bands of all time, on account of the fact that Kim's voice—her physical singing and speaking voice—is one of my favorite musical instruments on this planet. There is a dark allure, a giddy and sinister sort of children's-librarian warmth to her voice even at its coldest.

Kim Deal, as you may recall, started out as the bassist and (very) occasional lead singer of the Pixies, the legendary Boston band whose initial run from 1987 to 1991 more or less defined alternative rock as the 1990s would understand it. (One of the coolest things about me in junior high is I saw the Pixies live, opening for U2 on their fabled Zoo TV tour; one of the least cool things about me in junior high is I thought the Pixies sucked.) You have the Pixies to thank for the whole Deceptively Quiet Verses + Incredibly Loud Choruses formula; Kurt Cobain, as you may recall, cites the Pixies as a key inspiration for Nirvana's "Smells Like Teen Spirit," which defined the 1990s as the 1990s understood the 1990s.

But the Breeders are better than the Pixies. Trust me on this, and trust me that many a frigid Ohio winter has been thawed by the dulcet strains of "Cannonball," off the Breeders' 1993 breakout album *Last Splash*. The killer bassline courtesy of bassist Josephine Wiggs. The Deal sisters' audible switchblade smiles as they harmonize on the line "Spitting in a wishing well." The split-second of dead air right after the Deals harmonize extra-sweetly on the line "the bong in this reggae song." The giddy insubordination of that silence, which packs more personality than any other band's noise.

Anyway, that "Shocker in Gloomtown" video is just the Breeders playing the song in a literal garage while the actual members of Guided by Voices leer at them through the windows, and this is really all the commentary on being a Woman in (or of) Rock that you should really need the Breeders to provide. Though it's always fun, when Kim does elaborate. She did a really long and rad and combative interview with *SPIN* magazine's Charles Aaron for a 1995 cover story where she complained about this notion that all Women in Rock could really do is imitate men, or be protected by men like, huh, that one guy from Fugazi. "Now you've got guys like Ian MacKaye 'saving' girls from the mosh pit," she scoffed. "Hey man, fuck you. Girls know what they're doing when they get in the pit. They don't need you to save them."

Hey man, fuck you. I can so clearly hear these words in Kim Deal's voice, just as I can so clearly hear them in TLC's cacophony of voices, on every song they ever did, even the cheery ones, even the horny ones, even the not-at-all-confrontational ones. *Hey man, fuck you. We know what we're doing. We don't need you to save us.* And they didn't, but we (the actual we this time) sure as hell needed them. The Atlanta pop trio of Tionne "T-Boz" Watkins, Lisa "Left Eye" Lopes, and Rozonda "Chilli" Thomas is, by the numbers and also by the *feelings*, the biggest girl group of all time, which in retrospect was pretty obvious just based on the riotous video for their 1992 debut single "Ain't Too Proud to Beg": the exuberant primary colors, the giant hats, the baggy pants, the overalls, and of course, the glasses with a condom over the left eye that gave Lisa Lopes her nickname. This was clearly a group with 750,001 emotions and a hit song—and an entirely distinct and sumptuous *look*—for each of them.

Lisa's condom glasses are a provocation, sure, but they're the furthest thing from empty provocation. This is *strikingly wholesome* provocation. *Hey man, put this on*, she is saying, with her glasses. As the stakes get higher for TLC—as they sell way more records and generate way more controversy—bear in mind that these are not women content with mere shock value. Their biggest hits are explicitly *about* something. "Waterfalls," the ungodly smash from 1994's Diamond-selling *CrazySexyCool*, devotes its second verse to the HIV crisis: "Three letters took him to his final resting place." "Waterfalls" is *extra*-wholesome provocation, a gigantic karaoke supernova anthem about *restraint*, about *caution*. It's called

67

"Waterfalls" because TLC are advising you not to chase them. *Don't do that* is just such a bizarre message for a huge pop song, a cautionary tale all the more effective for being totally subliminal, given that everyone listening is too busy doing the dance from the video where TLC are turned into *Avatar*-via-1994 water people. The song's as "conscious" as any conscious rap you'd care to name, and like 50,000 times more fun than conscious rap. TLC are cutting-edge pop music now. Their every move is the new tradition. Also: *CrazySexyCool* came out in November 1994, four months or so after Left Eye burned down her NFL superstar boyfriend Andre Rison's house.

A way better headline: "TLC Fires It Up." *Vibe* magazine, November 1994. They're wearing firefighter outfits. (The inside headline for the story itself is "The Fire This Time," which is even better.) The group, in this moment, have more control over their narrative than usual, and are engaging in some slightly less wholesome provocation. But the *Vibe* article also details the troubling relationship between Lopes and Rison, their confrontations, and her accusations of abuse leading up to the fire. Lisa also pushes back against the notion that she's "the crazy one," an idea mistakenly conveyed by the group's own album title. "*Crazysexycool* is a word we created to describe what's in every woman," Lisa says. "Every woman has a crazy side, a sexy side, a cool side. A lot of our producers misunderstood us when we told them the idea—they'd do a crazy song for me, a sexy song for Chilli, and a cool song for Tionne. We had to explain that *CrazySexyCool* doesn't just describe us individually, it describes all the parts of every woman."

What's *really* crazy, if you don't mind my saying, is the thought of some crap dude driving around—it's not even his car—and seeing one of these three international superstars walking down the street, and having the audacity to think, *I'm gonna yell something out the window that'll make her want to have sex with me.* Who the hell are you? What the hell are you doing? At the time, "Waterfalls" struck me as absolutely the hugest pop song imaginable, but "No Scrubs," from 1999's sleek and sultry *Fanmail*, has emerged as the one TLC smash to rule them all, which makes it extra funny that it's a song about broke rando dumbasses ineptly flirting with TLC. *Don't do that*, the song says, a little less gently this time.

"No Scrubs" is also my personal favorite TLC hit for the admittedly selfish reason that the song defines the word *scrub* immediately: "A scrub is a guy that thinks he's fly," Chilli advises, "And is also known as a busta." Incredibly helpful. I'm serious. Every pop song that uses slang in the song title should be required, by law, to define the slang term within the first four lines of the song. They should amend the Constitution. Call it the Scrubs Doctrine. It also helps that as Chilli defines this term, she is swinging on that giant white swing on the giant spaceship in which the "No Scrubs" video is set, a futuristic vision that defines, for me, the best-case-scenario for 1999's vision of the 21st century. We get a new dance to learn; we get a fascinating new Kubrick-does-*Barbarella* visual tableau to associate with another fantastic hit song for the rest of our lives.

Lisa Lopes died in a car crash in Honduras on April 25, 2002; the 21st century is so much emptier without her in it, without TLC at full power guiding it. When VH1 premiered the biopic *Crazy-SexyCool* in 2013, it was the highest-rated cable movie of the year, and VH1's highest-rated program ever, and that's partly due to the prurient thrill of watching rapper-actress Lil Mama as she fully embodies Left Eye and dumps a bunch of shoes that suspiciously aren't her size into Movie Andre Rison's bathtub and lights them on fire. But in summer 1994, that fire started out as one of those occasional celebrity scandals that play out in real time almost as slapstick tabloid comedy, just something for CNN and MTV News to chuckle about and dismiss as *crazy pop star does crazy thing* without much concern for *why* she might have done it.

Which brings to mind Sinéad O'Connor's own brush with harrowing tabloid infamy, and over far less destructive an incident. All *she* did was tear up a photo. Of the pope. On *Saturday Night Live*.

IT'S ALMOST EMBARRASSING NOW to admit how *astounded* I was by the video for Sinéad O'Connor's "Nothing Compares 2 U" in 1990. There's scrub 12-year-old me gawking at the unflinching close-ups of this self-possessed Irish woman with the shaved head and the black turtleneck and the tears rolling down her cheeks. And she's just *singing*: no explosions, no quick cuts, none of that hyperactive "MTV-style editing" everybody was always complaining about. Just the stillness, the gravity, the gorgeous *severity* of it. How many televisions did I see blow up on MTV during the first 10 years of MTV? How many dudes in tight pants trying to *shock* me? But none of those dudes shocked me half as much as her palpable contempt as she sang about the doctor whose big advice was, "Girl you better try to have fun no matter what you do."

Per her brutal 2021 memoir *Rememberings*, Sinéad shaved her head before the release of her debut album, 1987's *The Lion and the Cobra*, after her label handlers told her to "stop cutting my hair short and start dressing like a girl." She accused them of trying to make her look like their mistresses; the Greek barber who shaved her head cried. The label also didn't like the way Sinéad looked on the cover of *The Lion and the Cobra*, her head of course freshly shaved, her mouth wide open. They thought she looked angry, like she was screaming. But she insists she wasn't: She's just singing. That's just the way it looks when she sings. Sinéad O'Connor is "Hey man, fuck you" incarnate.

Enter Prince. "Nothing Compares 2 U" is a Prince song in the sense that he wrote it, and first recorded it himself in 1984, and first released it with his side project the Family in '85, enlisting his protégé Paul "St. Paul" Peterson to sing the hell out of it. But really, "Nothing Compares 2 U" *was* a Prince song; Sinéad made it a Sinéad O'Connor song the moment she sang it. And this is her greatest act of defiance, of confrontation, of self-possession. This is a hostile takeover. She embodies this song on a molecular level. She changes the fundamental meaning of the song. She steals this song. She *owns* this song now. Just the *audacity* of that. The greatness and the fearlessness that requires. Sinéad O'Connor saying, "I'm gonna steal a song from Prince" is like Nicolas Cage saying, "I'm gonna steal the Declaration of Independence." But that's what she did.

The song hit No. 1 on the *Billboard* Hot 100 pop chart the same week its parent album, 1990's *I Do Not Want What I Haven't Got*, hit No. 1 on the album chart. She cried when she got the news, and not tears of happiness. Another great song on that album is the faster, poppier "The Emperor's New Clothes," which vibrates with boy-kicking energy: "Maybe it sounds mean," she sings. "But I really don't think so." Fantastic. "You asked for the truth," she adds, "And I told you."

In *Rememberings*, Sinéad tells a lengthy, bizarre, upsetting story

71

about a confrontation between her and Prince roughly nine months after "Nothing Compares 2 U" topped the charts. She is summoned to his place in L.A. He tells her to stop using foul language in her interviews. She tells him he can fuck himself. He tries to make her eat soup. She refuses. He proposes a pillow fight; he's clearly got some sort of heavy object stuffed in the pillowcase. She runs out the front door. He chases her. It's nighttime, she's alone, she has no idea where she is, she has no way to get back to her own place other than to run. She runs into the woods. Eventually she makes it to a road, but then Prince shows up driving a car, and gets out, and they chase each other for a brief spell, and then she runs to a nearby house and rings the doorbell frantically, and finally he drives off. She concludes, "I never want to see that devil again."

I can't tell you how to feel about any of this. I can't tell you how it should change the way you feel about him, or about her, or about this song. There is no true, clean, definitive way to Separate the Art from the Artist. Art fully separated from the artist ceases, in a fundamental way, to be art at all. The artist gives the art *meaning*. I'm the sort of guy inclined to tear up, even now, just typing the words, "Prince died of an accidental fentanyl overdose on April 16, 2016." I can mourn the artist. I can mourn the person, to the extent you can mourn a person you never met. But I can also mourn my naïve, saintly image of that person, when I'm given yet more compelling evidence that being one of the Greatest Artists of Your Generation does not automatically make you one of the Greatest Humans of Your Generation.

In 1992, for her second song as the musical guest during her second appearance on *Saturday Night Live*, Sinéad O'Connor sang

Bob Marley's "War" a cappella, and after singing the last line—"We have confidence in the victory of good over evil"—she tore up a picture of Pope John Paul II and yelled, "Fight the real enemy." *Her mother's* photo of Pope John Paul II, as it turns out. The photo Sinéad pulled off her mother's bedroom wall on the day her mother died. She did this to protest child abuse within the Catholic church. However you feel about this—maybe *especially* if it upsets you—this was, inarguably, the single most punk rock gesture of the 1990s. In her book she writes about going back to her hotel afterward and turning on the TV. "The matter is being discussed on the news and we learn I am banned from NBC for life," she writes. "This hurts me a lot less than rapes hurt those Irish children."

You asked for the truth, and she told you.

Another confrontational pop star, another prominent stage, another poorly received truth we asked for and need to hear: Yes, there is Fiona Apple, accepting Best New Artist in a Video at the 1997 MTV Video Music Awards, declaring that "this world is bullshit." She quickly adds that "you shouldn't model your life about what you think that we think is cool and what we're wearing and what we're saying and everything. Go with yourself. Go with yourself." But mostly everyone just remembers the bullshit part.

I don't recommend rewatching the "Criminal" video now. As you may recall, it's just Fiona Apple—NYC native, piano prodigy, jazz aficionado, hip-hop fan, wounding singer-songwriter, and architect of the sweltering 1996 debut album *Tidal*— writhing and scowling and sulking and semi-flirting amid faceless, passed-out heroin-chic models. This isn't a moral objection or anything. It's just that nowadays the "Criminal" video plays like the Joker directing an Abercrombie & Fitch ad, and the hell with it. (The video's actual director, Mark Romanek, also made the video for Johnny Cash's cover of "Hurt" that makes me cry every time I watch it, so overall he's totally cool with me.) I am exhausted by the rhetorical labyrinth of whether this clip is exploiting then-19-year-old Fiona Apple or if it's a shrewd satire of the world's attempt to exploit Fiona Apple.

In 1997, Fiona joined the inaugural lineup of Lilith Fair, the all-female-artist summer festival created by Canadian star Sarah McLachlan, who headlined along with a rotating crew that included Sheryl Crow, Tracy Chapman, Jewel, Paula Cole, and Lisa Loeb; 1998's lineup included Sinéad O'Connor, Erykah Badu, Missy Elliott, Bonnie Raitt, and Liz Phair. To my mind, McLachlan's 1993 hit "Possession"—a spectral, driving rock song inspired by disturbing letters she'd received from a stalker who then tried to sue her for quoting him—sets the tone for Fiona's work, specifically the issue of songs as therapy, and songs as weaponry. Songs you write that are then used to attack you; songs that you then write to defend yourself against the attacks triggered by your earlier songs. This problem of mistaken intent. Of misunderstanding. Of misappropriation. The first way Fiona Apple tried to fight back against it all was by singing searingly unmistakable words as forcefully as possible.

And so there's Fiona thundering, "I have never been so insulted in all my life" on the *Tidal* single "Sleep to Dream," yet another thrilling evisceration of yet another crap dude. But "Criminal" was the clear breakout moment: the percussive clatter, the accelerated pace amid *Tidal*'s myriad unearthly ballads, and the thrilling cliff dive of the song's bridge when she howls, "What would an angel say? / The devil wants to know." But "Criminal" the phenomenal song had to constantly contend with "Criminal" the controversial video, and Fiona Apple the songwriter had to constantly contend with Fiona Apple the blunt and unfiltered interview subject who'd tell you the truth if you asked her.

Fiona, too, wrote about her experience with rape; in a 1998 *Rolling Stone* cover story, her description of that experience spans six, seven, eight paragraphs of vivid and unsettling detail, down to the number of locks on her apartment door. Her conclusion: "I thought that ultimately, no matter what happens, if I lie about this, I don't like what that says." And she brought that commitment to the truth to every conversation, about anything, with anyone, even if it hurt her, even if she was wildly misconstrued at every turn, even if it depleted and exhausted her to know that everyone was listening to her, not to mention leering at her.

"If you want to see me cry, come to a photo shoot," she told *SPIN* magazine in 1997. "They treat me like I'm a hotel room; they make a mess, and then they just leave it." That'd be the *SPIN* cover story with the headline "Fiona Apple: She's Been a Bad, Bad Girl." Also, this is "The Girl Issue," which includes "Alanis, Ani, Gwen, Xena, Chloe, Chelsea, Daria, the WNBA, & many more." Also, this is the infamous *SPIN* story that leaves Fiona feeling so misinterpreted and sensationalized that she writes a poem about it and uses that poem as the title of her next album, which is, indeed, called (yes, this is happening): *When the Pawn Hits the Conflicts He Thinks Like a King What He Knows Throws the Blows When He Goes to the Fight and He'll Win the Whole Thing 'fore He Enters the Ring There's No Body to Batter When Your Mind Is Your Might So When You Go Solo, You Hold Your Own Hand and Remember That Depth Is the*

Greatest of Heights and If You Know Where You Stand, Then You Know Where to Land and If You Fall It Won't Matter, Cuz You'll Know That You're Right. The Women in Rock cycle continues. It is *I have never felt so insulted in all my life* in perpetuity.

One last bombastic young star, one last necessary truth, one last phenomenal jump-scare chorus: "If it makes you happy / It can't be that bad." Merely typing out the words to the chorus does not do the chorus, or the song, or Sheryl Crow justice. I remember my first time hearing "If It Makes You Happy," the slow-burn arena-caliber exorcism from her self-titled 1996 sophomore album; I remember the electrifying rasp of her voice when that chorus hits, a terrifying burst of pure, righteous, gnarly vocal firepower that once again was not expected by 18-year-old me.

How does this fantastic shit keep sneaking up on me like this? This song is yet another of the 12 billion songs with Deceptively Quiet Verses and Incredibly Loud Choruses, and on first contact, I totally saw the chorus coming, right? I *had* to have seen it coming. And yet the rapturous shotgun blast of Sheryl wailing, "IF IT MAKES YOU HAPPY" laid me out on the floor, laid me out on the *ceiling.* I have read tens of thousands of words about this person, including the *Rolling Stone* feature with the cover line "Sheryl Crow: Why the Hell Is She So Sad?" And I have watched her, too, navigate the absurdist gauntlet of fame and too much attention and wanton misinterpretation, and Women in/of Rock compartmentalization. But her greatness, her *necessity* was never more apparent to me than when she rhymed *bad* with *sad.* Once again, in the snarky-rock-critic section of my brain, I briefly wondered if there were a clever-er way to put it, and once again I quickly realized that *clever-er* is neither the goal in songwriting nor in rock criticism nor in life, and once again I succumbed to a truly phenomenal song that truly shocked me and sent me tumbling once again down Badass Condescension Mountain, another well-meaning but wayward boy who needed, once again, to be kicked.

VIVID GEOGRAPHY, OR, EVERYBODY HATES A TOURIST

SONGS DISCUSSED:

Wu-Tang Clan, "C.R.E.A.M."
Mobb Deep, "Shook Ones, Pt. II"
Nas, "N.Y. State of Mind"
Pulp, "Common People"
Björk, "Hyperballad"
Missy Elliott, "The Rain (Supa Dupa Fly)"
Outkast, "Elevators (Me & You)"
Juvenile, "Back That Azz Up"
Jane's Addiction, "Been Caught Stealing"
Soundgarden, "Black Hole Sun"
Luniz, "I Got 5 on It"

Y OU'RE A WIDE-EYED TEENAGER. You live
wherever you live. Your allowance (or your minimum-
wage job, or whatever) rules everything around you. It's
the winter of 1993 bleeding into '94. You are informed—by a magazine, by *Yo! MTV Raps*, by the coolest kid in your homeroom—that
the coolest record you could possibly listen to is *Enter the Wu-Tang
(36 Chambers)* by the Wu-Tang Clan, a sprawling Staten Island
crew consisting of (as one song's intro informs you) "the RZA, the
GZA, Ol' Dirty Bastard, Inspectah Deck, Raekwon the Chef,
U-God, Ghostface Killah, and Method Man." (Plus Masta Killa
and, eventually, Cappadonna.) This is a pleasantly chaotic series of
words, numbers, aliases, and parentheses that you most likely do
not understand. But that chaos, that confusion, only makes it all
sound cooler.

So you scrounge up the cash and buy the thing, and you spend
45 minutes just staring at the eerie faceless dudes on the cover,
and when you finally put the record on, the first words you hear—
"Shaolin shadowboxing! And the Wu-Tang sword style!"—are
sampled from a 1983 Hong Kong grindhouse flick called *Shaolin and Wu Tang* that you most likely haven't seen. But the music
sounds as grimy and exquisitely gloomy and elegantly ultraviolent
as you imagine that movie looks, and suddenly nearly a dozen dis-
parate voices—rappers, combatants, vibrant personalities, *stars*—
are all fighting for oxygen, for your attention, for your adoration.

"Bring Da Ruckus." "Wu-Tang Clan Ain't Nuthing ta F' Wit."
"Protect Ya Neck." "Method Man," the song. Method Man, the
human. It's overwhelming, it's aggressive, it's filthy, it's blunt, it's

vicious, it's exuberant, it's winter all the time, it's electrifying, it's baffling, it's *fun*. And it's arguably more fun the more baffled you are, and the overall relentless frigidity sounds colder the warmer you are, the more *comfortable* you are.

And then there's "C.R.E.A.M.," which you are quickly informed is an acronym for "Cash Rules Everything Around Me," a blunt but legitimately beautiful song in which these guys tell you where they're from, and what it's like where they're from, and what it's like for them to know how clueless you might be about where they're from. And what they really want you to know is that whatever your age or location or circumstances, the less cash you have, the more it rules everything around you.

The Wu-Tang Clan are one of the biggest rap groups in history, and the Wu-Tang *logo*, that superheroic black-and-yellow W, is one of the best logos in history, full stop. And once *Enter the Wu-Tang* blew up, that logo was everywhere: scrawled on notebooks, carved into school desks, and emblazoned on, like, 10 billion T-shirts. But prior to "C.R.E.A.M.," a goodly percentage of the fans who'd soon be wearing those T-shirts—a lotta suburban teenagers, for starters—had no idea what winter in Staten Island was like for a young, poor, Black person. This disconnect between artist and fan got to be a huge problem for the group, and maybe for all of rap music the more popular, the more *dominant* the genre became. Not everybody got the point[*] right away.

---

[*] For example, I initially thought of *Enter the Wu-Tang* as a collection of excellent outgoing answering-machine messages, including the one right after "C.R.E.A.M." where Raekwon and Method Man jovially compare methods of torture: "Yeah, I'll fuckin' lay your nuts on the fuckin' dresser, just your nuts layin' on the fuckin' dresser, and bang them shits with a spike fuckin' bat. Wussuh: BLAOOW". *Beep*. Hilarious. Absolutely hilarious.

In his 2009 book *The Tao of Wu*, the RZA—the Wu-Tang Clan's spiritual leader, primary producer, and fearless cat-herder—writes about how crucial it was, when the Wu-Tang Clan formed, that Staten Island was a physical island. "When you watch a movie like *Godzilla*, you see them go out to one of these tiny remote islands and find Mothra," he explains. "It was the same way with us. A nine-man hip-hop crew based on Mathematics, chess, comics, and kung-fu flicks wasn't springing up in the middle of a Manhattan art scene.* Only on a remote island can something like King Kong grow to his full capacity." He also advises everyone to "find an island in this life" (which is almost a beer slogan) and "turn off the electromagnetic waves being forced up on you" (which is not).

The sample RZA built "C.R.E.A.M." around—pulled from the opening seconds of an ethereal 1967 soul song called "As Long as I've Got You," written and produced by Isaac Hayes and David Porter, and performed by a Stax Records girl group called the Charmels—has a strikingly ghostly and archaeological quality, less a feat of crate-digging than reverent tomb-raiding. It's eerie, it's gorgeous, it's unforgettable. But the beauty only heightens the pain in Raekwon's voice as he describes growing up poor on "the crime side, the *New York Times* side," and the pain in Inspectah Deck's voice too when uses the word *depressed* twice in two seconds and announces that "Survival got me buggin', but I'm alive on arrival." (The other guys all loved that line.)

---

* RZA, born Robert Fitzgerald Diggs, technically made his big debut under the name Prince Rakeem on the very silly 1991 novelty goof "Ooh I Love You Rakeem," which was a very "Manhattan art scene" idea that badly misread his appeal and potential. Because apparently, even if you lived in *Manhattan* in the early '90s, then Staten Island, which was physically only 20-25 miles away, might as well have been a mountain in China.

VIVID GEOGRAPHY, OR, EVERYBODY HATES A TOURIST

Enter the Wu-Tang famously came out on November 9, 1993, the same day as A Tribe Called Quest's *Midnight Marauders*, a warmer and less combative all-time-classic rap record. Tribe hailed from Queens, and those two records constituted East Coast hip-hop's valiant attempt to strike back against the empire of Dr. Dre's gleaming, white-hot 1992 G-funk monolith *The Chronic*, which conquered the suburbs and threatened to make Compton the new capital of hip-hop. Meanwhile, the Wu-Tang Clan quickly sprawled into its own multiverse of solo stars and all-time-classic solo albums. But following the extra-sprawling triumph of the 1997 all-hands double album *Wu-Tang Forever*, the center has only intermittently held. The group nearly collapsed that year while on tour with the even more suburban-friendly rap-metal behemoths Rage Against the Machine. ("I didn't want to go," Method Man explained in the 2019 Showtime documentary *Wu-Tang Clan: Of Mics and Men*. "'Cause for me, the Black audience was the core, and I seen different guys go over to the white audience and never get to come back and shit, so I was a little scared.") And then, after Old Dirty Bastard's death of a drug overdose in 2004, they'd never quite be whole again. The phase where you've taken over the world feels much different from the phase where you create your own.

But any dissonance between the artists and their audience only heightens the greatness of *Enter the Wu-Tang*, which is full of raucous street-brawl anthems that are also, very much by design, chilly to the point of lethally frigid. They pull you in by detailing, so precisely, how it feels to be shut out in the cold. Per the RZA, "C.R.E.A.M." was recorded four or five times; one of its working titles was "Lifestyles of the Mega Rich," back when nobody involved in the song's creation qualified. The Wu-Tang Clan were

83

imagining their way out; a substantial percentage of their initial fanbase had to imagine its way in. And they know that you know that if you don't know, you don't know.

YOU'RE A WEARY FORTY-SOMETHING parent. You live wherever you live. Wait, okay, sorry: We're talking pretty specifically about me, now. We're talking about the time I spent a whole Memorial Day weekend—sunny and 80 degrees for the most part—listening to Mobb Deep's whole catalog on headphones while chasing my 1-year-old daughter around the bucolic midwestern suburbs. Various sidewalks, various parks, various patriotic heartland tableaus, all soundtracked by stupendously grim, iron-gray, bitter-winter-wind, bullet-ridden Queensbridge crime rap.

Pushing my kid on the swings while listening to Mobb Deep. Watching her trundle through a solid acre of billowing American flags while listening to Mobb Deep. Retrieving various toys and balls from the street while listening to Mobb Deep. She keeps throwing shit in the street. I can't get her to stop throwing shit in the street. *Throw the ball to me, pup. Don't throw it in the street.* And I'm doing the thing where I'm tremendously amused with myself, surrounded by all these other doofy dads who basically look just like me and have no idea that I'm listening to a Mobb Deep album called *Murda Muzik*. Sunny and 80 degrees and I'm listening to a bleak and tempestuous Mobb Deep song called "Quiet Storm." And I feel *dangerous*. And I think, *I am the coolest fuckin' dude in this park.* And then I cringe and feel absolutely ridiculous. The luscious, lethal ominousness of this music pulls me closer just to remind me of how impossibly far I am, in any physical or emotional or existential sense, from the danger itself.

All of which to say I am approaching "Shook Ones, Pt. II"—one of the greatest rap songs of all time—very much from the perspective of a Shook One.

The immortal duo of Prodigy (born Albert Johnson in Hempstead on Long Island) and Havoc (born Kejuan Muchita in Brooklyn) meets at the High School of Art and Design in Manhattan. Specifically, they meet (a) right after a knife fight, which (b) Havoc wins despite (c) not bringing the knife. They both rap in a dead-eyed, piercingly malevolent monotone; depending on what you read, they both stand somewhere between 5-foot-3 and 5-foot-6, which is not intimidating until you think about it for a while and then suddenly it gets super intimidating. They get to talking after the knife fight and decided to start a rap duo called Poetical Prophets, which is a *terrible* name for a crime-rap duo that met at a knife fight.

Pretty soon they change their name to Mobb Deep: much better. In 1993, they put out their debut album, *Juvenile Hell*, which is impressively hellish and understandably juvenile; in the video for the single "Peer Pressure," Prodigy and Havoc are two inexplicably scythe-wielding teenagers roaming the Queensbridge Projects, the largest public housing project in the United States, spanning six blocks, 96 buildings, and more than 3,000 units housing roughly 7,000-plus people. Great song, unnerving video, okay album. *Juvenile Hell* flops. In 1994, their fellow Queensbridge rapper Nas releases his debut album, *Illmatic*, which is universally hailed as an all-time classic to the thorough embarrassment of Mobb Deep. "We refused to be the laughingstock of the 'hood," Prodigy writes in his 2011 memoir *My Infamous Life*. "They were like, 'Look what Nas did, y'all suck.'"

Illmatic endures, of course, as one of the most deified rap records of all time, lithe and lucid, a master class in crystal-clear scene-setting from the rumbling subway train of the first five seconds onward.

Nas himself has never quite topped it, and will always live partly in its shadow, but few shadows emit a warmer, purer, more luxurious light. You ever do the thing, when you're listening to a rap album you listen to a lot, and you're also doing whatever else—you're walking, you're cooking, you're vacuuming, you're chasing the tennis ball your 1-year-old keeps throwing in the street—and it's getting close to your favorite line in your favorite song, and you stop what you're doing and stand perfectly still and filter out all other distractions so you can more purely *receive* your favorite line in your favorite song? I do that with *Illmatic*, on the song "N.Y. State of Mind," at the part where most of DJ Premier's rumbling beat drops out as Nas raps, "Never put me in your box if your shit eats tapes."

If you're going to let somebody else's album embarrass you, let it be *Illmatic*. Mobb Deep are embarrassed. They regroup. For their sophomore record, 1995's *The Infamous*, their hardness and darkness doubles, triples, quadruples. They sound as though they've somehow aged four decades in just two years, and spent that whole period fighting in every war in United States history simultaneously. "I'm only 19," Prodigy raps on "Shook Ones, Pt. II," as you stop whatever you're doing to more purely receive him. "But my mind is old."

Both Prodigy and Havoc (who doubles as the album's main producer) lean into the Queensbridge of it all throughout *The Infamous*, and foreground their alluring bleakness, their malevolence, the savage murmur of their voices. These guys don't sound exactly alike—there's an extra-serrated edge to Prodigy's voice—but they both sound disturbingly *unbothered*. You know in *The Silence of the Lambs*, how Hannibal Lecter's pulse never rises even when he's committing acts of unimaginable violence? "His pulse never got above 85, even when he ate her tongue"? I think about that when

86

VIVID GEOGRAPHY, OR, EVERYBODY HATES A TOURIST

I listen to these guys. How vicious and how calm and how insular and how foreboding they sound. How small their world has gotten, but also how infinite that world feels. Six blocks of Queensbridge are all they need. Even the scythes are extraneous now.

The scythe-free music video for "Shook Ones, Part II" implies that the song's skittering high-hat is actually a sample of a clicking gas-stove burner; Havoc let that rumor circulate for years without shooting it down, reasoning that it only fueled the song's almost mythic sense of place.* The song can freeze the very air you're breathing, freeze time, freeze the very blood your heart is pumping. It can make you want to run through a brick wall; it can make you want to dig your own grave. "For every rhyme I write / It's 25 to life," Havoc raps, shortly before rhyming "no hesitation" with "incarceration" with "You don't know me, there's no relation." And he's almost certainly right.

This song made Mobb Deep for life. Mobb Deep made two more fantastic albums in the '90s: *Hell on Earth* in 1997 and (yes!) *Murda Muzik* in 1999. There's a feud with Tupac. There's a feud with Jay-Z. Prodigy goes solo. "Shook Ones" plays a huge part in Eminem's *8 Mile*. Mobb Deep hook up with 50 Cent for a while. Prodigy goes to jail for a while. Prodigy and Havoc feud on Twitter, in stupendously ugly fashion. Prodigy passes away in 2017, after a nearly lifelong battle with sickle-cell anemia. But it's also so tempting to freeze everything right here with "Shook Ones, Part II," if only because

---

* The song's primary screwed-down piano riff went unidentified for 16 years, until a random dude on a message board traced it to a 1969 Herbie Hancock record called *Fat Albert Rotunda*. This is both a great argument for the internet (you can find out anything!) and an even better argument *against* the internet. (You can drain the mystique out of anything!)

to aficionados of a certain ultra-grimy type of rap music, rap music proudly freezes, forever, right here, with this song. And so do you, whoever you are, and whatever the temperature is wherever you are.

B UT WHAT HAPPENS IF you actively pretend to be someone or something you're not, from somewhere you're not? Disaster, humiliation, and abject failure, though maybe you'll also get to hop in the sack with someone *fascinating*. "You will *never* understand," bellows Pulp frontman Jarvis Cocker, "How it *feels* to live your life / With no *meaning or control*." This is the moment when "Common People," his mega-English band's Britpop anthem and infectious Glastonbury-sized taunt and eternal battle hymn, truly takes flight, or really one of a solid half-dozen times this fuckin' incredible song takes flight. Listen to all five minutes and 51 seconds of "Common People" and you'll end up on the ceiling, on the roof, on the moon. Everywhere but on the dole, assuming you weren't already there.

Jarvis Cocker: okay. He is tall, and lanky, and dignified, and yet visibly louche. He's got the giant glasses. He's got the vaguely pornographic beard, often. He's got the *extremely* pornographic rockstar cheekbones going, in his younger years. He is much smarter than you, or anyway much *wittier* than you, which also makes him much gloomier and more amusingly cynical than you (funny how that works). Jarvis is far from the only important member of Pulp—which he formed, at 15, in Sheffield, England, all the way back in *1978*—but he is the band's avatar and spokesman and frontman, in part because he looks the part, which is to say he looks like the guy who invented the "private browsing" tab.

"Common People" hails from the band's fifth and long-awaited breakout album, 1995's *Different Class*; in brief, it's a song about a posh, rich, sheltered, condescending young Greek woman attempting to slum it with the working class because she thinks working-class people are cooler, and nobler, and more vibrant, and she is right about a lot of that, but she is wrong in believing that this coolness and nobility and vibrance will rub off on her if she slums it with the working class long enough. She enlists our friend Jarvis to help her sleep with common people; his response, in a mockingly casual baritone, is "I'll see what I can do."

Rock critics overuse the word *anthemic* for a living, but it's the only appropriate word here: "Common People" is an all-time anthem about poseurs who haven't earned the right to sing it. The miracle of this song is that it makes the common extraordinary, and makes the mundane miraculous, and makes a debtor's prison feel like a palace, and makes despair feel triumphant, and makes a brutal lack of options feel like total freedom, because for the space of five minutes and 51 seconds, it is. We're stuck with what we've got, and you can't have it, even if you pretend it's all *you've* got.

The other miracle of "Common People" is that Cocker sketches out this universe with so much loving detail—you can taste the rum and Coca-Cola, hear the roaches climbing the wall, feel the chip stains and grease seeping into your skin—that you feel like you're really there even though the whole point of the song is that you can't be there no matter how hard you pretend to be. You're not really there *even if you're there.*

That same sense of exquisite unknowable specificity animates Björk's "Hyperballad," off the mega-Icelandic pop star's 1995 album *Post*, but now it's her total isolation you can't penetrate. This is a battle hymn for one, but she transports you there anyway, *there* in this case being the top of a mountain where Björk lives her with her lover, though every morning she sneaks off alone to throw shit off the mountain—"Like car parts, bottles and cutlery / Or whatever I find lying around"—to blow off steam.

As one does. You can so clearly picture the mega-Icelandic pop star chucking a muffler off a cliff; you can practically hear that muffler hitting the ground far below. (She listens, too, and then imagines it's her body crushed on those rocks instead.) That's all an illusion, of course, but when Björk sings anything, her universe suddenly becomes more real to you than your own.

Seriously, though, that's what "Hyperballad" is about. It's about how in a healthy long-term relationship, you have to treat your lover sweetly but find some outlet for all your wildness and rage. "Because I believe that all people have got both sides," she explained in a 1995 AOL chat (seriously). "So you end up having to unload your aggressions at a bar or by throwing cutlery off cliffs. So you can come back to your loved one, kiss him sweet on his cheek, and say happily, 'Hi honey.'"

This explanation is, quite frankly, Björk as hell. *Post*, her second solo album, is a delicate barrage of trip-hop, big-band jazz, amniotic lullabies, and industrial ferocity, a pleasantly chaotic series of bleeps, thumps, coos, howls, and ecstatic ululations that you perhaps did not, at first, fully understand. But don't let her world-renowned eccentricity blind you to her fundamental humanity. You gotta reconcile two conflicting ideas here: Björk is not of this earth, and yet Björk is very much of this earth. Very few people in history are more of this earth than she is. In my NYC years, I lived in Björk's neighborhood in Brooklyn Heights, but I never would've put it that way at the time: I would've insisted that Björk lived on the moon, or on the rings of Saturn. But this does her a disservice; this is a fundamental misunderstanding of her art. There's a difference between respecting her as an outlandish visionary and dismissing her as some sort of baffling space alien.

That's the needle to thread. As a generator of madcap ideas and highfalutin concepts, she's superhuman, but as a singer of songs, as a fount of emotions, she is *profoundly* human. I heard "Hyperballad" for the very first time as a forlorn 19-year-old college freshman staring forlornly out the third-floor window of my dorm room, and the utter mundanity of that memory is what makes it so precious to me: I was transfixed and *transported* by Björk, and Björk's private stormy mountaintop reverie. "'Cause everybody hates a tourist," leers Jarvis Cocker on "Common People," so I try to minimize that hatred by staying silent, and respectful, and cognizant of what I know I don't know about where I've been taken.

Another woman, another profoundly human galaxy-builder, another mountain, another battle hymn for one. "Beep beep!" declares Missy "Misdemeanor" Elliott. "Who got the keys to the jeep? *Vrooooom.*" And that's all it takes: You're bewildered, delighted, transported, and devoted to her for life. In the mesmerizing Hype Williams video for her 1997 debut single "The Rain (Supa Dupa Fly)," Missy—rapper, songwriter, producer, fashion icon, avant-garde worldbuilder—sits on a nuclear-green hill wearing a green tracksuit, her eyes rolling back into her head, swaying erratically like she's in a hurricane, pawing vacantly at the straight hair of her wig. "We wanted to make fun of the ways record companies try to make Black women look white," is how she explained it to *New Yorker* writer Hilton Als in 1997. "Fake hair, fake music."

The green tracksuit is not her most famous outfit from this

video, of course: That'd be the black blowup vinyl suit concocted by her longtime stylist, June Ambrose. It's a space suit.* It's a super-hero outfit. It's supposed to shock you, maybe even unnerve you. As Missy told *Elle* magazine in 2017, "To me, the outfit was a way to mask my shyness behind all the chaos of the look." Fair enough, but never forget: Astronauts are people, too.

Missy is from Portsmouth, Virginia; she cut her debut album, 1997's *Supa Dupa Fly*, in just two weeks with her childhood friend and budding superproducer Timothy Mosely, a/k/a Timbaland. By summer 1997—with both Tupac Shakur and the Notorious B.I.G. shot and killed within the past year—hip-hop was, if not in a state of crisis, then certainly a prolonged period of mourning and unease. This also created somewhat of a power vacuum, or at least a *star* vacuum. We needed a few new heroes, and the more colorful and flamboyant and relatively peaceful and exuberant those new heroes, the better. Virginia is not quite the South, the way we think of Atlanta or Houston or New Orleans as the South, but it's not quite Puff Daddy's conception of the East Coast either, and thus not quite part of Puff's burgeoning poppy and hyper-commercial Shiny Suit Era, either. Missy found shiny suits too boring. She was her own region. She was her own galaxy.

But what makes *Supa Dupa Fly* so incredible, and so immersive, is that Missy and Timbaland are in their own galaxy *together*, and that galaxy feels alive, it feels *populated*. There are growling dogs, meowing cats, beatboxing chipmunks, whooshing helicopters, and

---

* Not a garbage bag. But, according to Clover Hope's wonderful book *The Mother-lode: 100+ Women Who Made Hip-Hop*, Ambrose had to inflate the suit, with Missy still in it, at a gas station in Queens a block from the soundstage, a lovely collision of the interstellar and the mundane.

most importantly, sonorously chirping crickets that ground "The Rain (Supa Dupa Fly)" in a swampy sumptuousness even as Missy pushes the song airborne, skyward, heavenward. Without Missy's colossal earthbound presence, all these little zoological production touches would feel a little too goofy, too whimsical. But she's a flagrantly three-dimensional figure, and the sound of *Supa Dupa Fly*—part Quiet Storm, part New Jack Swing, part P-Funk, part electro-rap—is outrageous enough that it's tactile, it has a scent, it's *visible*. She merges her galaxy with ours, and she expands our sense of the possible: the what, the who, the how, the where.

THERE WAS A CERTAIN feeling there—and I don't have that feeling no more," lamented André 3000, of the deified Atlanta hip-hop duo Outkast, in 2001. "I wanna have that nostalgic feeling of how the Dungeon smelled, the way certain beats made you feel. It smelled like dirt, like a mildewy basement when it rains. Crickets."

He is referring to the south Atlanta headquarters of the sprawling hip-hop collective known as the Dungeon Family, who in the early '90s built a home studio in the basement of producer Rico Wade's mother's house.* A crawlspace under the kitchen. Dirt floor. Red clay walls. Pipes over your head. The moisture in the air fucked with the drum machines. It was rough. It was perfect. You go down there, you make music all night, you never come out. Hence: the Dungeon. Hence: the Dungeon Family. And this is where André and Antwan

---

* Wade is part of the epochal production trio Organized Noize: He's the big-picture guy, Ray Murray's the rap guy, and Sleepy Brown's the hook-singing R&B guy. If Sleepy Brown has any acting talent/ambition at all, he should win an Oscar someday for playing the lead in a Curtis Mayfield biopic.

"Big Boi" Patton, who as teenagers chose the name Outkast because *Misfits* was already taken, launched their spectacular charm offensive, further redefining what globally dominant rap music could look and sound like, and where it could come from.

The crickets, and the dirt, and the moisture in the air are all palpable on Outkast's 1994 debut, the triumphantly self-explanatory *Southernplayalisticadillacmuzik.* That record famously resulted in Outkast winning New Artist of the Year—Group at the infamously combative 1995 Source Awards in New York City, where André and Big Boi were infamously booed by the close-minded hometown crowd, and André, in defiant response, famously announced, "The South got somethin' to say." Even if you've heard that story 10,000 times already, you really oughta hop on YouTube to revisit that fiasco every so often just to hear *him* say it. The whole point of what the South has to say is that I, for one, can't say *The South* the way he says it.

And then Outkast called their next album *ATLiens*, released in 1996 and perfectly encapsulating their Georgia-as-outer-space ethos with the phenomenally eerie "Elevators (Me & You)," in which every little detail matters. The deep echo of the rimshots. The eerie little organ and chilly dub bass. The dial tones or elevator beeps or space-shuttle warning sirens or whatever reverberating out into nothingness. *ATLiens* is only the second of the group's four or five or six straight masterpieces, but that's the record, and "Elevators (Me & You)" is the song, that sums up Outkast's singular combination of south Atlanta basement grit and cosmic genius.

It's fun to pretend that these guys came out of nowhere—that they really were deviants, pariahs, aliens. But what's truly miraculous to me about Outkast is that they so obviously *came from somewhere*. Somewhere tangible and recognizable. They came from somewhere a lot of other people came from.* They heard, and loved, music that a lot of other people heard and loved. But then, miraculously, André and Big Boi built, out of that familiarity, another intoxicatingly unfamiliar universe. Something extraordinary, something *extraterrestrial.* Identifiable origins, supernatural destinations.

New Orleans, to the hapless tourist, carries that same sense of daunting otherworldliness.

With apologies to *Saving Private Ryan* or *Fargo* or *Ace Ventura: Pet Detective* or whatever, the best cinematography of the 1990s can be found in the first 10 seconds of the "Back That Azz Up" video: the two dudes (one in a wheelchair) playing violins in the middle of the street, the huge trees looming overhead with sunlight poking through the leaves, and the whole scene tinted the stately gunmetal-green color of dollar bills that have perhaps been thrown at a few strip-club stages in their time. And then we behold Terius Gray, a/k/a Juvenile, New Orleans rapper/ambassador extraordinaire, commanding the same spot, emerging from a cloud of smoke, as though he's a force of nature, as though the very atmosphere of his city manifested him.

Raised in the Magnolia Projects in the city's 11th Ward, Juvenile started out as a brash, underage shit-talking rapper with a malevolent but mellifluous voice: Get a load of him at 17 years old on hometown pioneer DJ Jimi's local 1993 hit "Bounce for the Juvenile," leading a chant of "Where the virgins at?" and then somehow

---

* In 1992, for example, the serene Atlanta-based rap crew Arrested Development had a monster crossover hit called "Tennessee." If you set foot on a college campus in the mid-'90s, you definitely heard it, or, more accurately, if you heard the song "Tennessee" in the mid-'90s, a college campus would spontaneously erupt around you.

turning a young lady's Popeye's order (three-piece white, small fries, red beans, biscuit, small drink) into a deliriously vicious insult.

He, uh, honed his craft from there, and indeed, in 1998, on his fantastic third solo album, *400 Degreez*, Juvenile gifted the world with an all-universe anthem called "Back That Azz Up." Specifically, it is the Strip-Club National Anthem. The Awkward Moment at Your Cousin's Wedding National Anthem. The Got a Detention at My Junior High After-School Dance National Anthem. The "Ma'am, I'm Gonna Have to Ask You to Leave" National Anthem. But it's also one of the seemingly dozens of foundational New Orleans National Anthems, this one produced by local god Mannie Fresh (who also raps a little, as does a 16-year-old prodigy named Lil Wayne) and emblematic of the lewd greatness of bounce music, in which a xylophone riff from New York City (swiped from "Drag Rap," a/k/a "Triggerman," a 1986 track from a Queens group called the Showboys) collided with a minimal breakbeat from San Francisco (swiped from "Brown Beats," a 1987 track by revered Bay Area DJ Cameron Paul) and produced a beat infectious and durable enough to power a whole-ass subgenre down in Louisiana.

By the mid-'90s, Mannie Fresh was the in-house producer for New Orleans monolith Cash Money Records, which ruled the city rap-wise alongside Master P's No Limit empire. The rapper and Master P affiliate Mia X tells really lovely and idyllic stories about growing up with Mannie Fresh in the 7th Ward: the way the streetlights came on at night, the smell of ammonia and bleach from mothers scrubbing their front porches. Mannie Fresh, steeped in the city's singularly dazzling panoply of sensory detail, was instrumental in helping New Orleans bounce music invade the whole entire world without sacrificing its inherent ultra-regional weirdness, its lewdness, its greatness. He made drum machines sound like miniature second-line parades. He made live instrumentation—real drums, real keyboards—sound truly live. He made New Orleans swagger palpable. He made New Orleans *sweat* palpable. You can *smell* the sweat. You can smell the bleach. You can feel the electricity that turns those streetlights on.

And then Juvenile jumps on "Back That Azz Up" and raps every last line—"Girl you working with some ass, yeah / You're bad, yeah"—like it's the chorus, like it's the best chorus ever written, like every last word should be etched onto your family's coat of arms. "It's the song that I didn't think would make it because it's bounce music," he told *Complex* in 2012. "I didn't think people in New York and L.A.—people that weren't from my area or are used to this kind of music—would like it. It just blew up. I was shocked." But not as shocked as your grandparents will be when this song comes on at your next family reunion.

A S A TREMBLING TEENAGER I dreamt, uneasily, of Los Angeles. I don't usually subscribe to the You Had to Be There philosophy of rock 'n' roll history, where a band's true appeal is fundamentally unknowable if you weren't a young person living in the band's hometown at the precise moment the band blew up. But I do suspect that the mid-'80s L.A. of it all—Black Flag, X, the Go-Go's, the Minutemen, Fishbone, Mötley Crüe, and pre-empire Red Hot Chili Peppers—means a great deal to the glam-turned-alternative legacy of Jane's Addiction, who were genuinely *frightening* to me in the early '90s, hence all the trembling.

Grimy and regal frontman Perry Farrell was born in Queens, and he still sounds like it; at 17 he ran away to California "with a surfboard, some art supplies, an ounce of weed, and one phone number," and he still looks like it. He formed Jane's Addiction in 1985, and they played a bunch of rad L.A. clubs with names that definitely mean something to you if you lived in L.A. at the time, and they didn't get kicked out of all of them. "As long as I could whip out my dick," he explained of his performing philosophy at the time, "I knew I was alive."

But somehow, by 1990, Perry's voice—the piercing, whining, slurring, slicing libidinousness of it—was the single most obscene element on midwestern rock radio. Usually the Jane's Addiction song on the radio was either the lovely, acoustic "Jane Says" or the goofy, ramshackle "Been Caught Stealing," but regardless, Perry sounded like if a Parental Advisory sticker could sing. "Been Caught Stealing," from the introductory barking dogs and the rubbery cartoon bassline on down, is a goofy outlier in a catalog that otherwise exactly splits the difference between absurd '80s hair-metal sleaze (shout-out lead guitarist Dave Navarro, a magnificent shredder and prime example of the "Live Más" mentality) and steely '90s alternative-rock crunch; I've always imagined this band as a Trojan Horse for both the proud subversion and the shameless commodification of the imminent MTV Buzz Bin generation, but I can't work out what the Trojan Horse looks like on the outside versus what's hiding on the inside, if that makes any sense. I've lost track of what's the subversive part and what's the commodified part.

Maybe the commodification is the subversive part—you ever think of that? Regardless, Jane's Addiction scared the hell out of me. The cracked supermarket sweep of the "Been Caught Stealing" video scared me, the porno-clown grandeur of Perry's voice scared me, and the Lollapalooza Tour—launched by Farrell as a traveling summer festival in '91 to both promote his band and spread the

Alternative Nation gospel o'er the land—scared me most of all. I found it all a little too *subcultural*, maybe. But then the subculture became just normal, dominant, above-ground culture, and Mötley Crüe gave way to Nirvana, and the funky '80s Red Hot Chili Peppers gave way to the soulfully funky '90s Red Hot Chili Peppers, who headlined Lollapalooza 1992 along with Pearl Jam and Soundgarden, and I spent the next 10 years or so as a trembling teenager dreaming, desperately, of Seattle.

I wore the ratty flannel shirts. I wore the ratty T-shirts underneath the flannel shirts. I watched the videos for "Smells Like Teen Spirit" and "Jeremy" and "Down in a Hole" 10 million times apiece. I bought the CDs those songs came from and listened to 'em in full 20 million times apiece. I rented the Seattle-deifying 1992 Cameron Crowe romcom *Singles* from Blockbuster. And I deified Seattle in turn: It was the coolest, loudest, and greatest city on earth, even if Nirvana were really from Aberdeen. But the closest I could get to the hallowed Pacific Northwest was to put on Soundgarden's 1994 monolith *Superunknown* again and thrash around to "Spoonman," mope around to "Fell on Black Days," grunt along to "Mailman," thrash-mope-grunt along to "The Day I Tried to Live," and bask in the malignant psychedelic glory of "Black Hole Sun," which inspired a trippy and discomfiting video that *really* scared me.

But I watched the "Black Hole Sun" video 10 million times anyway, because of the colossal snarling beauty of frontman Chris Cornell, because of lead guitarist Kim Thayil's thrashing Live Más solo, and because I wanted to be bassist Ben Shepherd when I grew up, all pummeling low-end, all cool alternate tunings, all magnetic contempt. As a trembling teenager too skittish to actually *attend* Lollapalooza, I worshiped Soundgarden, and by proxy Seattle, from

2,400 miles and a dozen cultural epochs away. I could never wail like Chris, or shred like Kim, or radiate contempt like Ben, but I vicariously stood alongside them anyway, shoulder to shoulder, at all the rad Seattle clubs with names that definitely mean something to you if you lived there at the time.

And then about a decade later, in 2003, as a professional rock critic and only slightly less tremulous adult, I moved to Oakland, California, and quickly acquainted myself with the Luniz logo, which is not quite as famous as the Wu-Tang Clan logo, though it is, to its credit, way grosser.

Luniz are an Oakland hip-hop duo consisting of the rappers Yukmouth and Numskull; the Luniz logo is a walking condom. Or a standing condom. The condom has a face: The condom is meanmugging you, essentially. In subsequent iterations the condom often wears an eyepatch, to better echo the Oakland Raiders logo; the condom is holding a handgun in one hand and a beverage of some sort in the other. I don't want to speculate. Also: okay. The tip of the condom is the head, obviously, and so it's open at the bottom, and gushing out of the condom—it's a *used* condom, okay? I'm trying to be delicate here. The condom is wearing Air Maxes and standing in a substantial white puddle of its own creation. How do you even clean that? Don't answer that. It's *gross*, alright? It's striking. It's effective.

Now imagine yourself walking down bustling Telegraph Avenue in Oakland, and you are accosted by an armed condom standing in a white puddle. Imagine the reaction—the *series* of reactions you would have to this. You'd be like, *Oh shit.* And then you'd be like, *What the fuck?* And then you'd be like, *Wow, that's hilarious.* And then you'd be like, *Eeeeeugh.* And then you'd be like, *That's awesome, actually.* And that's what it's like to listen to Bay Area rap.

VIVID GEOGRAPHY, OR, EVERYBODY HATES A TOURIST

"I Got 5 on It," which appears on Luniz's 1995 debut album *Oper-ation Stackola* and features an indelibly bellowed hook from San Francisco R&B king Michael Marshall, is arguably the greatest Bay Area rap song of all time. Or the *biggest* Bay Area rap song of all time. Or the greatest weed-rap song of all time, from *anywhere*. Or all three of those. Whatever the case, I evoke it here as a Trojan Horse for the whole of '90s Bay Area rap, because it is fantastic, and deliriously weird, and quite striking, and/or menacing, and/or surreal, and/or alarmingly beautiful. The dulcet obscenity of Too $hort, the daffy lingo of E-40, the delightful "Humpty Dance" hey-day of Digital Underground, the confounding magnetism of Mac Dre, Keak Da Sneak, Suga-T, Andre Nickatina, Spice 1, Latyrx, the Conscious Daughters, Souls of Mischief, and a few hundred oth-ers. I spent three years in Oakland* driving wide-eyed around Lake Merritt and listening to shit this weird and wonderful *on the radio*. I couldn't believe it. I still can't. That music, in that three-year period, was as close as I ever felt, musically, to where I was physically.

Of course, I was never truly *living* this music or its deliriously weird lingo. I was not riding sideways. I was not ghost-riding the whip. I was not personally acquainted with the thizz face. I never had 5 on it even once, not really. I was just another dopey kid along for the ride, feeling electrified, feeling grateful, feeling infinite. I knew what I didn't know. I wasn't really there even when I was there. But I was physically *there* enough that I could lean forward and turn the car radio up. So that's what I did.

---

* I also caught a reunited Jane's Addiction headlining Lollapalooza at a South Bay amphitheater, finally fully reveling in the geographical majesty of songs called "Ocean Size" and "Mountain Song" and "Summertime Rolls," and I thought to myself, *So this is what California is like.*

VILLAINS + ADVERSARIES

SONGS DISCUSSED:

Third Eye Blind, "Semi-Charmed Life"
Oasis, "Wonderwall"
Blur, "Song 2"
A Tribe Called Quest, "Check the Rhime"
Pavement, "Range Life"
Smashing Pumpkins, "Cherub Rock"
Limp Bizkit, "Nookie"
Offspring, "Pretty Fly (For a White Guy)"
DMX, "Ruff Ryder's Anthem"
Brandy + Monica, "The Boy Is Mine"

AND NOW, a few words on Third Eye Blind frontman Stephan Jenkins, from some of the people who know him best but wish they didn't.

"Stephan Jenkins is a total megalomaniac freak. He's so narcissistic that he's not really capable of rational thought."
—Kevin Cadogan, former lead guitarist and Stephan Jenkins bandmate, Third Eye Blind (*SPIN* magazine, June 2000)

"There's a few bands that we just don't like touring with. Your Third Eye Blinds of the world. I wouldn't go near Stephan Jenkins and that band. The guy's a douchebag. You know? You can put that on camera. 'Cause I really don't care. But he is. He's not a good person. That's all I'll say about that."
—Steve Harwell, frontman, Smash Mouth (Interview with *South Florida Insider*, 2010)

"Stephan Jenkins is such a fucking creepy douchebag (I feel so much better now)."
—Zach Lind, drummer, Jimmy Eat World (Twitter, August 2019)

"He made fun of me. Called me a fat guy. Screw you! He has no soul whatsoever. He and his band got into a fight once

because he wanted to put just his picture on their T-shirt. I just think, *You are walking, breathing, living cheese!*"
——Rob Thomas, frontman, Matchbox 20 (*SPIN*,
January 1999)

"I don't hate him, I just don't like him. He has no soul. He's really just a cock."
——Rob Thomas, Matchbox 20 frontman and also now the immortal singer of Santana's "Smooth" (*Rolling Stone*, 2009, *10 years after the Walking Cheese thing*)

"I was hip to Stephan's bullshit a long time ago. I wanted to have a career in music for the rest of my life and I knew if I was associated with that guy, I would not be allowed to do so. He was the inspiration for a lot of the songs on this record. The song 'Somebody Hates You' is entirely about him."
——Jason Slater, former bassist and Stephan Jenkins band-mate, Third Eye Blind, talking up his new band, Snake River Conspiracy (*San Francisco Chronicle*, July 2000)

"Stephan Jenkins has caused a lot of misery in his lifetime. He's a net negative as a person."
——John Vanderslice, San Francisco singer-songwriter and producer (the *Onion A/V Club*, June 2013)

"After the Third Eye Blind guy told me he fucked my girl-friend he told me I was 'A wordsmith like Jim Morrison.'"
——Max Collins, frontman, Eve 6 (Twitter, December 2020)

What's the deal here? Why do so many people hate Stephan Jenkins? To what do we owe the world's displeasure? Lotsa megalomaniac walking-cheese douchebag rock stars in the world. What makes this guy special? What makes this guy the great unifier? I suppose you'd have to start with what makes him great.

Let me clarify immediately that "Semi-Charmed Life," the runaway hit from Third Eye Blind's self-titled 1997 debut album, is awesome. It's catchy, it's gritty, it's subversive, it's ridiculous, it's incandescent, and it forced pop radio to unartfully censor the words *crystal meth*. I heard this song for the first time on midwestern college radio in 1997—I was *oblivious*, and *I was the DJ*. So I'm standing in the DJ booth, and my friend Maya walks in and tells me to play this song I'd never heard of called "Semi-Charmed Life," and I do, and Maya starts *dancing*, immediately, when that guitar riff kicks in. I spent four years basically *living* in my college-radio DJ booth, and this is the one and only time I can recall anybody dancing in it. And I'm just bewildered, dumbfounded, stupefied, and filled with a profound grudging respect for whatever the deal is here.

Quick overview of major guitar-rock bands in 1997: Pretty much nobody wants to be a major guitar-rock band in 1997. Or, nobody wants to *only* be a guitar-rock band. You got Radiohead's *OK Computer*: fewer guitars, more ennui. You got U2's *Pop*: fewer guitars, more irony. You got *Be Here Now* by Oasis: same amount of guitars, more helicopters. You got the Foo Fighters if you're still obsessed with "alternative rock," and Built to Spill if you're getting into "indie rock," and the Verve if you're sticking with Britpop. But the big whoop with rock critics is "electronica," and the theory anyway is that the new rock stars are the Chemical Brothers, or the Crystal Method, or the Prodigy. Rock is dead. Again. For real this time. All of which to say that the most subversive part of "Semi-Charmed Life" isn't the oral sex or the crystal meth: It's a bunch of grown men from San Francisco with shiny guitars singing, *Doot doot doot, doot doot doot doo.* That and Stephan's walking-cheeseball falsetto when he declares, "Not listening when you say / *Good-byyyyye.*"

Quick overview of Stephan Jenkins: Born in Indio, California; grows up in Palo Alto. High school yearbook quote: "Success: All it takes is all you've got." Forms the frat-rap duo Puck and Natty (Shakespeare reference), who land a doofy song called "Just Wanna Be Your Friend" on a *Beverly Hills 90210* soundtrack in 1992. Forms Third Eye Blind (it's ironic) in San Francisco. Classic original lineup: Stephan Jenkins on vocals and guitar; Kevin Cadogan (yeah, that guy) on lead guitar; Arion Salazar on bass; and Brad Hargreaves on drums. *Third Eye Blind* comes out in 1997 and kicks major ass, with 13 songs spanning from pretty good to fuckin' stupendous, *and then also "Semi-Charmed Life."*

We're talking majestic pop-rock songs—"Losing a Whole Year" for the busted-up lovers, "Graduate" for the losers, "Jumper" a legitimately tender balm for the despondent, and "How's It Gonna Be" for the despondent busted-up lovers post-graduation—that make you want to rumble down the interstate on water skis while tied to the bumper of a Camaro just so you can break your leg, just so you can scrawl the lyrics on your own cast. We're talking red-flag Tinder bios. We're talking *sonic manspreading.* We're talking songs that make you want to smooch your also-married-to-someone-else high school sweetheart in the back of your minivan in the parking lot at your 15-year high school reunion. Every single song on this record is *so much.* The least obnoxious song on this record is called "Burning Man." It's wonderful. All of it. Don't fight it. Come on. Fall in love with the Bad Boy for once. Fall in love with the Sad Literary Boy with the cheeseball falsetto who thinks he's the Bad Boy. Luxuriate in his shakiness, his semi-tunefulness, his semi-charm, his peppiness, his lasciviousness, his pretentiousness, his rap-adjacency, his *cocksurety.* Not a word. Now it's a word. He made it a word.

Stephan Jenkins all quoting Heidegger in *Rolling Stone.* Stephan Jenkins all chatting with *Spin* about his model-actress girlfriend, Charlize Theron. Stephan Jenkins: He's well-read, he's alarmingly self-actualized, he's vulnerable, he's brash, he's insufferable, he's irresistible. He's the kinda rock-star frontman where in press photos your eyes are drawn straight toward him and all the other dudes behind him just automatically get blurrier.* It's not his fault. It's mostly not his fault. It's not entirely his fault. Okay, it's his fault, but *that's the job.* Success: All it takes is everything you've got.

The deal here, quite simply, is that if you write/sing a pop song as pristine as "Semi-Charmed Life," everyone has to listen to everything you say about everything, forever. So allow him to retort, in a brief but action-packed March 1999 *Rolling Stone* interview that I enjoy very much.

Stephan Jenkins on his feud with Pearl Jam frontman Eddie Vedder, who'd recently criticized Third Eye Blind for covering the Who: "This is Eddie, as usual, starting something he can't

---

* Third Eye Blind have put out seven records total (Jenkins wanted to call one *Crystal Baller*; it's a play on words) and are still kicking ass on the nostalgia-tour circuit, but only Dr. Manspreading and drummer Brad Hargreaves remain. In 2017, to celebrate the self-titled debut's 20th anniversary, Cadogan and Salazar toured small clubs with yet another 3EB castoff (guitarist Tony Fredianelli, Cadogan's original replacement) as XEB. Great name.

finish—like Ticketmaster. So to have him policing who can play Who covers makes him a power-hungry cop. He wants to wear mirrored sunglasses and write tickets."

Boom! Roasted.

Stephan Jenkins on his feud with the band Live: "We were playing a festival, and their crew was harassing people. I called 'em on it, and the band did the Hollywood hide-behind-the-bouncer thing. The band is a bunch of pussies. Once you've got guys clearing the hallway for you, you're a karaoke band."

Boom! Roasted.

Stephan Jenkins on his feud with Green Day: There is no feud. Third Eye Blind's bassist playfully tackled Green Day's bassist. This is why you don't let bassists out of the van or the tour bus or the plane or whatever. They should build slightly larger dog crates for bassists. They hugged it out, presumably.

Stephan Jenkins on his feud with Rob Thomas: "He's obsessed; he won't shut up about me. I don't know him."

Boom! Roasted.

Stephan is asked if he once called Rob fat. "I have no idea. But if I blew up to Elvis-like proportions, I would expect *Rolling Stone* to make fun of me, and I would take it in stride."

Boom! Roasted.

Stephan is informed that Rob Thomas called him "a good archenemy." "He's not my archenemy—I don't know him. I don't have any idea what he weighs."

Boom! Roasted.

Stephan is informed that Rob Thomas called him *walking, breathing, living cheese*. "See? Even when he's talking about me, he has to use food references."

Oh my God. *I don't have any idea what he weighs.* Look: Rock 'n' roll needs jerks. Not just jerks: *jerkoffs.* Honor them. Cherish them. But don't form bands with them. Maybe just don't talk to them at all. And if you do, just know that they're not listening, especially when you say goodbye.

> "Women have had me over. It's happened twice in the last month. After I've bopped 'em, they've gone and sold it to the papers and made money out of it. Fair play. But I've just come in their gob (mouth) and gone off, so therefore I've had them over. Tied 1-all, baby."
>
> —Liam Gallagher, lead singer, Oasis
> (*Rolling Stone*, May 1996)

Oh my God. *After I've bopped 'em.* I can't believe it. I can't believe the magazine's (reasonable! helpful!) decision to clarify, parenthetically, the meaning of the word *gob.* I can't believe these are the first words of Oasis's *Rolling Stone* cover story. The deal here, quite simply, is that if you write/sing a pop song as pristine as "Wonderwall," everyone has to listen to everything you say about everything, forever; specifically, everyone has to listen to every mean thing the songwriter says about the singer, and vice versa.

In this corner! Wearing various parkas, pullovers, anoraks, pea coats, etc. Majestic sensible outerwear. Dressed for a torrential downpour even when indoors. Dressed as though a Man City match might break out at any time. The guy with the John Lennon glasses. The guy with the nose. The guy with the thousand-yard sneer. The singer. Not frontman. *Singer.* In his humbler moments he will concede that his brother, Noel—who writes all the songs and makes all the decisions and even sings a few of the songs he himself wrote—is arguably the true frontman of Oasis. But then again, this is not a guy burdened by humility. It's Liam Gallagher, singer, Oasis! *And in this corner…* vowels!

The vowels are getting knocked the fuck out. The vowels will *submit.* The vowels are destined for relegation. Majestic, elongated, luxuriantly contemptuous vowels. Those long *ehhhhh*s and *eeeeee*s and *ahhhhhh*s. "You make me laaaaauugh / Gimme your auto-graaaaaaaph." Each Liam vowel gets its own little bespoke parka and thousand-yard sneer and pair of brass knuckles. Even on the ballads. Even on *The Ballad.* Each Liam vowel ignites its own miniature drunken brawl.

So let's get Liam a new challenger. *Replacing the vowels in this corner,* Liam's older brother, Noel! Older by five years. The genius songwriter. The domineering bandleader. The far more musically adept but far less dashing Gallagher brother. Oasis formed in the Gallagher brothers' homebase of Manchester, England, in 1991 and broke up messily in Paris in 2009; Liam and Noel have been estranged pretty much ever since, though they insult one another constantly in the media and on the internet. Can I be honest and say that I find Liam and Noel's insults to be more vibrant, to be more *musical,* to be of *greater lasting sociocultural value* than most other bands' songs? For example, in a May 2020 episode of the podcast *Matt Morgan's Funny How?,* Noel observed how much weight Liam had gained during the initial days of COVID-19 self-quarantine. Specifically, Noel said, "He's not fucking isolating from the sweet trolley, is he?"

Oh my God. *Fucking isolating from the sweet trolley.* Stupendous.

The first major iteration of Oasis—Liam on vocals (and tambourine), Noel on guitar (and occasional vocals), Paul "Bonehead" Arthurs on guitar (thus nicknamed after he got a bad haircut), Paul McGuigan on bass guitar (better known as Guigsy), and Tony McCarroll on drums (soon replaced by Alan White)—are a one-band Rock-Star Jerkoff battle royale, so vicious, so puerile, so riotously quotable in their enmity for one other and for the world at large that they'd be one of the greatest rock 'n' roll bands ever born if they'd never played one song. *Definitely Maybe*, their gloriously cacophonous 1994 debut album, announces its jerkoffishness, its will to power, its *cocksurety* in its very song titles: "Rock 'n' Roll Star," "Supersonic," "Up in the Sky," "Cigarettes and Alcohol," and, yes, "Live Forever."

And meanwhile the hills are alive with the sound of Britpop, which as an unworldly Ohioan teen I mostly understand as a rad new subgenre in which English rock stars are *talking just absolutely wild shit in the media all the time.* Talking wild shit, often, about *America.* We got Suede frontman Brett Anderson, in the *NME*, calling Bruce Springsteen a dullard and announcing that "I find the idea of British bands singing in American accents horrifying" and hypothesizing that "that claustrophobic, stifled Englishness is conducive to great art," whereas "in America, there's no tragedy, no failure, no impotence, no premature ejaculation." We got Elastica leader (and Brett Anderson ex) Justine Frischmann, also in the *NME*, declaring that "I can't think of anything better than 16-year-old boys wanking and looking at a poster of me, but don't quote me on that 'cos I'll kick your head in." We got Blur frontman (and future Justine Frischmann ex) Damon Albarn threatening to name one of his band's albums *England vs. America* and bragging—in the

NME, of course—that "if punk was about getting rid of hippies, then I'm getting rid of grunge."

Worthy adversaries, all. Britpop was lousy with adversaries; that was the whole point. But Oasis crushed all of them with their second album, 1995's *What's the Story, Morning Glory*, featuring the 1.6-billion-Spotify-streams-and-counting monolith that is "Wonderwall." "At first I didn't like it," Liam conceded to *Rolling Stone* in 2020. "'What the fuck is this tune?' I said, 'I don't like this—it's a bit fonky.' I got Police vibes. It was a bit Sting. I like the heavier stuff. I said, 'This doesn't suit me, man.'" What you hear, on "Wonderwall," in real time, is Liam Gallagher realizing that even if it is a bit Sting, this song suits him just fine. What you hear is Liam and Noel setting their differences aside and delivering the greatest power ballad of their generation, in which Oasis ascend, and *transcend*, and ultimately explode in hilarious contemptuous megalomania. Remember when Liam described Radiohead as a "boring bunch of fuck-king stoodents"? Remember when the band's ludicrously overblown 1997 album *Be Here Now* loaded up on helicopters and cocaine? You think I'm joking? "It was an album mixed on cocaine," Noel conceded. "Loads and loads of trebly guitars." Meanwhile, Liam made a few concessions of his own: "In 1996," he declared, "I was doing as much cocaine as anyone you've ever heard of."*

Cocaine: the Devil's Reverb. Cocaine: the Other Third Gallagher Brother. Cocaine: the sweetest sweet in the Sweet Trolley.

---

* Both those quotes come from John Harris's splendid 2004 book *Britpop! Cool Britannia and the Spectacular Demise of English Rock*, and yes, as you suspected, *Be Here Now* is explicitly the spectacular demise in question.

Cocaine: the mortar in the Wonderwall. Jerkoffs need power bal-lads too, and in fact need them more than anybody.

As a conflict-averse person myself, I'd rather not wallow in the muck of the Blur-Oasis feud,* which always felt like a pretty obvi-ous divide to me: The artier and posher Blur wanted to live like Common People, whereas Oasis actually *were* Common Peo-ple. Damon Albarn did not get rid of grunge, no, but he cer-tainly *outlasted* grunge, and in 1997, amid the Gallagher brothers' lamentable cocaine whirlwind, Blur graced the world—yes, even America—with one of the great semi-contemptuous grunge jams of our time.

Oh, yes. "Song 2." The *woo-hoo* song. Great song. It's stuck in your head now. I'm not sorry and you're not even mad. We will all hear "Song 2" at every sporting event we attend for the rest of our lives—*woo-hoo*—and I, for one, will always get a little thrill from the audible smirk in Albarn's voice as he sings about what-ever the hell he's singing about. Blur's catalog is full of verbose and wickedly clever and stylistically fearless jams, but "Song 2" is, by streaming metrics anyway, far and away the band's biggest hit, and that is endlessly amusing to me, a funny little joke not so much on the band as on the band's Common People-ass listeners. "Song 2," to my mind, is the most exhilaratingly condescending jock jam ever born, unclever and obvious and blunt in its lowest-common-denominator magnificence, every *woo-hoo* another punctuation

---

* Suffice it to say Noel says some truly vile shit and then gets sassed by his mother; Steven Hyden's splendid 2016 book *Your Favorite Band Is Killing Me: What Pop Music Rivalries Reveal About the Meaning of Life* is way more thoughtful in its analysis than any of the actual combatants were at the time.

mark as Damon dumps another shovelful of slop into the pig trough. *My* pig trough. *Woo-hoo.* Very amusing. Sometimes a hit song is the most deliciously villainous act of all.

> "Why you always gotta be the center of attention? You know what I'm sayin'? And in the midst of being the center of attention, that's cool if you want to play Michael, but stop tryin' to front like I'm Tito or some shit. You know what I'm sayin'? And no disrespect to Tito, but it's just the whole, Tito played the background, so Phife's just supposed to play the background and shut the fuck up."
> —Phife Dawg, in Michael Rapaport's 2011 documentary *Beats, Rhymes & Life: The Travels of A Tribe Called Quest*

I hate watching people fight. And even though "No disrespect to Tito" is also very amusing, I *especially* hate watching Q-Tip and Phife Dawg fight, given that A Tribe Called Quest is one of the greatest rap groups ever, and "Check the Rhime" off the Queens group's 1991 masterpiece *The Low End Theory* features the greatest exchange between two rappers in recorded history. "You on point, Tip?" Just that question and this answer: "All the time, Phife." And then, the reverse: "You on point, Phife?" Zero question this is the best shit ever. "All the time, Tip." Don't tell me they fought sometimes, hated each other sometimes, regarded each other more as adversaries than allies sometimes. My heart can't bear it.

In truth, Q-Tip was, indeed, often the Michael Jackson of ATCQ, the co-producer (alongside Ali Shaheed Muhammad) and visionary and dominant voice, particularly on the group's radiant debut, 1990's *People's Instinctive Travels and the Paths of Rhythm.** But what makes *The Low-End Theory* superior is the stark contrast between Tip (cerebral, loquacious, literally nicknamed "The Abstract") and Phife Dawg, whose best line on the record is somehow "Go get yourself some toilet paper 'cause your lyrics is butt." For all the talk about A Tribe Called Quest as conscious and sleek and jazzy—as canonized, as *deified* as these guys rightfully are now as Golden Era standard-bearers—it is important, and in fact *necessary*, that they also have lines that stupid. The wise 23-year-old man cannot exist without the dopey 13-year-old boy. The highbrow cannot exist without the lowbrow. The abstract cannot exist without the unpleasantly concrete.

And so I do not want to listen to the ecstatic congeniality of "Check the Rhime" and think about all the times Tip and Phife were at each other's throats. I do not want to revisit *The Low End Theory*'s riotous climactic posse cut "Scenario"—featuring Charlie Brown, Dinco D, and most notably Busta Rhymes from the Long Island group Leaders of the New School—and think about how *those* guys basically broke up on camera on *Yo! MTV Raps*, such was the velocity of Busta's imminent blockbuster solo career. "Scenario" is a world-historically fantastic song about rapping your ass off with your friends, and as a conflict-averse person, I'm hellbent on blocking out the adversity of it, even though there's no friendship—or certainly *no beloved rap group*—without that adversity.

---

* Still, my favorite part of that record is on the slick-talking love song "Bonita Applebaum" where Q-Tip raps, "And if you need 'em I got crazy prophylactics," and the small crowd of dudes egging him on just goes, "WHOOOA." I want to live in that "WHOOOA." I want to cultivate, in my personal life, a group of friends who together constitute, in our own modest way, that "WHOOOA."

But another key facet of the Q-Tip and Phife bond is that you can totally tell—you can *hear*—when it's dissolving. Tribe put out one more bulletproof classic (1993's *Midnight Marauders*) and then, uh, two more albums, *Beats, Rhymes and Life* in '96 and *The Love Movement* in '98, both desultory and disappointing,* and the latter released a month after the group broke up. Phife struggled with diabetes for his entire run with Tribe, and for the rest of his life; Q-Tip went on to a respectable solo career, but he wasn't the same without Phife, and Phife often was nowhere to be found. The group reunited for the 2008 Rock the Bells Festival, primarily to help Phife pay his medical bills, and that experience, as depicted in Rapaport's 2011 documentary, only left everyone further dismayed. "When we see Tribe onstage, we want to believe that it's love," explains Dave from De La Soul, while we're talking about deified rap groups with tumultuous histories. "And if it's really not, and behind the scenes there's some BS going on, I'd rather they not be up there."

Phife Dawg died on March 22, 2016, of complications due to diabetes. His voice, naturally, jars you at first whenever you hear it on the final Tribe record, the reinvigorated *We Got It from Here…* *Thank You 4 Your Service*, released that November. "I had no idea that his days were numbered," Q-Tip told *The New York Times* a few weeks before the album came out, openly sobbing, his face buried in his hands. "I just want to celebrate him, you know?"

---

* The great poet/critic/Ohioan Hanif Abdurraqib's great 2019 book *Go Ahead in the Rain: Notes to A Tribe Called Quest* is the authority on their catalog, particularly the heartbreaking section where he describes taking the grave bodily risk of pulling his gloves off during the winter of '96 to fast-forward his Walkman past the lousier parts of *Beats, Rhymes and Life.*

Ah, God. I'm sorry that got so heavy. We gotta lighten the mood in here. Wait a minute. Okay. Here we go.

"Out on tour / With the Smashing Pumpkins / Nature kids / I-they don't have no function / I don't understand what they mean / And I could really give a fuck."
—Stephen Malkmus, Pavement frontman, on the band's almighty 1994 spite-country jam "Range Life"

Much better. Holy shit. Throughout the mid-'90s, as an alt-rockin' (and conflict-averse) teen, my Top 5 favorite bands, in no particular order, were Nine Inch Nails, Pearl Jam, They Might Be Giants, Smashing Pumpkins, and Pavement, and immediately you see the problem. One of 'em. One of several. The problem: Two of my musical dads are fighting. Two of several.

I fell for Billy first. William Patrick Corgan Jr. Lead singer, lead guitarist, rhythm guitarist, possibly-all-other-guitars guitarist, maybe bassist as well, frontman, primary songwriter, mastermind, and dictator of Chicago rock band the Smashing Pumpkins. A band that also featured, at the height of its powers, guitarist James Iha, bassist D'Arcy Wretzky, and drummer Jimmy Chamberlain, though you got the sense, from Billy anyway, that only Billy mattered. A bit of a Grumpy Gus, this guy, as his lyrics indicate. "I'm all by myself / As I've always felt," he wailed on "Soma," an extra-grumpy jam on the Pumpkins' transcendent 1993 album *Siamese Dream*, before uncorking the whiniest, gnarliest, raddest guitar solo my 13-year-old ass had ever heard. Here was a sentiment—a *worldview*—I could get behind. *I'm invincible. I'm alone. I'm super sad, but at least I'm the best at sadness. No one can touch me, but why won't anybody try?*

Billy is a '70s-rock-star sorta guy, and not the punk parts of the '70s: Think Yes (for the prog), think Alice Cooper (for the cheese-ball glam), think Cheap Trick (for the defiantly uncool power pop). No time to play it cool; no time to *be* cool. Billy schemed. He whined. He took himself ultra-seriously; he embraced the pro-wrestling-heel silliness inherent to taking yourself that seriously. He was enraged. He was enraging. People talked a lot of shit about him, and he talked a lot of shit right back. He talked a lot of shit about *his own bandmates.* "You know, I gave them a year and a half to prepare for this record," he grumbled to *SPIN* in 1993, address-ing rumors that he insisted on playing all the guitar and bass parts on *Siamese Dream* himself. "I'm surrounded by these people who I care about very much, yet they continue to keep failing me. I say, 'I need this, I need that,' and they don't do the job, and what it does is it makes me feel the same abandonment I felt as a child. And then what it says to me is, 'You're not worth the trouble.'"

He was a Michael surrounded by Titos, you might say, if you were him. And the result, on a grouchy and colossal and pulverizing jam like *Siamese Dream* opener "Cherub Rock," is a rock band that sounds 200 feet tall but also doesn't quite sound like a function-ing rock band at all. Instead, it sounds like a morbid, tyrannical, self-consciously villainous, outrageously talented person imagining a rock band in his head. There's an unembarrassed magnificence, but also a crushing loneliness radiating from the guy who wants you to know that he's almost single-handedly responsible for that magnificence.

And then, in 1994, Pavement—the Stockton, California, uber-indie-rock band that played it cool for a living—inexplicably sassed Billy Corgan into oblivion. Those DGAF lines on "Range

Life"—an otherwise disconcertingly lovely Dirtbag Eagles jam off Pavement's sophomore album, *Crooked Rain, Crooked Rain*—came out of absolutely nowhere, a baffling cheap shot brought to you by Pavement frontman and fellow supervillain Stephen Malkmus.

Stephen's a handsome fella. A droll and erudite and Scrabble-playing and confrontationally aloof sort. In 1997 *Rolling Stone* asked him—this isn't even a question—"People say you're arrogant and mean." And Stephen very politely responded, "It's not true. It's part of the act." Though he did add, "I'm a pretty icy performer. I'm nice at the bottom of my heart, but I like the tough-love, bitchy-performer thing."

On "Range Life," Stephen does indeed invest the hard K at the end of the line "I could really give a fuck" with a truly fearsome amount of iciness and bitchiness, and his target responded in kind. "How about let's start with jealousy?" Billy groused to *Rolling Stone* in 1995. "There's always been flak from certain bands—the Mud-honeys and Pavements of this world—that somehow we cheated our way to the top and deceived the public into getting where we were." Furthermore: "You have the football team, except the foot-ball team is the guys in Pavement and Mudhoney. And they're all patting themselves on the back for how cool they are instead of healthily challenging themselves to greater heights."

In Billy's defense, at the time he was promoting the Pumpkins' 1995 double-CD monstrosity *Mellon Collie and the Infinite Sadness*, which is a stupid title for an album I loved with all my blackened teenaged heart. I loved its unembarrassed excess, its maudlin gran-diosity, its rad-as-hell guitar solos. (His best guitar solo is a rad little joybomb on a song called "Here Is No Why.") But by then I adored Pavement as well, after I caught the agreeably silly "Cut

Your Hair" video on MTV and convinced my buddy Scott to boost the *Crooked Rain, Crooked Rain* cassette for me from our local Super Kmart. I knew Pavement were much cooler than Smashing Pumpkins, but I saw no contradiction, no need to take sides. "Range Life" was a little uncouth, yes, but it also felt *right*—it felt true to their respective selves—for Pavement to be so intolerably smug, and Billy Corgan to be so intolerably aggrieved by that smugness. We need bands that care as little as Pavement; we *desperately* need bands like Smashing Pumpkins that care too much.

"Everybody was saying, 'Limp Bizkit is shit.' So we said, 'OK, we'll be shit. We'll make a gigantic toilet and come out of it like five turds.' We got their attention. They were watchin' the show and they were buyin' the records. You gotta do that sometimes, man."
—Fred Durst, Limp Bizkit frontman
(*Rolling Stone*, 1999)

I regret to inform you that we have reached the Woodstock '99 portion of our program, in which the '90s themselves turn heel and embrace utter sonic/moral turpitude. Tough break for everybody.

The five-turd situation precedes Woodstock '99, though. I had forgotten about the 30-foot-high onstage toilet from which—*through which*—the Jacksonville, Florida, rap-rock band Limp Bizkit would emerge to begin every set during their stint on Ozzfest 1998, *climbing out of the lid* of this gnarly gargantuan beast to (presumably) *applause*, whereupon, having emerged from the 30-foot toilet, the boys would then launch into a song called "Pollution." I do greatly enjoy photos of Fred atop the mega-toilet—holding

121

court, as it were—though depending on the camera angle, it can look like a regular-sized toilet with a Fred Durst action figure posed on the lid.

Limp Bizkit's 1997 debut album, *Three Dollar Bill, Y'All*, is best known for its phenomenally disrespectful cover of the 1987 George Michael pop classic "Faith," which gets my vote for the all-time cover song that most rigorously despises the original. Limp Bizkit covers George Michael the way Atilla the Hun covered Europe. And then came 1999's *Significant Other*, featuring the hellacious tag team of "Nookie" (a song about doing it for the nookie) and "Break Stuff" (a song about breaking stuff just to break stuff). Rage—the noun, verb, fellow canonical rap-rock band, and state of mind—is huge again. Angry white men are huge again, if indeed they've ever *not* been huge; the '90s movie with the greatest cultural impact on the 21st century is probably *Fight Club*, which is also a tough break for everybody.

Which brings us, regrettably, to July 1999, when the ordinarily bucolic hamlet of Rome, New York, plays reluctant host to the infamous dipshit rage-fest that is Woodstock '99, characterized by its sheer corporate greed, its epidemic of sexual assault and violence against women, its penchant for arson and destruction, its total disregard for private property and human life. Limp Bizkit's ultra-chaotic performance of "Break Stuff" is the moment, roughly mid-way through this horrific three-day societal nadir, when the '90s break bad, when the '90s break, when the '90s die. But is "Break Stuff" the cause or the effect? Do all the dipshits at Woodstock '99 break stuff because "Break Stuff" makes them want to break stuff? Or do they like "Break Stuff" because it articulates their pre-existing urge to break stuff? Is Fred Durst history's greatest scoundrel, or an unfairly maligned generational patsy? We all know why Limp Bizkit did it. But is Limp Bizkit really why *we* did it?

Related question: Did Orange County punk-rockers the Off-spring once make me, a conflict-averse and well-adjusted and happily married fortysomething father of three, joyously scream the words, "You stupid dumbshit goddamn motherfucker," into the crisp spring evening air in a seething crowd of 20,000-odd people in a soccer stadium in Columbus, Ohio, or did they simply articulate my preexisting urge to scream the words, "You stupid dumbshit goddamn motherfucker?" The song is "Bad Habit," a road-rage anthem from the band's colossal 1994 breakout album *Smash*,* which also includes a jaunty song about urban gun violence ("Come Out and Play") and an even jauntier song about a friend-zoned simp cruelly mistreated by a mean sexy lady ("Self Esteem"). Awesome. Also, yikes.

A goofy, gleeful villainy comes natural to these fellas, and so it's not that the Offspring merely *play* Woodstock '99 so much as Woodstock '99 somehow *manifests* them, and soon they're regaling a world-historically seething crowd of 250,000-odd peo-ple with their latest irresistibly odious hit single, 1998's "Pretty Fly (for a White Guy)." Which is a song about a white kid who gets so into rap music that he starts dressing and acting like a rap-per, i.e., a Black guy. "Now cruising in his Pinto, he sees homies as he pass," sings impressively shrill Offspring frontman Dexter

---

* *Smash*, released on feted SoCal indie label Epitaph Records, is the non-sellout '94 mirror twin to Green Day's *Dookie*. Those two records are generally credited with kickstarting the national mainstream punk-rock boom, though if you ask me, I, personally, should get the credit for kickstarting the national mainstream punk-rock boom because *I bought both those records and many other punk records as well.*

Holland. "But if he looks twice, they're gonna kick his lily ass." Awesome. Yikes.

Dexter, in addition to fronting the Offspring throughout their 10-album, nearly 40-year career, got his Ph.D. in molecular biology in 2017, and thus I've always thought of him as a self-aware guy who writes very smart very stupid songs. And as "Pretty Fly (For a White Guy)" blossomed into somewhat of a surprise hit, Holland seemed to realize that this song mocking white kids for embracing Black culture was just stupid enough to be dangerous, and so he took pains to reroute the song's animosity toward "poseurs of any kind," as he explained to *SPIN* magazine, which explains why now we've got Dexter, onstage with the band at Woodstock '99, wielding a giant red toy bat and delivering a lusty beatdown to five full-size effigies of the Backstreet Boys. Ah yes. Teen pop. A much safer and less racially divisive topic. Big yikes. It is, indeed, exhausting always rooting for the antihero. But the Offspring's songs are just *that good*, that triumphant in their repulsion, that aspirational in their glorious stupidity.

One more foundational Woodstock '99 memory triggered by one more joy- and rage-inducing blur of red, this time in the form of Yonkers rapper DMX's bright red overalls as he thunders through the electrifying "Ruff Ryder's Anthem," one of the biggest hits from *It's Dark and Hell Is Hot*, the first of his *two* chart-topping 1998 albums of sacred and profane crime rap. Rap along if you like: "All I know is pain / All I feel is rain / How can I maintain / With mad shit on my brain?" But maybe stop rapping along once he starts describing all that mad shit in lurid detail. The vast majority of DMX's songs involve him robbing and/or shooting people;

let's not turn this into an analytics thing, but he robs and/or shoots a disconcerting, action-movie-body-count number of people.

And then he ends every album—and every riveting live show—with a prayer. Humble, penitent, supplicant, devout. And the first miracle of DMX is how genuine both the shootout and the prayer sound, coming from his mouth, delivered in such an authoritative, such a terribly vulnerable but also triumphantly invulnerable voice. He knows his death is always in the air. He knows God will protect him for exactly as long as he needs protection. He knows he's immortal for precisely as long as he needs to be.

DMX, a/k/a Dark Man X, a/k/a Earl Simmons, died on April 9, 2021, of a cocaine-induced heart attack. He was 50, and had suffered enough for 100 lifetimes. Brutal child abuse. Abandonment. Isolation. A lot of time living on the street, turning to crime so he had enough money to eat, sleeping in Salvation Army donation bins, learning to prefer dogs to people, for their loyalty and if necessary their viciousness. He could rely on dogs. When he was 14, a trusted mentor turned Earl on to rap music, but also handed Earl a blunt without letting on that it was laced with crack cocaine. "A monster was born," Earl would explain in 2020, on the podcast *People's Party With Talib Kweli*, his pain and sense of betrayal still palpable, still unbearable.

And so DMX, on record, could be the ultimate antagonist, the remorseless antihero, steeped in ultraviolence, not all of it fictional. But DMX also, objectively, *prays better* than anyone in rap history. And this is the aching contradiction he embodies, and transforms, miraculously, into Not a Contradiction at All. The hurt, and the violent anger—the wildly entertaining stories of X hurting others—fuel the grace, and the humility, of these prayers, which in turn makes the hurt bearable.

Sometimes he's in a full-blown clash with the devil, as depicted in a famous trilogy of songs beginning with *It's Dark and Hell Is Hot*'s eerie and utterly believable "Damien." Sometimes he's raging at *God himself*: "Lord you left me stranded / And I don't know why," he laments on "Ready to Meet Him," yet another essential 1998 track. "Told me to live my life / Now I'm ready to die." But at the end of every last blockbuster album, we find DMX once again penitent, purified, imperfect and yet saved. In his prayers he is present tense for me, always, no matter the facts, no matter what spiritual beliefs anyone might hold. But do me a favor. Even if you're not the type to ever consider praying for yourself, don't ever stop praying for him.

"We didn't even know each other. I had never even seen her before, because I listen to a lot of Gospel music. From the time she was released and I was released, instantly people compared us, and we never understood it. It's like they chose the two of us out of the bunch to put at odds. They never did it with me and Aaliyah, or Brandy and Aaliyah. It was always Brandy and Monica."

—Monica, as quoted in Fred Bronson's 2003 book *The Billboard Book of No. 1 Hits*, discussing the monster No. 1 *Billboard* hit "The Boy Is Mine"

I don't know him. I don't have any idea what he weighs. Brandy Norwood was born in McComb, Mississippi, in 1979; her mother, Sonja, once told *People* magazine, "I knew Brandy was going to be a star the day she was born." The family moved to L.A. when she was

4 years old to help make her a star, and soon she was, first in the sitcoms *Thea* and *Moesha*, then in R&B. Brandy's self-titled debut album—released in 1994, when she was 15 years old—revealed that she was not a belter, not an octave-swooping walking-volcano diva a la Mariah Carey, not a raging waterfall of defiant vulnerability a la Mary J. Blige. What I hear most, on *Brandy*, is the smooth and sultry and electrifyingly laid-back insinuation of Janet Jackson, and I'm saying this as a person who *loves* Janet Jackson. It's a triumph of vibe. On Brandy's debut single, "I Wanna Be Down," it's a level of chill that burns hotter than the sun.

Monica Denise Arnold was born in Atlanta in 1980. She started singing in a traveling Gospel choir when she was 10. To my mind, somewhat like Brandy, the real action in Monica's voice has always been at the low end—the darkness, the depth, the *soul*. Plus her comfort with rap music, or at least the beat-heavy propulsion of rap music, to rival Mary J. Blige herself, particularly on Monica's debut single, "Don't Take It Personal (Just One of Dem Days)," from her own debut album, 1995's *Miss Thang*.

So both these singers, both these young *stars*, are poised to make huge leaps, artistic and otherwise, with their respective second albums in 1998, and it just so happens that Brandy is co-writing and co-producing a diaphanous and sweetly contentious potential hit called "The Boy Is Mine," and she hunts down Monica to join up and turn it into a duet, and what results is *the* signature song for them both, and, unsurprisingly, a durable source of gossip and innuendo and Cold War Superpower tension and outright hostility between them both. Because no matter how splendidly their voices might blend together, and no matter how huge this song still is, it's clear that this town still ain't big enough for the two of 'em.

For a song in which two teenage girls argue over a boy who is clearly seriously dating both of them, "The Boy Is Mine" is deceptively serene. They hardly raise their voices; it's like they'd be screaming at each other if they weren't stuck in a crowded library. It's like they're trying not to wake up a sleeping baby. It's a knife fight with no knives, just side-eyes. This is the Coldest War. This is liquid nitrogen incarnate. They trade off lines, but their voices intertwine so exquisitely that sometimes it doesn't feel like a duet at all.

"The Boy Is Mine" was released as a single in May 1998, and reigned as the No. 1 song in America for the entire summer of 1998. Brandy's second album, *Never Say Never*, came out in June 1998: "The Boy Is Mine" was track three. Monica's second album came out in July 1998: "The Boy Is Mine" was track two. Also, and this is important: Monica's second album was called *The Boy Is Mine*. Yikes. Brandy was reportedly greatly displeased to hear this, though in Monica's defense, Monica was reportedly greatly displeased when Brandy performed "The Boy Is Mine" *without her* on Jay Leno's *Tonight Show* in May, featuring several backup singers, one of whom was remarkably out of tune. Yikes. In September, during rehearsals for their joint performance of "The Boy Is Mine" at the MTV Video Music Awards, Monica allegedly (according to the song's coproducer Dallas Austin) punched Brandy in the face backstage.

The VMAs performance of "The Boy Is Mine" is, indeed, a sort of architectural marvel. Brandy and Monica are isolated high up on giant platforms on opposite sides of the stage, with giant staircases leading down, and a dozen or so backup dancers in pajamas (I think) providing most of, y'know, the movement. It's like they're yelling at each other from third-story apartment windows across a highway from each other; the distance between them feels court-ordered. They both sing the hell out of the song, but that physical distance between them is the main attraction: The song only works if you truly believe that they can't stand to be even six feet away from each other. When they finally do walk down their respective staircases and take center stage and risk any sort of proximity, it's an electric moment whether you believe all the rumors or not. Monica sings, "Not yours." Brandy sings, "But mine." You decide what they're really saying.

FLUKES + COMEBACKS + SPECTACULAR WEIRDOS

SONGS DISCUSSED:

Los Del Río, "Macarena (Bayside Boys Remix)"
Billy Ray Cyrus, "Achy Breaky Heart"
The New Radicals, "You Get What You Give"
The Cherry Poppin' Daddies, "Zoot Suit Riot"
Cher, "Believe"
Chumbawamba, "Tubthumping"
Tag Team, "Whoomp! (There It Is)"
Mark Morrison, "Return of the Mack"
Santana + Rob Thomas, "Smooth"
Vanilla Ice, "Ice Ice Baby"
Natalie Imbruglia, "Torn"

F UCK IT. We're doing "Macarena." And we will not tolerate, in this or any other venue, the unseemly specter of Performative "Macarena" Hatred. Nor will we tolerate, while we're busy not tolerating things, dismissive use of the term *one-hit wonder*. I am morally and philosophically opposed to this term, as I find it to be *rude*, and furthermore, I've found there is quite a bit of wiggliness to the term *hit*, if you'll forgive the term *wiggliness*. And so let us instead embrace the (I feel much better about this term) *wondrousness* of the supposed one-hit wonders, the flukes, the oddballs, the improbable comebacks, the covers of covers, the remixes of remixes, the pre-Peak Internet viral sensations. And let us begin with, yes, the extra-fluky (and extra-wondrous) "Macarena." Fuck it.

Antonio Romero and Rafael Ruiz were both 14 years old when they formed the duo Los Del Río, meaning "Those From the River," in the Spanish city of Dos Hermanas in *1962*. Yo: Los Del Río formed the year before the first Beatles record came out. Los Del Río put out records for *30 years*. That's how this story *starts*. Los Del Río are Flamenco singers, primarily. They are, by and large, traditionalists. Nostalgists. They are regional stars. Even *regional stars* might be overstating it. They are working. They are successful. They put out tons of records, in Spain. They tour. They tour internationally. But they do not aspire to global pop stardom in the traditional sense, or the non-traditional sense. By the 1990s what we got here, in essence, are two sweet fortysomething dudes making their Flamenco tunes and wearing their suits and dancing their rumbas and minding their own goddamn business. Their success is modest and sustainable, and their ambitions as well.

And then, in 1992, while touring South America, they find themselves in Venezuela, at a fancy party attended by Venezuelan President Carlos Andrés Pérez and, more importantly, a dancer named Diana Patricia Cubillan. Diana dances for the party, and Antonio improvises a little song to encourage her, a song about a woman named Madelena. The lyrics to Antonio's little song translate roughly to "Give your body joy, Madelena / Your body is made for happiness and good things."

"When Antonio saw me dance, the words just came out," Diana told the Associated Press in 1996. "His inspiration was me. Why would that be—because of the shape of my body? The way I danced? What do I know?" You can find Diana on Instagram under the name La Macarena Del Mundo because Los Del Río changed the lady's name in the song and also, therefore, the song's title.

It is a reliable source of semi-viral internet content to assert that the lyrics to "Macarena"—a song named after Antonio's daughter, as well as the Basílica de la Macarena Catholic church in Seville—are hella dirty, which requires jumping to the horniest possible interpretation of the phrase *give your body joy*. (In defense of Team Horny, in the song Macarena has a boyfriend, Vittorino, who's serving in the military, so while he's gone she hooks up with two of his friends. But let's maybe not jump to the horniest possible interpretation of the term *hooks up with*.) But what really strikes me about the original song—which kicks off Los Del Rio's 1993 album *A mí me gusta*—is how delightful and genial and *chill* it is. All the elements are in place: the relentless handclaps, the buoyant percussion, the supernatural blending of Antonio's and Rafael's voices, the humble propulsion of it all. Plus the little flourish at the end of every fourth line of the chorus—"Heyyyy Macarena

(AYYYYY)"—that keeps the song looping in your head. The song's enormous appeal doesn't require much translation, nor does it require much *embellishment*.

But look out: Here come the embellishments. First "Macarena" gets a deliciously gaudy remix from the Spanish dance-music duo Fangoria, who electrify the beat and add the insidious two-chord bouncing-ball keyboard riff that's probably stuck in your head right now. That (admittedly much hornier) remix blows up in clubs throughout Latin America, kicks off an infectious line-dance craze, and creeps northward until it hits Miami, where a local radio DJ named Jammin Johnny Caride* commissions *another* remix because he knows that to go truly viral—to go full-blown monocultural in America—he needs a version of "Macarena" that isn't *entirely* in Spanish. So he gives his Miami buddies Carlos de Yarza and Mike "In the Night" Triay—who own a local label called Bayside Records—72 hours to do the job. Carlos writes some new lyrics of the straightforward "Move with me / Dance with me" variety, his friend Patti Alfaro sings them, and 1995's "Macarena (Bayside Boys Remix)"—which spends 14 weeks as the No. 1 song in America—is born.

If you still hate it, I get it. I do. But I do also encourage you to rewatch the "Macarena" video sometime, even if it's on mute. There are a few different versions, but *attractive, half-dressed young people dancing the Macarena* is the unifying theme, and yet the real

---

* "It was like the bubonic plague," Caride says in Leila Cobo's 2021 book *Decoding "Despacito": An Oral History of Latin Music*, recalling his first public exposure to the "Macarena" dance. "The dance floor clears out, people fall in line like an army, and they start to do that little dance. The ones who didn't know it, they learn it on the spot." He means the bubonic plague in the positive sense.

attraction is the Los Del Río fellas themselves in their natty suits, delivering the indelible refrain, perhaps dancing themselves for like 1.5 seconds at a time, perhaps twirling an umbrella, perhaps singing into one of those old-timey hanging microphones, and for sure generally still minding their own goddamn business.

There's something quite charming about the inherent culture clash, the *generational* clash here: It's like a relentlessly youth-targeted Gap ad that inexplicably includes the two middle-aged Gap executives who green-lit the ad. Because Antonio and Rafael themselves are just unwitting cogs in their own machine now, the unlikeliest of pop stars with, happily, little control over the remix chicanery and other industry machinations that made "Macarena" truly viral, monocultural, inescapable, immortal. By this point Los Del Río are not-so-modestly successful, but their modesty, their *geniality* shines through. Their geniality *survives*. They don't even do the dance. Everyone else does it for them.

Billy Ray Cyrus does the dance, or at least *a* dance, a series of tight-pantsed, spin-heavy, rubber-legged gyrations that further enliven the already quite rowdy video for his 1992 country-pop smash "Achy Breaky Heart," the overwhelmingly female and remarkably *adult* crowd line-dancing with evident delight as our hero and his somehow gloriously audible mullet soak up the spotlight. Here we've got another fluke '90s hit best remembered now for its baffling, crushing ubiquity: Billy Ray's debut album *Some Gave All* was the No. 1 album in America for 17 weeks, and this song was *everywhere, all the time*, for months on end. But don't let that oversaturation blind you to what an oddball underdog story this was, from the unknown guy who wrote it (Vietnam veteran and Tennessee family man Don Von Tress*) to the unknown guy who sang it (Miley Cyrus' dad).

Miley's dad was born in Flatwoods, Kentucky, in 1961, and switched his life's aspiration from baseball pro (he got a scholarship to Kentucky's Georgetown College but dropped out) to pop superstar after catching a Neil Diamond concert (reasonable). He led a country-and-rock cover band called Sly Dog for a while; he lived in his Chevy Baretta out in L.A. for a while. And then he caught pretty much the biggest break you can legally catch. Billy Ray didn't even get to "Achy Breaky Heart" first: That honor goes to the Marcy Brothers, a country-pop trio of actual brothers from Oroville, California, who released the song in 1991 with a different title ("Don't Tell My Heart") and different pronunciation (*achy breakin'*, not *achy breaky*) and some frankly pretty dope guitar-solo action, all of which added up to jack shit, chart-wise. I feel bad about that: The Marcy Brothers version is inferior, to be clear, but it's not, like, "The difference between selling jack shit and having the No. 1 album in America for 17 straight weeks" inferior. There's just no logic to music.

What I can tell you about Billy Ray's version of "Achy Breaky Heart" is that the way he sings the line, "You can tell your dog to bite my leg," is country as hell. He sings that line like it's the funniest joke ever told, and that's how you gotta sing every line, so that's how he sings every line. But no matter how jovial and unthreatening Billy

---

* "Once I started writing, it went so quickly the song just fell out of the air," Don told *The North Indiana Times* in October '92 as "Achy Breaky Heart" climbed the charts. "I love the abstract factor. There's just no logic to music." That article's headline, BTW, was "Country Songwriter Not Quitting His Day Job," on account of the fact that Don was hanging wallpaper in an Indiana nursing home at the time.

Ray might've been, there's no getting around the fact that this song achieved the sort of blockbuster oversaturation that inspires Performative Hatred in even the kindest and most open-minded among us. Even the inevitable delightful "Weird Al" Yankovic parody, 1993's "Achy Breaky Song," is much grouchier than his usual, expertly rhyming "you know I hate that song a bunch" with "it might just make me lose my lunch." If you're like Al and you still hate this one, too, I get it. But Billy Ray's audible mullet will still reverberate forever.

THE SINGLE GREATEST PERFORMANCE of Performative One-Hit-Wonder Hatred I have ever witnessed in person transpired in December 1998 in Cleveland, Ohio, at a bizarre alt-rock-radio-station music festival and canned-food drive co-headlined by Gainesville, Florida, ska-punk lifers Less Than Jake and glorious L.A. one-hit-wonders the New Radicals. Someone should write a whole-ass book on Less Than Jake, and I can't guarantee you it won't be me: These dudes were into ska-punk both way before it was cool and (even more impressively) long after, and they have my enduring respect. Less Than Jake fans *love* Less Than Jake. Also, anecdotally, Less Than Jake fans *hate* the New Radicals.

"You Get What You Give." That's the New Radicals' one hit. I feel less rude than usual, stating this plainly, because it sure seems like the New Radicals planned on having just the one. They are led by singer-songwriter, multi-instrumentalist, charming Only Guy on the Album Cover narcissist, and bucket-hat enthusiast Gregg Alexander, who I would've sworn to you was English (it's the hat), but who apparently grew up in Grosse Pointe, Michigan. Sure. Gregg was raised a Jehovah's Witness, used to drive around with his mom listening to Motown, and vowed, after hearing Prince's

137

"The Beautiful Ones" as a teenager, to run away to California and become a rock star (reasonable). And then, briefly, he became one.

I suspect you do not require a lengthy, obnoxious description of "You Get What You Give," an upbeat piano jam with a phenomenal pre-chorus that sounds like peak Billy Joel discovering cocaine and Jesus simultaneously. (At least that description wasn't *lengthy*.) So in Cleveland, at this bizarre canned-food-drive situation, the New Radicals take the stage second-to-last, with only Less Than Jake left to go, and among the more cynical among us, already there's a sense that "You Get What You Give" is gonna be it for these fellas, hit-wise, very much by design. But in this moment, Gregg and his pals are still very much Going For It in terms of chasing pop stardom, Going For It here defined as *willing to play a canned-food drive in Cleveland a week before Christmas.* Gregg does not, in my estimation, seem happy to be here, in Cleveland, a week before Christmas. The New Radicals play some songs, to broad crowd indifference. Halfway through the set, they play "You Get What You Give." The crowd perks up. The New Radicals proceed to play other, far less popular New Radicals songs; the crowd once again grows indifferent. The set ends, blessedly. No encore is requested, and yet the band returns for an encore anyway. The encore consists of "You Get What You Give," again.

And suddenly Cleveland, in my estimation, doesn't seem too happy that the New Radicals are still here. "Somebody find a power outlet!" someone yells. And then I watch in amazement as a sizable group of Less Than Jake fans, huddled together in the middle of the crowd, stand silently, with their middle fingers raised toward the stage, for the entirety of "You Get What You Give," again. Not a great time to be surrounded by canned food.

This image—a bird-flipping flock of peeved Less Than Jake fans—pops into my head whenever I revisit the New Radicals' debut (and farewell) album, 1998's *Maybe You've Been Brainwashed Too*, which has, just in case you weren't aware, other songs, most notably an impressively goopy ballad called "Someday We'll Know" during which Gregg bellows, "DID THE CAPTAIN OF THE TITANIC CRY?," which I am rendering here in all caps because *that's how he sings it*. The whole album is as chaotic and pompous and ideologically convoluted as subversive major-label pop gets, a sunny hellscape of dystopian post-Motown cocaine melodramas; sometimes, by design, Gregg sounds like an incoherently mumbling hot mess, and sometimes he sounds like a focused L.A. studio pro with a surprisingly affecting falsetto who's just totally Going For It. Third Eye Blind's "Semi-Charmed Life" bears mentioning here, I suppose, in terms of maximum dorky pop as a delivery system for maximum drug-binge shock value; I also suspect that Gregg and 3EB frontman Stephan Jenkins would really get along, and that you don't want to be around when they do.

And then the band flamed out, and Gregg worked behind the scenes on some blockbuster pop songs you've probably heard (including the 2002 Santana and Michelle Branch jam "The Game of Love") but otherwise stayed out of sight until, quite unexpectedly, Joe Biden's 2021 virtual inauguration spectacular, wherein Gregg and his pals reunited to play "You Get What You Give" again.* It was great to see Gregg's face again. And if any of those

---

* The song meant a great deal to Joe as his son, Beau Biden, battled brain cancer: The lines "This whole damn world / Can break your heart / Don't be afraid / Follow your heart" especially. Beau died in 2015. Even the silliest, most flamboyant pop flukes are unimaginably important to somebody.

pissed-off Less Than Jake fans were watching, I hope they gave him a second chance, and gave his song a third.

Is the New Radicals vs. Less Than Jake the weirdest show I've ever seen? Is it the *most '90s* show I've ever seen? What's the single most '90s sentence I could write? Let's try this: In college I saw both Big Bad Voodoo Daddy and the Cherry Poppin' Daddies live. Separate shows. Separate cities. Tight window of opportunity. The mid-to-late-'90s swing revival gets my vote as the decade's most surreal and transcendently disreputable subgenre, ennobled by the horn-heavy emergence of third-wave ska and turbocharged by Jon Favreau's canonical 1996 comedy *Swingers*, which climaxes with Big Bad Voodoo Daddy—stylish Southern California gents who'd already been at it since 1989—helping our boy Jon get the girl, the girl in this case being Heather Graham. Impressive! Cut to Cleveland in 1998, and BBVD are commanding a stylish and exuberant crowd eager, for some reason, to wild out to a song called "Go Daddy O" and exuberantly time-warp themselves back to the Great Depression. It made perfect sense at the time.

As for the disreputably named Cherry Poppin' Daddies, they hailed from Eugene, Oregon, which makes as much sense as anyplace else would; front man Steve Perry had the sort of booming voice and vivid lyrical flair ("pull a comb through your coal-black hair") that allowed you to overlook, for the length of a peppy hit 1997 song called "Zoot Suit Riot," the fact that the actual Zoot Suit Riots were racist attacks on Latino teenagers in World War II-era Los Angeles. I told you this was weird.

Did neo-swing make perfect sense at the time? It probably didn't. Did I enjoy the occasional tune from the Squirrel Nut Zippers or the Brian Setzer Orchestra anyway? Hell yes I did. Does

"Zoot Suit Riot" hold up now as a double-nostalgic pop song? Hell yes it does. Just now, did I make it all the way through a second Cherry Poppin' Daddies track? Hell no I didn't, but only because I picked a song called "Here Comes the Snake" before deciding I didn't want any part of the Snake. Was this music *escapist*, in the classic pop-music sense? I guess, but don't ask me to explain why sexy young people in 1997 sought to escape to the halcyon days of, like, 1927 or 1937. I can't decide if this stuff is *timeless* in the classic pop-music sense, or if the whole appeal is that it's proudly, explicitly dated. Either works, but either way it's way more fun if you do the goddamn dance, even if the goddamn dance is like 20 times harder to do than the Macarena.

You want to talk truly *timeless*? Did you know Cher was born in 1946, which was *the year after World War II ended*? I don't say that to be rude, but to more effectively convey my awe that Cher, at 52, had a massive pop hit the year after "Zoot Suit Riot" came out with 1998's "Believe," an AutoTune exaltation that divided the 1990s from the 2000s just as surely as God divided the light from the darkness.

"Some years I'm the coolest thing that ever happened," she told *Rolling Stone* in 1999, shortly after "Believe" became her fourth No. 1 *Billboard* single and her first *since 1974*. "And then the next year everyone's so over me." As a snotty alt-rockin' early-'90s teenager I knew her primarily as the infomercial lady who slapped Nicolas Cage and called David Letterman an asshole and wore That One Outfit on That One Battleship. The notion of Cher as a present-tense hitmaker struck me—seemingly struck *everyone*—as ridiculous, and yet "Believe," in its dance-pop effervescence and invigorating post-heartbreak bravado and wine-dark-sea depth of defiantly human vocal tone, is the one song from the 20th century that defines the 21st century for me, a brassy voice from the distant past who graciously stopped selling moisturizing shampoo on television long enough to point us toward our transcendent android future.

AutoTune, as the 2000s rumbled onward, was dismissed as a cheat, a crutch, an abomination, an anti-art and anti-human scourge publicly reviled by everyone from Steve Albini to Christina Aguilera to Jay-Z. But there's *Cher*, of all people, in *1998* of all years, stretching the word *sad* into four electrifyingly melodramatic syllables—*It's so sa-a-a-ad that you're leavin'*—that breathe life back into the ghost in the machine. She perfected this polarizing technology years before its loudest and pissiest detractors had even heard of it; Cher, 25 years ago now, is still the only Artificial Intelligence I ever want to hear about. I caught her alleged Farewell Tour in 2002 at a hockey arena in Columbus, Ohio, and whatever I wrote about her is mercifully lost to the pre-Peak Internet mists of time, but I'm guessing it was just *oh* and *wow* alternating for 600 words. And my descendants will revere her as well, centuries hence, delighted to welcome their robot overlords so long as they speak with her voice.

P ERFORMATIVELY HATE 'EM WHILE you can, by the way, because the very concept of the one-hit wonder is dying. They've done studies; they've compiled *data*.* The biggest songs spend more time overall in the Hot 100 now—months as opposed to weeks—so there's less room for newer shit, plus Taylor

---

* The website *Priceonomics* raised a ruckus with a 2015 post literally titled "The Death of the One-Hit Wonder," bolstered by a graph of artists who only ever had one song chart in the *Billboard* Hot 100, showing a steady downward curve from 1965 to 2015. Cher was back on tour by then, FYI.

Swift, for example, can put out a new, mid Taylor Swift record, and suddenly the whole Top 10 is new, mid Taylor Swift songs. It's like how Film People complain that Marvel movies are clogging up all the movie theaters.

The consequence for pop music is that you get fewer delightfully arbitrary thunderbolts like Dexy's Midnight Runners' "Come on Eileen" (No. 1 in 1983) or a-ha's "Take on Me" (No. 1 in 1985) or Cutting Crew's "(I Just) Died in Your Arms" (No. 1 in 1987, love the parentheses). And precisely *because* the artists in question did not endure as pop stars in the years to come (sorry), those hit songs come to define, and also perhaps *explain*, the years and indeed the whole decade in which they were briefly hit songs and those artists were briefly pop stars. This phrase *one-hit wonder*, despite being hella rude, is itself growing archaic, and we will miss it when it's gone, and miss the one-hit wonders when they're gone.

You'll miss the Chumbawambas when they're gone. Chumbawamba: British anarchist collective. Put out their debut album in 1986 and called it *Pictures of Starving Children Sell Records* just to puncture the pompousness of Live Aid. Put out six more records (including one in 1994 called *Anarchy*), all of which righteous and energetic and pugnacious, none of which *mainstream* in any traditional sense of the term. And then, in 1997, out of approximately fucking nowhere, they hit No. 6 in America with "Tubthumping," an exuberant Molotov cocktail of pub battle cries, trumpet solos, whiskey drinks, vodka drinks, lager drinks, cider drinks, and dulcet odes to "pissing the night away."

Did "Tubthumping"—with its less dulcet but very necessary refrain of "I GET KNOCKED DOWN / BUT I GET UP AGAIN," very much bellowed in all caps—inspire a generation of

143

alt-rockin' American teens to embrace true utopian pro-union and anti-fascist anarchy? Not really. Was the song instead co-opted as a dreaded Jock Jam, a genre animated by the sort of vacuous apolitical boorishness antithetical to much of what Chumbawamba stood for? Kinda. Still a great song though, right? Fuck yeah.

That sense of hard-fought exuberance—irrational, fleeting, tempered by the subversion-proof mainstream, and yet mercifully undimmed by the merciless passage of time—is what we can't afford to lose, no matter how silly that exuberance often sounds and feels. You'll miss the Tag Teams when they're gone. Tag Team: Atlanta pop-rap duo of DC the Brain Supreme and Steve Rolln. Hit No. 2 in 1993 with a bumptious and mostly family-friendly Miami Bass hybrid called "Whoomp! (There It Is)." Prevailed, chart-wise, in a gritted-teeth feud with 95 South, a Miami Bass crew way closer to Miami (Jacksonville) who had a remarkably similar (but notably less popular) hit song at the same time called "Whoot, There It Is."* Snuck a song with the line "I crave skin"—a remarkably gnarly way to convey the sentiment that DC the Brain Supreme is conveying there, i.e., he's horny—into a song that'll charmingly corrupt every family reunion you attend for the rest of your life.

"Whoomp! (There It Is)" has no political ideology beyond an unflagging allegiance to the "B-double-O-T-Y oh my," and yet it conjures up a remarkably Chumbawambian sense of rapturous anarchy. As for Tag Team's 1993 debut album, also called *Whoomp! (There*

---

* They shoulda used parentheses. "Whoomp!" came out shortly after "Whoot," but Tag Team insisted they'd recorded it earlier; the two groups performed their respective hits back-to-back on *The Arsenio Hall Show* in July '93 and let callers vote for their favorite, and 95 South won that battle but very much lost the war. ("Whoot" peaked at No. 11; *Billboard* eventually named "Whoomp!" *the second-biggest song of 1993.*)

It Is), I can report that it has, just in case you weren't aware, other songs, including one in which DC the Brain Supreme announces, "Nubian ham is what I want," which is an even gnarlier way to convey the sentiment that he's horny. But this story ends the only way it could: with no further Tag Team hits, with Steve Rolln arrested in 1997 while in possession of 600 pounds of Mexican marijuana (he got out of prison in 2001), and the fellas triumphantly reunited in 2021 for a viral Geico ad in which they chant, "Scoop! There it is!" while making ice-cream sundaes in some lady's kitchen.

You'll miss absurd shit like this. You'll miss the Mark Morrisons when they're gone. Mark Morrison: the "Return of the Mack" guy. Born in 1974 in Germany to parents who emigrated to the U.K. from Barbados and mostly raised him in Leicester, England. Grew up rough and learned to sing R&B with the deftness, the lasciviousness, the rhythmic and melodic swagger of a G-funk superstar rapper, albeit with a remarkably nasal voice that can make the word *freaky* sound extra freaky. Says he wrote "Return of the Mack" in the Leicester prison on Welford Road. Recorded the allegedly slow, staid, toothless original version of "Return of the Mack" that very few people have heard and that apparently no one liked; handed the song over to Joe Belmaati and Cutfather, two Danish producers who cranked the tempo, added the drums from the immortal 1981 Tom Tom Club smash "Genius of Love," added bright new chords from a 1992 R&B tune called "Games" from an L.A. singer named Chuckii Booker, tossed in a bunch of other li'l samples from the likes of Run-DMC and the French disco giant Cerrone, and wound up with the 1996 version of "Return of the Mack" that pretty much everyone has heard and absolutely everyone thinks is the best song ever made while they're listening to it.

It's the way Mark sings the words, "Oh my god," with that ultra-nasal ultra-swagger. There is a sweetness, a tartness to his voice that is inextricable from his nasal-ness, to his huh-I-didn't-know-he-was-Englishness, to his bad-boy-ness. And he's a pop star now, and he puts out a 1996 album also called *Return of the Mack*, which has, just in case you weren't aware, other songs, including the one where he chants *freaky freaky freaky* a whole lot, and I dig the soft-core nasal braggadocio of this record quite a lot, actually, but the Mack will only be returning for a limited time. In 1994, Mark was involved in a nightclub brawl that ended with a man named Julian Leong stabbed to death; four years later, in a newspaper article in the *Scottish Daily Record*, it says, "The singer punched Mr. Leong in the face and smashed a bottle. He told police he did it to calm the situation." The trick, I think, is to avoid situations where it becomes necessary to smash a bottle and punch someone in the face just to calm the situation.

Mark was not the guy with the knife in that brawl, and he gets arrested but is ultimately sentenced to community service, which he then blows off by sending a bodyguard to do it for him,* and this scheme fails, obviously, and only nets Mark more prison time, according to another *Scottish Daily Record* article that describes Mark as both a *yob* and a *sod*. Both those terms are insults, so far as I can tell, and while I can't tell you exactly what a *yob* or a *sod* is or what differentiates the two, I do know that you want to try to avoid doing anything that might compel a Scottish newspaper to call you

---

* I must admit that I am delighted by this scheme, in which Mark just gave his sunglasses to the bodyguard and hoped that would suffice, in terms of a disguise. *Yes, hello, I am English pop star Mark Morrison, as you can tell from these sunglasses, and I'm here to clean these toilets.*

a *yob* and a *sod* in the same article. My point here is that "Return of the Mack" is Mark Morrison's only American hit.

You'll miss shit like this the most.

W HAT IS THE SINGLE greatest opening line of the 1990s? Let's figure this out. To expedite the process of figuring this out, let's narrow the field down to two choices. Your choices are "Alright stop, collaborate and listen" or "Man, it's a hot one." You pick.

"Man, it's a hot one" is not from a one-hit wonder, just in case you weren't aware. Santana, the eponymous rock band led by Mexican-born guitar god Carlos Santana, racked up two Top 10 hits, "Evil Ways" and "Black Magic Woman," back in, huh, look at that, 1970. Wow. Santana played *fuckin' Woodstock*. Not Limp Bizkit and Brian Setzer Orchestra and societal-collapse Woodstock. The original, legit 1969 Woodstock. This is the guy whose shrewdly eponymous rock band finally landed a No. 1 hit in, huh, look at that, 1999. Wow. That song is "Smooth," and Rob Thomas, professional Stephan Jenkins antagonist and frontman for ascendant Orlando pop-rockers Matchbox 20, is on lead vocals, and Rob's legit-genius first line is "Man, it's a hot one," as you might be aware.

What's the deal with "Man, it's a hot one"? What elevates this blithe, half-muttered, temperature-based remark to the pantheon? Could part of the attraction be *doubt?* "When I listened to the lyrics and heard, 'It's a hot one,' those lyrics are outside of time and gravity," Carlos himself observed to *Rolling Stone* in 2019. "I thought we had entered a place of immortality. But with all respect to Rob, I said, 'I'm having a little challenge believing you that what you're singing is true.'"

Wow. Is it *really* a hot one, Rob? And who exactly are you to say? *Don't mansplain the weather to me, Rob.* Let's not discount the role of gentle derision here, and irony, and sarcasm. *Your* sarcasm, though, not the singer's. Rob Thomas sings the line "Man, it's a hot one" like he's hot. He sounds *sweaty*. Grant him that. And anyway pop-song immortality often starts as somewhat of a joke. *Ha ha ha, "Man, it's a hot one." That's so dumb. I'll never forget it as long as I live.*

But to my mind, the true greatness of "Smooth" lies in the whiplash pivot from the nonchalant generality of "Man it's a hot one" to the remarkable specificity of "My muñequita / My Spanish Harlem Mona Lisa." Incredible. *Muñequita* means "little doll"; Rob wrote this song for his girlfriend, Marisol Maldonado, who is of Spanish and Puerto Rican descent and grew up in Queens (close enough). They got married in 1999, and they're still married, and she stars in the "Smooth" video—it's really all terribly sweet. "When I met Carlos," Rob told Leila Cobo for her book, "the first thing he said was, 'Hey, you must be married to a Latin woman; that's the kind of thing a white guy married to a Latin woman would say.'"

Fantastic. "Smooth" was the last No. 1 song of the 20th century and the first No. 1 song of the 21st century; it topped the charts for 12 weeks, total, but it felt like two whole centuries. This song somehow sounds, today, like it's still the No. 1 song in America, today. *Supernatural* generated another No. 1 hit ("Maria Maria"!), sold approximately 10 billion copies, won approximately 200 Grammys, and made fifty-something Carlos Santana a present-tense pop hitmaker; probably all of that happens even if "Smooth" doesn't begin the way it begins, but what I know for certain is that when Rob half-mutters That Line, that's the precise moment when this song moves outside of time and gravity.

That's your first option. Your second option arrives courtesy of Robert Van Winkle, the Dallas-born white-rapper dynamo better known to the world as Vanilla Ice, who in 1990 enraptured us with just five words: "Alright stop, collaborate and listen." He says, "Alright stop," and you stop. He says, "Collaborate," and you go, *What?* He says, "And listen," and you listen.

So, listen. Cards on the table. In 1990, as a dimwit 13-year-old, I owned six cassette tapes. You ready for this shit? Six tapes. *Hysteria* by Def Leppard, *New Jersey* by Bon Jovi, *Gonna Make You Sweat* by C+C Music Factory, *Pump Up the Jam* by Technotronic, *Please Hammer Don't Hurt 'Em* by MC Hammer, and *To the Extreme* by Vanilla Ice. And what I know for a fact is that Vanilla Ice's "Ice Ice Baby" is the platonic ideal of your first rap song, or at least the first rap song you ever loved.* It's a better song the less hip-hop you're familiar with, the less context you have in general, the younger and more naïve you are. It's the best rap song imaginable if you are but an adorable newborn foal, your shaky legs tottering adorably on the Disneyfied ice of late childhood or early pre-adolescence. It's better if you don't know shit about shit.

"Ice Ice Baby" is a way better song, for example, if you're unaware that it samples the absolute bejesus out of the 1981 Queen and David Bowie arena-rock masterpiece "Under Pressure"; it's a better song if you've never seen that exquisitely mortifying MTV clip of Vanilla Ice attempting to explain that "Ice Ice Baby" doesn't sample "Under

---

* This idea is explored at great length in the rap critic Jeff Weiss' great 2020 *Ringer* feature "The (Mostly) True Story of Vanilla Ice, Hip-Hop, and the American Dream," and also the much taller rap critic Tom Breihan's splendid 2022 book *The Number Ones: Twenty Chart-Topping Hits That Reveal the History of Pop Music*. Please read any article or book mentioned in any of these footnotes. Thank you.

Pressure." It's better if you're unaware that the lines, "Police on the scene / You know what I mean / They pass me up / Confronted all the dope fiends," is the purest expression of white privilege in the history of American song. It's better if you're unaware that Vanilla Ice is gonna get roasted to a crisp by Arsenio Hall on *The Arsenio Hall Show*, and Kevin Bacon on *Saturday Night Live*, and (even worse) by Jim Carrey on *In Living Color*. It's better if you're unaware that Vanilla Ice was born in Dallas, not Miami as he often implied, and that his real name is indeed Robert Van Winkle, not literally anything else.

It's better (last one, promise) if you didn't catch Vanilla Ice at the 1991 American Music Awards, concluding his acceptance speech for Best Pop/Rock Artist with an ill-advised message for the haters: "Word to your mother. And the people who try to hold me down and talk bad about me, *kiss my white butt*. Word to your mother."* It's better (*this* is the last one, honest) if you just stop the song, and your personal development, and Vanilla Ice's whole *career* after "Alright stop / Collaborate and listen." So let's do that, actually. Let's do what he says, but do what he says in reverse. Listen. Then collaborate. (*Huh?*) Then stop.

That's your second option. You pick. Mmm. I sense you are dissatisfied. Fine. Fine. I'll give you one more candidate for the single greatest opening line of the 1990s, and that candidate is, "I thought I saw a man brought to life," from Australian pop star Natalie Imbruglia's 1997 smash hit "Torn," which is—possibly it's better if you don't know this—a cover song. Technically, it's a cover of a Norwegian cover (by pop star Trine Rein) of an American cover (by the rad L.A. alt-rock band Ednaswap) of a Danish remake (by Lis

---

* I do enjoy how he brackets every statement with "Word to your mother." It's like he's speaking in HTML. <wordtoyourmother> *I'll take a ham and cheese omelet, hash browns, and rye toast* </wordtoyourmother>.

Sørsenson) of a song co-written by two of the Americans (Anne Preven and Scott Cutler of Ednaswap, cowriting with former Cure bassist Phil Thornalley, who produced both Trine's and Natalie's versions; sorry, I'm simplifying this the best I can). And this, too, is a reliable source of semi-viral internet content, to shout, "Natalie Imbruglia's 'Torn' is a cover!" in a crowded theater and run.

But let me suggest to you that Natalie—a teenage veteran of the Australian soap opera *Neighbours* who fled to Britpop-mad London in search of pop stardom, and seized it with her 1997 debut *Left of the Middle*, most of the rest of which she co-wrote herself—wipes out all this convoluted prehistory when she sings, "I thought a saw a man brought to life," imbuing these semi-innocuous words with a soap-opera veteran's expert combination of yearning, exasperation, destitution, and hidden resolve. (The video, in which Natalie radiates yearning exasperation as her failing relationship is stage-managed by a soap-opera-type film crew, is pretty dope, too.)

It's *her* song now, is what I'm saying, and what she's politely saying as well. "It seems like everyone else is obsessed with that," Natalie told *The Independent* in 2022, still hashing out the cover-of-a-cover-of-a-cover-of-a-remake thing. "I think, you know, some songs marry with the person. And it's my truth and how I related to what's in the lyrics and how I communicate that—the authenticity of that— that people connect with. And that's valid." Even if Natalie never had another monster hit song again—there's a rude and wiggly term for that, though it escapes me now—a pop star she will always remain because *that's how that works*. Natalie Imbruglia sings, "Illusion never changed / Into something real," and majestically contradicts herself, because pop music changes illusions into something real, something *wondrous*, all the time. And sometimes one song is all it takes.

TEENAGE HIJINX

SONGS DISCUSSED:

Rage Against the Machine, "Killing in the Name"
Body Count, "Cop Killer"
Guns N' Roses, "November Rain"
Red Hot Chili Peppers, "Under the Bridge"
Alice in Chains, "Would?"
They Might Be Giants, "Particle Man"
Cake, "The Distance"
Weezer, "Undone (The Sweater Song)"
Beastie Boys, "Sabotage"
Radiohead, "Creep"
Pearl Jam, "Yellow Ledbetter"

I'M PRETTY SURE I peaked as a teenager and hit rock bottom as a human being on the night I tried and failed to toilet-paper a suburban mailbox after a Rage Against the Machine concert. Summer 1996. *Evil Empire* tour. Akron, Ohio. Specifically, the University of Akron's basketball arena, a/k/a the JAR, a/k/a the James A. Rhodes Arena, named after the four-term Ohio governor who sent the National Guard into nearby Kent State to quash Vietnam War protests in May 1970. Four dead in O-HI-O. And then, 26 years later, Rage Against the Machine— the world's preeminent incendiary leftist rap-rock band—came to town and played a song called "Vietnow." If front man Zack de La Rocha addressed this bitter irony during his visit to literally the James A. Rhodes Arena, I was, at 18 years old, way too dumb to notice. I did love it when Zack would jump off the drum riser right when the drums kicked in and all the lights got really bright. Great show. Electrifying. You might even say *radicalizing*.

Then we drove around. Uh-oh. Nothing more dangerous than a carload of radicalized, over-testosteroned teenage boys cruising around the suburbs at 11:30 p.m. or so, hunting for a machine against which to rage. No machines were available, hence the mailbox. My attack on this mailbox was improvised. We're talking a standard U.S. Postal Service street-corner deal, one of them giant blue dudes with the rounded top—a shape utterly unconducive, as it turns out, to the act of toilet-papering. It was *diabolical*. I *tried*. I tried for probably 30 seconds, but it felt like three hours. I like to imagine "Know Your Enemy" by Rage Against the Machine blasting from the car stereo as my buddies watched my feeble and mortifyingly apolitical attempt at vandalism, flaccid strands of toilet paper drifting down harmlessly onto the verdant grass. How would I, personally, have characterized "The Machine" when I was 18? What did I think *raging* against this machine would entail? And who's this enemy I'm supposed to know,* anyway? I'm better off not thinking about any of it now because back then all I was thinking was *I can't get any toilet paper to stick to this fuckin' mailbox.*

What do I want, as a steakhead 18-year-old with a head full of nonsense and a trunk full of toilet paper? I want *excitement.* I want *adventure.* I want *intellectual stimulation.* I want *out.* Out of the suburbs. Out of the malaise. Out of my near-total ignorance of the world around me. I want to go where the action is; I want to *be* the action. I want to kick ass and take names. I want to be thought of as cool. All of which are American Dreams. All of which are American Dreams. All of which are American Dreams. All of which are American Dreams.

What do Rage Against the Machine want? To kick ass, take names, and provide intellectual stimulation to dopes like me. The band—Zack de la Rocha, weedly-deedly guitar god Tom Morello, bassist Tim Commerford, and drummer Brad Wilk—hailed from Los Angeles and put out their self-titled debut album in 1992, selecting, as their debut album cover, Malcolm Browne's famous 1963 photograph of the Vietnamese monk Thích Quảng Đức burning himself to death in the street in Saigon to protest the government's treatment of Buddhists. Rage tried their best to get through to me, further packing their lyrics and their videos and their interviews and their

---

* As Zack explains in the song, the enemy includes "Compromise / Conformity / Assimilation / Submission / Ignorance / Hypocrisy / Brutality / The Elite / All of which are American Dreams." (I'm pretty sure I was guilty of most of those, despite not remotely qualifying as The Elite.)

155

liner notes with oft-lengthy treatises on Leonard Peltier, the Shining Path, the Weather Underground, white supremacy, the Zapatistas, the Black Panthers, and countless other righteous causes and societal enemies. They put a whole-ass bibliography in the CD booklet for *Evil Empire*; they got kicked off *Saturday Night Live* mid-show for hanging American flags upside-down; they burned an American flag onstage at Woodstock '99 while playing (what else) "Killing in the Name," during the climactic part (where else) where Zack shouts, "Fuck you, I won't do what you tell me," repeatedly.

The eternal question is what percentage of this band's audience ever "got it," however you describe that audience, however you define the notion of *getting it*, however you characterize what Rage's *it* even was. "I've been on a warpath since my first gig in high school, and it's missionary work, in a way," Tom Morello told me when I interviewed him backstage in 2019 before his solo show at a giant raucous hard-rock music festival in Columbus, Ohio. "And one thing I want to be very clear about is that there's no political litmus test to being in the crowd. I come from an archly conservative town in Illinois, and it was music that reached me. So you play a few good guitar solos, people pay attention a little bit to the lyrics and the graphics on the screen, and you never know what might happen."

And once Tom and his band took the stage, one thing that I knew would happen is that everyone would wild the fuck out when they played "Killing in the Name." This song is forever twinned in my mind with Body Count's "Cop Killer," the notorious 1992 super-anti-police-brutality broadside from veteran rapper Ice-T's heavy-metal side project that found itself more or less censored out of existence once police unions and the George H. W. Bush administration caught wind of it. As a steakhead teen, I primarily understood "Cop Killer" as one of those songs that terrified adults and was therefore extremely cool, an overbroad and extra-oblivious personal category that also included 2 Live Crew's "Me So Horny" and Madonna's "Justify My Love." But what strikes me now about "Cop Killer"—a song that is still not officially streaming or available for sale today—is that it's unspinnable. "I'm 'bout to bust some shots off / I'm 'bout to dust some cops off." You cannot make this song mean something other than what Ice-T meant it to mean. That's what made "Cop Killer" so powerful, and therefore why it had to be, for all practical purposes, destroyed.

Whereas the great strength, and perhaps the ultimate weakness, of "Killing in the Name" is that "Some of those that work forces / Are the same that burn crosses" is unambiguous, but "Fuck you, I won't do what you tell me" is *deliciously* ambiguous. You need to experience this song live at least once, and when you do, as the song ramps up to its rapturous, ferocious conclusion, you might wonder what's going on with everyone around you, their hands also balling up into fists, their brains also emptying of all other thoughts, their feet also lifting off the ground.

Uh-oh. What percentage of these people are thinking about white supremacy, or police brutality, or Mumia Abu-Jamal, or Vietnam, or Vietnow? Maybe they're thinking about Joe Biden. "Fuck you, I won't do what you tell me." Maybe they're thinking about the CDC's Covid guidelines. "Fuck you, I won't do what you tell me." Maybe they're thinking about something they read on Twitter. *Definitely* "fuck you, I won't do what you tell me." Maybe they're thinking about Rage Against the Machine when Rage Against the Machine aren't playing "Killing in the Name." *No,* "fuck YOU, I won't do what YOU tell me." Maybe they're thinking about their mothers.

"Killing in the Name" doesn't judge. Anger is a gift, or so I've been told, and all Rage could ever ask is that you listen hard and get angry, but also that you be careful who you give that gift to, and who you accept it from. Beyond that, it's enough to scream those words in a giant crowd of people also screaming those words, enough to feel that ecstatic collective fury, enough to *belong*. Because that's an American Dream, too.

A NOTHER ORIGIN STORY. ANOTHER radicalizing moment. Another peak/nadir. Fall 1988. I am 10 years old, and I ask my parents to tape the MTV Video Music Awards because it's past my bedtime and Guns N' Roses will be performing. Arsenio Hall hosts, INXS win five awards, Michael Jackson wins the Video Vanguard Award, and Guns N' Roses perform a song called "Welcome to the Jungle." At the time I am attending Sacred Heart Elementary, a Catholic school in suburban Eureka, Missouri, if that's relevant, which I think it might be, because after *they* watch Guns N' Roses perform "Welcome to the Jungle," my parents are *unhappy*.

The next day, they sit me down. "Now, Robby,"* they say, choosing their words slowly, carefully. "We're just concerned... that you might get the idea... that drugs might be something you want to try." I had not gotten that idea. I am too naïve to even be impressionable. I want you to imagine that you are a fourth-grader at Sacred Heart Elementary, attempting to process the exact nature of the threat implied by tyrannical frontman Axl Rose's line, "If you got the money, honey, we got your disease." What, like chicken pox? For this reason, and 10,000 other extremely good reasons, my parents will not allow me to buy GNR's epochal 1987 debut

---

* Yeah, Robby with a Y. I changed it to just Rob in the sixth grade, *for the ladies.*

album, *Appetite for Destruction*, nor their shorter and even surlier 1988 release *G N' R Lies*, which features both an outrageously racist and homophobic song called "One in a Million" (I was unaware of this at the time), and a photo of a naked lady in the liner notes. (I was extremely aware of this at the time, thanks to reporting from my Catholic school classmates.)

The threat passes; the '80s give way to the '90s; the winds, uh, change. Now, the party line, amongst rock critics anyway, is that grunge killed hair metal. That doesn't look right to me in lowercase, actually. Grunge Killed Hair Metal. There. That's better. That's the party line. Late-'80s MTV, you get GNR, you get Poison, you get Def Leppard, you get Cinderella, you get (hooray!) Bon Jovi. You get Spandex. You get hairspray. They, at least, get a lot of chicks. But early-'90s MTV, you get Nirvana, you get Pearl Jam, you get Soundgarden, you get Alice in Chains. You get darkness, you get self-loathing, you get zero chicks, or at least zero chicks willing to tolerate dudes who use any variation of the phrase *getting chicks*.

So what are Guns N' Roses, probably the single biggest and most dangerous rock band of the '80s, doing to maintain their viability in 1991? They're unleashing the comically bloated *Use Your Illusion* saga, a 30-track, two-and-a-half-hour double album, the two halves sold separately at like $17 a pop, and all of it peaking with "November Rain,"* a 9-minute-long maximum-power ballad that features an orchestra, angelic-demonic backup singers, unambiguous Elton John vibes, multiple extra-bonkers guitar solos, and a blockbuster $1.5 million video that features both a wedding and a funeral, these two events bisected

---

* Which appears on *Use Your Illusion I*, though overall I'm partial to *Use Your Illusion II* because it has "You Could Be Mine," the original "Don't Cry," and (most importantly) "Get in the Ring."

by an unusually violent rainstorm that compels a random wedding guest to dive, full-extension, into the wedding cake.

Why did he do that? What the hell is going on? What disease is *he* suffering from? Is this sort of thing even cool anymore? Or does all this sort of music totally suck now?

My answer to this question, back in '91, is that I don't buy either *Use Your Illusion* album with my precious allowance money, even though I totally could, my parents having thrown up their hands at this point with regards to my moral development. I have the money, honey, but I no longer want their disease. Nowadays I think of the "November Rain" video—which in 2018 became the oldest music video on YouTube to surpass one billion views, which is a phenomenal backhanded compliment—as the end of something, a putting away of forbidden childish things, a last gasp of shameless amoral cheeseball hair-metal majesty before I submit to my true destiny of being an Alt-Rock Teenager.

Which means…what? It means that now that I like moody and sensitive and sophisticated bands like, uh, the Red Hot Chili Peppers. Oh, boy. What the hell is going on with *these* guys? What even *are* these guys? Funk-metal? Rap-rock? Alternative? Punk? *Unembarrassed.* That's what these guys are. Naked on album covers and/or magazine covers and/or onstage, perhaps with socks on their penises, perhaps not. Macho as all hell but with semi-benign neo-hippie wibbity-wabbity undertones. Flower-children Lakers fans with erections lasting longer than four hours. They contain multitudes. Multitudes of guitarists, for one thing. These fellas got an excessively virile way with words. There's a devil in their dicks and some demons in their semen. Oh, boy.

Forming in 1982 in, of course, Los Angeles—the city they live in, the City of Angels—the Red Hot Chili Peppers are already battle-scarred veterans by the dawn of the '90s, weathering multiple lineup changes and still reeling from the crushing loss of original guitarist Hillel Slovak, who died, of a drug overdose, on June 25, 1988. He was 26. And then—how should I put this? When I am not actively listening to the band's fifth album, 1991's *Blood Sugar Sex Magik*—featuring buoyant-mystic prodigal guitarist John Frusciante and overseen by funky-monk superproducer Rick Rubin—I will grudgingly concede that it's one of the 100 most important albums of the decade. Whereas when I am *actively listening* to *Blood Sugar Sex Magik*, I am also chasing strangers down the street either on foot or on a riding lawn mower to inform them that it's the best album ever made. I once referred to *Blood Sugar Sex Magik* in print as "a raucous Mountain Dew enema." Do I regret saying this? Well, I just said it again, so *clearly I don't.*

With apologies to Frusciante and superstar bassist Flea, the true MVP of this record is wibbity-wabbity frontman Anthony Keidis, who is a D+ singer but an A++ frontman precisely because he doesn't give a shit that he's a D+ singer. Furthermore, I will never get tired of the story my wife tells about going to a teenage sleepover, and her friend had the "Under the Bridge" video recorded on a worn blank VHS tape, and this girl would repeatedly rewind and rewatch the end of the video where Anthony sprints, shirtless, in slow motion just as the song gets to the climactic line "Under the bridge downtown / Is where I drew some blood," and there'd be tears running down the girl's face. That's A++ frontman behavior, right there. We are all managing our loneliness, and our abject horniness, as best we can, and that very much includes Anthony himself: On "Under the Bridge," as on no other song across his band's admirably chaotic 40-plus-year career, he perfectly harmonizes his taste for horndog reverie with his taste for goofball philosophy with his taste for exquisite melancholy. He's sad, he's horny, he's sorry, he's hornier, he's lonely but grateful for his city if nothing else, he's sorrier, he's horniest.

"Under the Bridge" is also a sumptuously mellow anthem about, well, drawing some blood under a bridge, and let just say that as a doofus 12-year-old who still didn't know enough to even want to try any drugs, I was in no position to wrap my head around the heroin of it all, and that goes for every '90s rock band I adored that occasionally or not-so-occasionally wrote hit songs about heroin, which was most of them. "Junkhead," "Sickman," "God Smack," "Down in a Hole," "Angry Chair,"* "Hate to Feel," "Would?" There, that's more than half the songs on *Dirt*, the pummeling 1992 sophomore album from ultra-growly Seattle rockers Alice in Chains, who do indeed personify for me the complications of the old Grunge Killed Hair Metal canard, given that these magnificently dour fellas sure do strike me as a fantastic hair metal band (their 1990 smash "Man in the Box" sounds like Very Angry Bon Jovi) that organically morphed into an even more fantastic grunge band. That lineage seemed pretty clear to me back in '92, though the opening line of "Would?"—"Know me / Broken by my master"—was unfortunately a little less clear to me,† in terms of who or what the master might've been.

---

* In a high school English class I wrote a weepy essay about my great grandma, who everyone adored and who was mostly confined to a rocking chair with various health problems, and I titled it, yes, "Angry Chair," and it's probably still stashed in a box somewhere in my parents' basement.

† Nor did I immediately grasp that "Would?" is a tribute to Andrew Wood, the charismatic Mother Love Bone frontman, also eulogized at great length by Temple of the Dog, who personified the flamboyant greatness of both grunge and hair metal better than any one human ever had or ever would.

162

"Would?" is vicious and cathartic enough to be the last song on an album as unrelentingly heavy as *Dirt*, but it's also catchy and thrilling and bizarrely *welcoming* enough to be the *first* song on the grunge-heavy soundtrack to Cameron Crowe's 1992 Seattle-rock-scene romcom *Singles*, which only further mythologized Seattle as the coolest city in rock 'n' roll history, especially if you'd never been there. "Would?" also exemplifies the mesmerizing chemistry between AIC's two singers and songwriters, pointy-bellowing frontman Layne Staley and power-murmuring guitarist Jerry Cantrell, whose voices meld into a jarring vulnerable-tough-guy close harmony worthy of the Louvin Brothers. Throughout *Dirt*, Staley's voice especially has this sort of Midnight Movie force and beautifully grotesque anguish and voluptuous ferociousness to it, and if you stack up a bunch of his vocal tracks—"What in God's name have you done? / Stick your arm for some real fun"—they warp together into something colossal and magnificently inhuman, or, I suppose, more human than human.

Wait—what the fuck did he just say? There I am, in high school, wallowing in my bedroom, despondently cataloging all my unrequited crushes while my stereo's blasting a song literally called "God Smack." That constant dissonance between why I was wallowing and why the singer might've been wallowing: Is that a testament to the universal power of the song, or the singular naivete of the listener? Is the song great or am I just oblivious? Probably both. Definitely both.

Just a little something to think about. You don't have to think about it, though. I'm still thinking about it enough for the both of us, in part to avoid thinking about much worse things.* There I

---

* Layne Staley died, at 34, of a drug overdose on April 5, 2002, eight years to the day after Kurt Cobain, though in Layne's case the exact day is estimated, as he reportedly died two weeks before his body was discovered.

am, during my spectacularly ill-advised collegiate open-mic-night years, brazenly stumbling through the delicate Alice in Chains acoustic tune "Don't Follow" and botching Layne's climatic high note: "Scared to death, no reason why / Do whatever to get me by." You could tell just by listening to me, I bet, that I had no idea what *do whatever to get me by* might've meant to him or any other rock star I worshiped as a teenager. You could tell just by the way my voice always cracked on the word *scared*.

I S HE A DOT?" Then there was the day my Cool Uncle Nick changed my life. "Or is he a speck?" Cool Uncle Nick had great taste and a cool stereo. "When he's underwater does he get wet?" Cool Uncle Nick told me this was a song he just thought I needed to hear. "Or does the water get him instead?" And then Cool Uncle Nick played me "Particle Man," by the immortal Brooklyn rock duo They Might Be Giants.* "Nobody knows." The accordion, the handclaps, the Saturday Morning Cartoons radiance and irreverence of it all. "Particle Man." It's a polka, kinda, but like a cool polka, and all the cooler for not trying too hard to be a "cool polka." You get me? Sure you do. Hearing this song for the first time changed my life. I am not joking or even slightly exaggerating.

John Flansburgh (who sings half the songs) wears glasses a lot and plays electric guitar with an exaggerated professorial air, as though smoking a pipe at all times; John Linnell (who sings the other half of the songs, including this one) wears a professorial expression of benign

---

* "Particle Man" is one of two songs from their epochal 1990 album *Flood* to be randomly and delightfully canonized in an episode of the semi-epochal cartoon series *Tiny Toon Adventures*, the other one being the band's jaunty cover of the 1950s goof "Istanbul (Not Constantinople)." If you know, you know.

amusement and mostly plays keyboards or the accordion. They are wildly prolific art-rockers and politely flamboyant weirdos perfectly calibrated to the sensibility of an oddball 12-year-old. This is a *Far Side* Cartoon-A-Day Calendar sensibility, a "Weird Al" Yankovic sensibility, a Pee-Wee Herman sensibility, a *ToeJam & Earl* sensibility, a Monty Python on VHS sensibility, a *Hitchhiker's Guide to the Galaxy* sensibility, a *Mystery Science Theater 3000* sensibility. This band will rearrange your brain like a *MAD* magazine fold-in.

They certainly rearranged mine. "Particle Man' *rewired* me, and specifically rewired my sense of what *cool* was, or could be, or should be. Who gets to be cool? Who decides? What did my fellow teenagers think was cool from 1990 onward? Is *coolness* solely the province of angst, and rage, and furious moping, and confrontation, and crunchy guitars, and rampant badassness? Or does one achieve True Coolness by subverting that angst and rage and punishing volume and by instead embracing exuberance, and surrealism, and the sort of shrewd and defiant silliness often dismissed as *quirky*? Is a song about the eternal struggle between Particle Man and Triangle Man—or a song about the comfort of a bluebird nightlight, or a song about being reincarnated as a bag of groceries, or a song called "The Statue Got Me High," or a song called "Fingertips" composed of 21 micro-songs designed to liven up your CD player's "track shuffle" feature—any less cathartic and important than yet another song about yet another furious dude still pissed at yet another ex-girlfriend?

I spent my Alt-Rock Teen years convinced that there were two kinds of music: the fun kind and the important kind. Silliness and seriousness. Kid stuff and adult stuff. Comedy and tragedy. They Might Be Giants and Alice in Chains. And so, glued now to my beloved alt-rock radio in the deep-cut dead of night and confronted by a crabby and very strange 1994 manifesto called "Rock 'n' Roll Life-style" by a truly bewildering Sacramento band literally called Cake, I immediately know what this is (delightful, hilarious) and what it isn't (tough, meaningful). And then the song berates me for what I think I know. "Excess ain't rebellion," bellows Cake boss John McCrea, a C+ singer and A++ front man. "You're drinkin' what they're sellin'."

Oh, dear. McCrea's deepish voice has the irreverent, gloriously punchable tone that's like a dog whistle for wise-ass teenagers with a Weird Al mentality, and yet *excess ain't rebellion* is a remarkably pro-found idea to convey to a clueless 16-year-old in a wacky but also alarm-ingly angry semi-pop song.* Is that true, that excess ain't rebellion? And if we consider all the excess, all the chaos, all the self-destruction of early-'90s alt-rock radio, what *is* rebellion, in an era where every-one else seems to think that excess is rebellion? Who gets to decide what's *sardonic* or *wacky*, for that matter? Is true rebellion presenting to the world as an "alternative rock" band but flirting constantly with country music, and mariachi music, and Middle Eastern music, and, like, opera? Is true rebellion a trumpet solo, or a pedal-steel solo, or a Bakersfield-style honky-tonk guitar solo? Is true rebellion a vibraslap?†

While I mulled all that over, in 1996 Cake scored themselves an honest-to-God MTV and radio hit called "The Distance," with a rubbery little bubble-funk bassline and a rad James Bond-style

---

* You can find "Rock 'n' Roll Lifestyle" on Cake's excellent first record, 1994's *Motor-cade of Generosity*, which also includes a magnificent guitar jam called "Jolene" that isn't quite as good as Dolly Parton's "Jolene," but it's, like, 80 percent as good, which is incredibly good.

† Cake's percussion instrument of choice, a *Far Side*-worthy contraption that looks like a cheese grater welded to the gear shift to a 1974 Camaro and makes a ridicu-lous but deeply satisfying rattling sound. Go listen to the first 15 seconds of Ozzy Osbourne's "Crazy Train" and you'll get the gist.

surf-guitar riff and an oddly iconic a cappella opening line ("Reluctantly crouched at the starting line") that primes you for John McCrae's whole *deal*. And here's how I'd summarize John's whole deal: He's a self-aware medium-funky white guy during a golden era for self-aware medium-funky white guys. Not a whole golden era, maybe, but okay certainly a golden *hour*. Bradley Nowell from Sublime. Mike Doughty from Soul Coughing. The Barenaked Ladies in their bolder moments. Beck. They're not quite full-time white rappers, in the Vanilla Ice sense, but they're very often not *not* rapping, if you get me. This sort of thing is an awfully strong spice—paradoxically, medium-funky white guys might be the strongest spice of them all. Weezer taught me that.

And here's where all these teenaged false binaries collide: fun and important, silly and serious, kid stuff and adult stuff, comedy and tragedy. "I seriously thought we were the next Nirvana," Weezer frontman Rivers Cuomo told *Rolling Stone* in 2019, reminiscing for the billionth time about his barbed power-pop band's self-titled 1994 debut, better known and loved as The Blue Album. "And I thought the world was going to perceive us that way, like a super-important, super-powerful, heartbreaking heavy rock band, and as serious artists. That's how I saw us." But then, via the highest possible rotation on MTV and alt-rock radio, the world got a load of Weezer's first crunchy-goofy hit single, "Undone (The Sweater Song)," which contained, according to Rivers himself, his "darkest thoughts," and yet, he laments, "It became clear everyone else who hears this song is going to think it's hilarious."

Everyone else had a point. Weezer were from L.A. but didn't look like it, which I appreciated. These four fellas did not exactly radiate glamor from the cover of the Blue Album: I would describe them as having accessible haircuts, and they're not slouching, exactly, but they look like someone just yelled at them to stand up straight. Shuffle in the Blue Album's various timeless knucklehead anthems amid all the super-important, super-powerful glowering stuff bouncing around my head in '94—your Soundgardens, your Tools, your Stone Temple Pilots—and Weezer felt like a spoof, like a Dr. Demento-born and WWF-raised parody of a tough-guy alt-rock band. And the better Weezer's songs got, the greater that disparity between Rivers' grim reality and our grimly kooky perception of his reality. "Undone" (The Sweater Song)" played his unraveling and eventual *nudity* for laughs, not pathos; "Buddy Holly" became the instant-nostalgia song with the majestic weedly-deedly guitar solo and the *Happy Days*-themed Spike Jonze video; "Say It Ain't So" is an aching slow burn about buried family trauma with an opening line so legitimately odd and poignant and heart-breaking and, yes, *heavy*—"Somebody's Heine / Is crowding my icebox / Somebody's cold one / Is giving me chills"—that you could easily dismiss it as merely hilarious.

How much time should we spend discussing all the other Wee-zer albums? Two seconds? Alright: I *loved* 1996's *Pinkerton* when I was 18. I proudly let that record *define* me. I don't need to tell you how *that* turned out. Actually, here's another question: Why do I keep describing my teenage self like this? *Steakhead, doo-fus, dumb, oblivious, naïve.* What's with all the extravagant self-deprecation? Is this just reverse-psychology narcissism? Am I negging myself as some sort of perverse subconscious pickup-artist scheme? You know what's another great song on the Blue Album? The fortress-of-solitude battle hymn "In the Garage," whose sec-ond verse begins thus:

I got electric guitar
I play my stupid songs
I write these stupid words

The way Rivers Cuomo talked about himself when I was 15 reminds me of me, now, talking about my sucky 15-year-old self. It's tempting to want to go back in time and tell him to be a little kinder to himself. But if I did that, he probably wouldn't have a career, and I wouldn't have an identity.

IPICTURE HEAVEN AS A Guitar Center. If you ever worked at a Guitar Center, I'm guessing you *don't* picture heaven this way, but I never worked there and don't have that problem. So I die, right, and I wake up in a Guitar Center. And I'm like, *Hmm.* Nobody's around, but I hear, y'know, noodling off in a far corner, over by the bass guitars. So I dust myself off and head over there, and I turn a corner, and there's Jesus.

Jesus Christ, I mean. The Big Man, or, I guess, the Son of the Big Man. Part of the original power trio.* He's got the long hair, the robe, the sandals: Jesus looks exactly the way they taught me to picture him back at Sacred Heart Elementary in Eureka, Missouri. And now he's sitting there, alone, on a giant amplifier, noodling on a bass. The bass is, I don't know—a Music Man? An Ibanez? What's the No. 1 bass in heaven? A Rickenbacker? I don't know. His bass is plugged into the amp he's sitting on so he can feel the rumble beneath him as he plays—it's not a sexual feeling, it's just a cool feeling.

And then Jesus notices me and stops noodling.

---

* Oh my God. My mom is gonna kick my ass up and down the street. At this point she probably wishes I'd gone ahead and tried drugs.

And I ask, *Am I dead?* And he says, *Yep.* And I say, *Ohhhh.*
And I ask, *Are you…Jesus?* And he says, *Yep.* And I say, *Oh?*
And I ask, *Uh, what're you doin', Jesus?* And he says, *This is what I'm fuckin' doin'.* And then he BUSTS OUT THE RIFF TO THE BEASTIE BOYS' "SABOTAGE."

Now might seem like a bad time to discuss hard-fought personal and spiritual growth, but don't worry, I'm not talking about *mine.* I am fascinated by the moral arc of the Beastie Boys, who formed as hardcore-obsessed teenagers in early-'80s New York City and first broke out locally with a 1983 prank-call goof called "Cooky Puss." Then they signed to Def Jam Records, kicked out their drummer and close friend Kate Schellenbach, and refashioned themselves as charismatic-asshole frat-rappers at the behest of label co-founder and young funky-monk superproducer Rick Rubin, who helped them sell 10 million copies of their irresistibly bratty debut album, 1986's *Licensed to Ill*, which featured an extra-bratty and assholish and irresistible little tune called "(You Gotta) Fight for Your Right (To Party!)"

Look at that song title. Look at it. Look at how hard the punctuation is working to convince you that "(You Gotta) Fight for Your Right (To Party!)" is a parody, a knowing wink, an in-on-the-joke evisceration of dickhead boorishness and not, y'know, a *celebration* of dickhead boorishness. But a dickhead celebration is what pretty much everyone assumed "Fight for Your Right" was, and therefore what it became, especially when the suddenly famous Beastie Boys—now and forever a trio of Adam Horovitz (a/k/a Ad-Rock), Adam Yauch (a/k/a MCA), and Michael Diamond (a/k/a Mike D)—played it live on a stage decorated with a 20-foot-tall hydraulic penis. "We are what we pretend to be," Kurt Vonnegut once wrote, "So we must be very careful about what we pretend to be."

He was not talking about performing onstage with a 20-foot-tall hydraulic penis, but the point stands.

And so the slow, arduous, but tremendously heartening redemption narrative began. The Beasties fled to L.A., put out the funkier and substantially less boorish *Paul's Boutique* in 1989, strode into a vibrant new decade with 1992's leaner and rawer *Check Your Head*, and peaked as both humans and alt-punk-rap-funk pioneers with 1994's *Ill Communication*, which features three tremendously important songs:

No. 1: "B-Boys Makin' With the Freak Freak," which samples standup comic Mantan Moreland's timeless declaration, "If this is gonna be that kinda party, I'm gonna stick my dick in the mashed potatoes." (Maturity is a slow process.)

No. 2: "Sure Shot," in which Yauch raps, "I want to say a little something that's long overdue / The disrespect to women has got to be through," an apology and rallying cry that meant a lot, truly, coming from the dudes who'd reveled in the casual dickishness of *Licensed to Ill* hits like "Paul Revere" and "Girls."*

No. 3: FUCKIN' "SABOTAGE." Which strikes me now as the enlightened or at least way less bro-y "(You Gotta) Fight for Your Right (To Party!)," reversing the doomed pretzel-logic curse of becoming the thing you're pretending to make fun of. "Sabotage" has the ferocity, the distortion, the screaming,

---

* Both dumb-but-great songs, by the way. This is not one of those deals where Enlightened Mature 2023 Guy impresses you with his maturity by denouncing the unenlightened antics of Immature 1986 Guys. It's just that the Beasties themselves have mostly set the *Licensed to Ill* era aside, and "Sure Shot" is the moment when they prove that ecstatic rowdiness and inclusive tenderness can coexist.

and the wanton pinching brattiness of the classic Beastie Boys experience—plus an iconic '70s-cop-show video directed by our guy Spike Jonze, who explained the '70s to the '90s better than anyone alive—but it also has the sense, no matter where you are or how you're listening to it, of an arena full of jubilant boys and girls and men and women alike all jumping in unison. It's this fantastic sense of aggression but drained of *menace*, of ugliness, of steakheaded gatekeeping assholerie.

The Beastie Boys made a bunch more great music, and brought a great deal more good* into the world, and then ceased to exist when Yauch died on May 4, 2012, after a three-year battle with cancer. He was 47. He was a rock star, and a superstar rapper, and a good person who spent his life trying to be a better one. He also played one of the raddest basslines devised.

And that's the goal for everybody—not the raddest-bassline part, usually, but the good-person-getting-better part. That commitment to constant spiritual and societal improvement is hard, frustrating, lifelong, but utterly necessary work. The poet Robert Browning once wrote, "A man's reach should exceed his grasp." And then he heard me, at 16, trying to play Radiohead songs on my cheap but nicer-than-I-deserved electric guitar, and he was like, *Not you, though. You, stop reaching. You can grasp these.*

Shit, we're back to the suspicious self-deprecation, but I blame "Creep" for making me this way. "But I'm a creep." Radiohead

---

* Yauch, in particular, became a practicing Buddhist and spearheaded a series of ultra-cool and tremendously influential Tibetan Freedom Concerts between 1996 and 2001, a too-easy counterpoint, maybe, to the epic nihilism of Woodstock '99, but the comparison's there to make.

formed in the town of Abingdon in Oxfordshire, England, in 1985 as a "boring bunch of fuck-king stoodents," as I believe Liam Gallagher once described them. "I'm a weirdo." No way can I convey to you now the colossal impact of "Creep," their debut single, which appeared on *Pablo Honey*, their endearingly generic alt-rockin' 1993 debut album. "What the hell am I doing here?" No offense to moaning tormented-by-fame rock-star frontman Thom Yorke, but my primary hurdle here is that the written word will not suffice to describe guitarist Jonny Greenwood's shuddering, jarring, cataclysmic *JOOT-JOOT JOOT* outburst right before this, the chorus to "Creep," and yeah, I am reduced to typing out a famous electric-guitar sound as *JOOT-JOOT JOOT.* "I don't belong here." This is humiliating. That *JOOT-JOOT JOOT* "is the sound of Jonny trying to fuck the song up," as fellow guitarist Ed O'Brien explained to the *NME* in 1992. "He really didn't like it, so he tried spoiling it, and it made the song."

We are what we pretend to be; we are the hostile guitar sounds— *JOOT-JOOT JOOT*—we improvise in a failed attempt to sabotage the songs about what we've become. Maybe that's pompous rock-star bullshit, but it's pompous rock-star bullshit that defined the next 10 years of my life. Here's the thing about me. Has this come up yet? Radiohead's next album, 1995's *The Bends*, very arguably ranks in my Top 10 albums of all time: the total shredding freakouts of "My Iron Lung" and "Just," Yorke's pulverizing falsetto on "Fake Plastic Trees" and "High and Dry," and the electrifying squeak of the acoustic-guitar strings deep into the moody ballad "Nice Dream," a split-second blip every bit as precious to me as *JOOT-JOOT JOOT.* And *OK Computer?* The third Radiohead album? Came out in 1997? *OK Computer* was My Absolute Favorite Album Ever for... half a decade? A full decade? Two decades? Is *OK Computer* still

My Absolute Favorite Album Ever? These are basic-ass White Male Rock Critic of a Certain Age opinions, and I don't care, but I also don't care to waste any time here trying to explain or justify these opinions. What do you want me to say?

Here's what I'll say; here's the half-memory that gets us closest to a coherent explanation. Summer 1997. I'm 19 years old. *OK Computer* only came out a few months ago, but I'm already obsessed. And I'm at a house party, or in any event, I'm hanging out in some dude's backyard. Suburban house. Trampoline in his backyard. I know a few people at this party, but not many. And I am distracted. I am glum. I am sulking. I'd gotten dumped recently, if I recall correctly, and of course I do. I'm gonna be fine. Totally mundane circumstances. But the memory I have now, I'm sulking in the backyard, and keeping my distance, and the only thing in my head is *OK Computer.* That's the memory. "Paranoid Android" or whatever, just, *bzzzzt,* in my head.

And my impulse now, right, is to embellish this memory with tons of florid, tragicomic detail. I want to paint a chemical sunset behind the house. I want 50 hot girls bouncing on the trampoline and ignoring me. I want to be humming "No Surprises" to myself, pathetically. I got a cowlick, I'm wearing cargo shorts, whatever. Hysterical and useless. *Bluh bluh bluh bluh.* None of that is real, of course. None of that is *true.* But what feels true is the fundamental idea of me, struggling in a social situation, less awkward than I imagine but still quite awkward, and I'm just *thinkin' real hard* about *OK Computer.* As one does; as I did, for years. That feels true, and true to me. And what I wonder now is whether this moment represents my world expanding, or my world contracting. I have thought and said and written and felt so much about this band that I don't know what else to say, and all I can think to ask is, did Radiohead open my mind or forcibly shut it? Did they show me a wondrous universe outside myself, or did they help me build a wondrous universe crammed inside my own head where I could spend the vast majority of my time to the near-total exclusion of the outside world? Fascinating, right? Yeah, maybe.

It is pretty much the same deal with Pearl Jam, the Seattle alt-rock gods whose debut album, 1991's *Ten*, was the third CD I ever owned, and which boasts eight Good Songs out of 11, for an exemplary Good Song Percentage of 73 percent. Don't overthink it. "Why Go," "Oceans," and "Garden." That's it. Every other song on *Ten* is a Good Song.* And what Pearl Jam frontman and voice-of-a-generation mumbler Eddie Vedder conveys to me, as a clueless 13-year-old with three CDs who's hanging on his every word, is how uncomfortable he is with the idea of millions of clueless 13-year-olds hanging on his every word. Pearl Jam's fame, in my teenage memory, is inextricable from Pearl Jam's intense discomfort with fame. Or Eddie Vedder's discomfort with fame, at least. Pearl Jam, for the rest of the '90s, are synonymous, for me, with rock-star self-negation. They retreat. They recoil. They refuse. So somewhere in high school some English teacher finally makes me read that 1853 Herman Melville short story "Bartleby, the Scrivener," about the guy who doesn't want to scriven anymore and so he just keeps saying, "I would prefer not to," and it's

---

* In lieu of our arguing about this, can I tell you my daddest dad joke? There's a company called Evenflo that makes strollers and car seats and such, and we have one of their baby gates in our house, and every time I walk by the Evenflo baby gate, I go, "EVEN FLOWWW / DON'T LET YOUR BABIES FALL DOWN THE STAIRS, YEAH" and *nobody ever laughs*. Nobody. That's why it's my daddest dad joke: I am alone in thinking that the Evenflo baby gate should include a little built-in speaker that blares the chorus to Pearl Jam's "Even Flow" every time it successfully restrains a baby.

all profound and literary.* *Pearl Jam, make more videos.* "I would prefer not to." *Pearl Jam, do more interviews and be on more magazine covers.* "I would prefer not to." *Pearl Jam, stop complaining about Ticketmaster.* "I would prefer not to." *Pearl Jam, quit hanging out with Neil Young all the time.* "I would prefer not to." *Pearl Jam, put your best songs on your full-length albums.* "I would fuckin' prefer not to."

Because it turns out that "Jeremy," one of the first Pearl Jam record's eight Good Songs, was also released as a three-track single that included what I am only now realizing is one of Pearl Jam's greatest Good Songs of all.

?? Unsealed on a porch a letter sat ??
?? Then you said, I wanna leave it again ??

Do not trust *anyone who claims to know the exact* words to "Yellow Ledbetter," a transcendently languid classic-rock jam built, as Pearl Jam lead guitarist Mike McCready more or less concedes, on the foundation of Jimi Hendrix's "Little Wing," and bolstered by Eddie Vedder's most transfixing bout of mumbling in the public domain.

?? On a weekend ??
?? Wanna wish it all away ??
?? And they called and I said that I want what I said ??
?? And then I call out again ??

---

* I hate to tell you this, but in high school, if a teacher ever made you write an essay about "Bartleby, the Scrivener," and you just turned in a single sheet of paper with "I would prefer not to" written on it, you would've automatically been named valedictorian. Balloons and confetti dropped from the ceiling. You got to graduate high school immediately. It was like a cheat code. I'm sorry you had to find out like this. I didn't know either.

Just roll with it. What makes "Yellow Ledbetter" so important is the gibberish, the mysteriousness, the bafflement, the sense of deep calm so absolute that you accept the idea that the song maybe isn't supposed to mean anything or consist of real English words.* It's supposed to sound like Pearl Jam recorded it five minutes before they wrote it. And there was something so comforting about hearing this song on the radio in, say, 1992, amid all those other blaring alt-rock songs trying so hard to achieve the emotionally resonant and lasting profundity that "Yellow Ledbetter" achieves just by existing.

And as Pearl Jam evolved into one of the most prolific and beloved rock bands of their generation, "Yellow Ledbetter" would emerge as the perfect encore. Last song of the night. The dramatic but serene conclusion. The light of the disco ball reflecting off all the half-deflated balloons drifting down to the dusty gymnasium floor. This song has the exhausted but thoroughly satisfied casual lope of 10,000 Pearl Jam fans all walking back to their cars. You ain't gotta go home, but you can't stay here, except this music is where I've stayed, where I've flourished and/or atrophied, for my whole life. And if die and wake up in a Guitar Center and Jesus is hanging out amid the guitars instead, I know what song I hope he's playing.

---

* Vedder has introduced the song live as an anti-war statement about a friend's brother killed in action during the Gulf War, and that's a tremendously Eddie Vedder sort of move, to sing about something so profound and tragic in a beautifully garbled tone almost designed to generate confusion.

ROMANCE + SEX + IMMATURITY

SONGS DISCUSSED:

Salt-N-Pepa, "Shoop"

Nine Inch Nails, "Closer"

Tool, "Stinkfist"

Prince, "Gett Off"

Boyz II Men, "End of the Road"

Liz Phair, "Fuck and Run"

Sunny Day Real Estate, "In Circles"

Bonnie Raitt, "I Can't Make You Love Me"

Dave Matthews Band, "Crash Into Me"

Blink-182, "What's My Age Again"?

I GOTTA TALK TO you for a second about the Eddie Money song "Take Me Home Tonight." Incredible song. Top 5 hit in 1986. PG-13 synth-pop erotica. Immaculate conception via sax solo. Plus Eddie Money looks like '80s Evan Dando. So the concept of "Take Me Home Tonight" is that Eddie is singing, amorously, to a lady friend, and imploring her to, y'know, take him home tonight. Whereupon none other than Ronnie Spector shows up and thunders, "Be my little baby," echoing an earlier, even more famous song where Ronnie sang that.

But here is my truth: As a kid I thought Ronnie was singing, "*FEED* my little baby." I learned about sex at the usual age, thank you very much, but for years afterward I thought this song was about a lady having a one-night stand with Eddie Money and getting pregnant and having a kid and *showing up on his doorstep with a newborn* nine months later demanding that Eddie feed the baby. I thought "Take Me Home Tonight" was a cautionary tale about premarital sex. I swear to God. "Feed my little baby." Unbelievable. Go listen to "Take Me Home Tonight" again: Does it sound, *at all*, like Ronnie Spector is singing, "Feed my little baby"? *No, it doesn't.*

There's 5-year-old me, buckled into a car seat in the back of my father's rusty Fiat in the early '80s and cheerfully assuming that Meat Loaf's bawdy 1977 dad-rock epic "Paradise by the Dashboard Light" is about a nice guy and a nice lady driving while listening to a baseball game who get into an argument about whether they should drive farther. I thought paradise was an external place: Six Flags, maybe, or the zoo.

There's 13-year-old me riding shotgun in my mom's Toyota, and the R-rated 1990 Bell Biv DeVoe* ditty "Do Me" pops on the radio, with a quite visceral opening five seconds I'd transcribe like so:

OHHHHH YEAHHH AHH

OHHHHH YEAHHH AHH

And my mom, like, *slaps* the radio off. Just, *WHAP*. And then *silence*, in the car, for an uncomfortably long time. Another time my mom asked me, point-blank, what the initials in the Naughty by Nature song "O.P.P." really stood for. *Can you imagine.* I panicked. I told her it stood for "Other People's Privates." I thought that would soften the blow. It did not. *Silence.*

"Do Me," it occurs to me now, bears a striking resemblance, in sound and transcription, to Salt-N-Pepa's timeless 1986 junior-high-gymnasium-dance classic "Push It." And yet I bopped along harmlessly to this song—"PUSH IT GOOD"—while driving around with my mom all the time, and I do recall watching all the junior high girls boisterously line-dance to this song—"PUSH IT REAL GOOD"—as I nervously pressed my back right up against the bleachers folded into the walls of the gym, not even blooming enough to qualify as a wallflower. "Push It" is not, it seems to me now, subtle. But somehow Salt-N-Pepa—the luminous Queens rap trio of Cheryl "Salt" James, Sandra "Pepa" Denton, and Deidra

---

* "Poison" is the best BBD song, obviously, even if the mega-uncouth line "Me and the crew used to do her" is both uncouth and grammatically incorrect. (It should be, "The crew and I used to do her.")

"Spinderella" Roper*—expertly glide across the line between *risqué* and *obscene*.

Maybe that's because Salt-N-Pepa themselves never thought of the song as risqué, let alone obscene. "For 30 years, we have been telling people that 'Push It' isn't about sex, but no one ever believes us," Pepa lamented to *The Guardian* in 2017. "Honestly, for us, as young girls, it was about dancing." I respect that, and I believe her; *You better respect and believe us* is the whole goddamn point of the Salt-N-Pepa catalog. But I do think Salt and Pepa are the only two people on earth who believe that. As Salt explained in that very same *Guardian* article, "An aquarium told us that when they put the song on, the sharks started mating."

Huh.

I believe the sharks, too. I am always tremendously delighted to hear Salt-N-Pepa on the radio—any song, at any age, in any mood, from mercurial teen to exasperated adult—and I credit the group's phenomenally shrewd sense of balance. Swaggering rap music with the light-footed exuberance of pure pop. Sexy songs about dancing; dance-floor-filling songs about not having sex. Y'know what's a truly fantastic Salt-N-Pepa song? "Do You Want Me," a slinking electro-funk gem from the group's third album, 1990's *Blacks' Magic*. The one with the chorus that starts like this:

Do you really want me, baby? Let me know
'Cause if you really like me I suggest you tell me so

---

* She's the DJ, obviously, though Roper is actually the second (and thereafter canonical) Spinderella; on "Push It" and the rest of the trio's 1986 debut *Hot, Cool & Vicious*, the role of Spinderella is played by Latoya Hanson, who left the group before the album even came out.

I'd somehow forgotten about "Do You Want Me" for *years*, and I was *ecstatic* to stumble across it again recently: the slurry boy-girl murmur of that chorus, the deft James Brown sample that sounds like nobody'd ever had the idea to sample James Brown before, and the sneak-attack provocation of a playfully lascivious young-lovers duet about abstinence, about restraint, about refusal. They're into each other, but Salt won't have sex with the guy yet. "I'd just be playing myself out / If I spent the night at your house," she decides, waving off his feeble complaints that she's a tease. It's a love song about not giving in to lust.

To wit, *Blacks' Magic* also has a song called "Let's Talk About Sex," a breezy and bumptious shuffle with one of the catchiest hooks Salt-N-Pepa ever devised—"Let's talk about all the good things / And the bad things / That may be"—that delves further into the love-versus-lust conundrum but never sounds like a lecture or a sermon or a junior-high health class. And the song held up as transcendent pop music even when the group explicitly rewrote it as a PSA called "Let's Talk About AIDS" for a 1992 Peter Jennings ABC News special about what by then was a harrowing global health crisis shrouded in fear and ignorance and misinformation.

All of this—the deadly seriousness, but the early total dance-floor frivolity, too—feeds directly into 1994's *Very Necessary*, Salt-N-Pepa's biggest and best record, which endearingly denounces pop-star gossip ("None of Your Business") even as it gives everyone plenty to talk about ("No One Does It Better," which includes the line "When the bugle is blown it's all tongue and no teeth"), and drops a song called "Sexy Noises Turn Me On" three tracks before an agonizing PSA closing sketch literally titled "I've Got AIDS." It also features the group's two highest-charting hits, both of them mildly lewd and entirely joyous and only deepened by Salt-N-Pepa's hard-fought wisdom, even if you can't hear a trace of the fight in the songs themselves. "Whatta Man," a remake of Laura Lyndell's 1968 Stax soul single, is a delectable summit with powerhouse Oakland girl group En Vogue, who absolutely crush one of the sweetest and coolest and most indestructible hooks mid-'90s pop had to offer, but yeah, no, "Shoop" is the one. "Shoop" is the one with the opening line that further betrays me as the corniest dude alive.

Here I go, here I go, here I go again
Girls, what's my weakness? (Men!)

Here is my truth: Every time I listen to this song, when Pepa raps, "Girls, what's my weakness?," I *physically point* to a corner of the room or the car or wherever, as if cueing the imaginary girls there to yell, "Men!" I look ridiculous. It's humiliating. I don't care. A song that compels you to gladly humiliate yourself is the mark of true greatness. "Shoop" is a marvel of male objectification, a gender-swapped catcall summit. "Don't know how you do the voo-doo that you do," Pepa raps, ribald and weightless; "I gotta know, how does it hang?" Salt inquires, and I hope you appreciate how ridiculous I felt even typing that out. This song is absurdly *fun*, this song is *silly*, this song is *free of consequence*, and that freedom is all the sweeter for how hard Salt-N-Pepa have always worked to teach us that *freedom from consequence* isn't a real thing.*

---

* I'm sorry, I'm still thinking about the sharks fucking to "Push It." *How was this discovered?* Did someone just happen to bring a boombox blasting "Push It" into the aquarium? Or were the aquarium people sitting around trying to figure out how to get the sharks horny, and this was some marine biologist's genius idea? Is this

My wife loves "Shoop." That's the other thing. Amid the utter early-morning chaos of getting our kids fed and clothed and acceptably groomed and out the door for school, my wife sometimes raps "Shoop" quietly to herself, or, better yet, not-so-quietly to me. And it is indeed quite flattering to have the love of my life inform me that "If looks could kill you would be an Uzi" at 8 a.m. on a Tuesday, but the truth is that I happily regress, in these moments, to my timid and naive and disastrously misinformed adolescence. As my wife merrily dances around the kitchen, I feel myself backing up, giving her space, pressing against our refrigerator, which might at any point transform into one of my junior high gymnasium's fold-in bleachers. The nervousness-around-girls is an old feeling; the utter contentment is a newer feeling that never gets old. This, it turns out, is paradise, and I'd take her home tonight, but we're already here.

M ISINTERPRET THIS, PAL:

I wanna fuck you like an animal
I wanna feel you from the inside

Or, as I heard it 600,000 times on the radio:

I wanna [   ] you like an animal
I wanna feel you from the inside

---

what marine biology *is*? Y'know how everyone in high school wants to be a marine biologist for like 10 minutes? I'd totally have gone through with it if I'd known this is what marine biologists did. Me all winning a Nobel Prize for playing Luther Vandross for some manatees. Okay, sorry. I've processed it now. Sorry.

Ah, yes, that's my shit. An all-time-great goofy radio edit. The delicate elision. The dead space. The offending word just snipped out of the fabric of existence. So *chaste*. Nine Inch Nails' "Closer" is a transcendent pop song as well: hooky, mesmerizing, and deliciously subversive. You know what's more subversive than writing and singing this song, though? *Playing this song on the radio.* The first DJ who cued up "Closer" violated more taboos and shattered more sociocultural norms than the guy who wrote and sang it. I don't care what radio edit you use. The chorus still says what it says and means what it means.

I don't mean to downplay the many transgressions of dictatorial Nine Inch Nails mastermind Trent Reznor, whom I worshiped in high school, and who often complained in interviews that modern rock stars have utterly demystified themselves: They talk too much, take too many photographs, and in general do too much *explaining*. They're ruining everything; they're ruining the *illusion*. As a kid, Trent never wanted to know what Pink Floyd or Supertramp really looked like. And so let's re-mystify him: Trent Reznor was a fucking alien-wizard who crash-landed on this planet in 1989 and invented industrial music* and descended from the burning mountaintop with two stone tablets, with SOUL carved on one and HOLE carved on the other.

And I worshiped him. I may never put on the 1994 Nine Inch Nails album *The Downward Spiral* ever again, because this is music

---

* Trent gladly admits that "Down in It," a frigid and disconcertingly danceable single from Nine Inch Nails' 1989 debut album *Pretty Hate Machine*, is directly inspired by the Vancouver industrial band Skinny Puppy's tune "Dig It," from their 1986 album *Mind: The Perpetual Intercourse*. And so one way to summarize Trent's outsized appeal is that *Pretty Hate Machine* is a way better album title, pop-star-marketing-wise, than *Mind: The Perpetual Intercourse*.

I no longer need to play out loud to hear. I can recite this record for you the same way I can recite my Social Security number. And my question for you is, how fucked up does that make me? "Reptile," the exquisitely grueling dirge that begins with the line, "She spreads herself wide open / To let the insects in"? "Heresy," the pulverizing death march with the chorus that goes, "God is dead / And no one cares," which didn't exactly harmonize with all the Catholicism? "The Downward Spiral," wherein Trent mutters, "He put the gun into his face / Bang / So much blood for such a tiny hole"? Yo: "Big Man With a Gun"? Remember when the biggest threat to my innocence was Meat Loaf?

You can have my isolation
You can have the hate that it brings

And I took it. Trent's isolation was my isolation; his hate was my hate. "Closer" ends with a lengthy, majestic industrial-funk keyboard breakdown, and I memorized every individual second the same way I memorized all those Civil War battles in history class, and let's just say I don't remember jack shit about the Civil War now. I wonder what *The Downward Spiral* was trying to teach me; I wonder what I learned. On the internet now it is way easier to find the *uncensored* version of the "Closer" video, which is too bad, because I suspect that the MTV edit, which as a teenager* I watched like 600,000 times, was *better*, not to mention more dangerous and subversive. In the edit, every frame MTV cut is replaced

---

* It's just now occurring to me that you can divide my life into two halves: There is *as a kid/teenager*, and then there is *on the internet*. That's it. That's the great divide. And I am so grateful, truly, that those two life phases never really intersected at all.

with a title card that says SCENE MISSING, and I guarantee you that whatever a corny 14-year-old kid *imagines* is in that missing scene is way more graphic and inappropriate than whatever's actually missing. I finally watched the uncensored version: There's a naked lady in it. *Eh*. In this way, and in only this way, the stuff in my teenage head was way gnarlier than the stuff in Trent Reznor's head. He could've used a little bit of *my* isolation, if you want to know the truth.

Whoa! If I could move my arm that fast, I'd never leave the house!

I almost died laughing the first time I watched Beavis and Butt-Head watch the mega-grody stop-motion video for Tool's punishing 1993 breakout hit "Sober," and I also almost died laughing when I watched them watch that video again *today*. Tool—a philosophical and scatological prog-metal band from Los Angeles, or maybe they're alien-wizards who crash-landed on this planet shortly after Trent Reznor did—are so grim, so badass, so intense, so profound (?!), and so disturbing that you might also find them—perhaps as a defense mechanism—hilarious. Tool excel at making you electrifyingly uncomfortable: After "Sober," their next big single/mega-grody video was called "Prison Sex." Either it ain't that deep or it's bottomless; these guys are either stupid as all hell or they're the most intellectually stimulating rock band born in the 20th century.

What a Tool song called "Stinkfist" presupposes is, *Why not both? Why not all of it?* They played "Stinkfist" on the radio; they played the mega-grody "Stinkfist" video on MTV, although MTV called it "Track #1"* because apparently you couldn't say "Stinkfist"

---

* Off Tool's 1996 tour de force *Ænima*, which also features a song called "Hooker With a Penis," which Spotify recently informed me was my most-played song of 2022.

on MTV. I'd argue now that the most provocative aspect of this song is that it's also beautiful in places. Melodically beautiful, and if you took it seriously enough maybe even philosophically beautiful: "Desensitized to everything / What became of subtlety?" frontman Maynard James Keenan bellows, amid an unsubtle prog-rock-ass barrage from drummer Danny Carey. I love this band so much.

Tool aren't much for interviews or other forms of demystification, but you can find, on the internet, a lovingly fan-curated Frequently Asked Questions file on the band, last updated in 2001 and running 16,594 words of arduously acquired factual information spiced up with bold fan conjecture. This FAQ addresses "Stinkfist" at some length: A Tool fan with an aol.com email address suggests that "It is using a fist-up-the-ass metaphor for the desensitizing of the public." Yes. Definitely. Maybe. A less whimsical anecdote: I saw Tool live in Columbus, Ohio, on September 14, 2001, and Maynard, a/k/a Mr. Stinkfist himself, gave a lengthy and thoughtful speech, right after they played "Prison Sex," about choosing compassion and love over fear, which inspired, much to his consternation, a full-arena chant of "USA! USA! USA!" You go to war with the emotional and sociopolitical army you have, not the army you might want or wish to have at a later time. Either it wasn't that deep or it was bottomless.

Alright, so picture a guitar-wielding man in a shredded, assless, canary-yellow bodysuit performing a porno-funk song called "Gett Off"—yes, two T's in "Gett," and you know why—at the 1991 MTV Video Music Awards, spinning around to emphasize the asslessness of his bodysuit right when he gets to the line, "Move your big ass 'round this way, so I can work on that zipper, baby." Is that more or less subversive than a prog-metal song called

"Stinkfist" or an industrial-rock chorus of "I wanna fuck you like an animal"?

What if the assless-bodysuit man is *literally Prince*?

All I know for sure is, if you play "Gett Off" in an aquarium, the sharks will start fucking *you*.

Another uncomfortable silence between me and my mother occurred in her Toyota when Prince's "Cream" came on the radio, and that song's intro isn't even tremendously porn-y: a few abstract moans, a cowbell, a simple boom-kick drumbeat, and a sultry and muted guitar riff that makes it sound like the guitar, also, is wearing an assless canary-yellow bodysuit, and okay, yeah, it's way pornier than I remember. And also the song's called "Cream." And also it's Prince, who would spend the rest of the '90s releasing a reliably great but hilariously indigestible amount of material—including the 1996 three-disc set called *Emancipation,* followed by the 1998 three- or four- or five-disc set called *Crystal Ball*—whilst also changing his name to an unpronounceable symbol and writing the word *slave* on his cheek, actions that seemed merely eccentric at the time but revealed themselves, with the fullness of time, to have far more troubling and vital exploitative-music-business explanations.* Take him seriously, always. He's earned it.

But please forgive me if that X-rated performance of "Gett Off"—a song I will describe here, in a professional capacity, as *horny Public Enemy*—is my dominant image of Prince in the '90s, though also, impressively, it's the first thing that pops into my head when I think about the VMAs in the '90s, and that's a show I

---

* He was fighting with his label. "When you stop a man from dreaming, he becomes a slave," Prince explained to *Rolling Stone* in 1996. "That's where I was. I don't own Prince's music. If you don't own your masters, your master owns you."

watched religiously (or I suppose sacrilegiously) as a teen. I actually have no idea why there are two T's in "Gett Off," and yep, that jumpsuit sure seems to be assless, and there I am watching this shit at like 13 years old, thunderstruck and intimidated and feeling more like a helpless little kid than I ever have, thinking, *Man, if this is what it takes to get a girl to dance with you, this is never gonna work.*

But then a girl danced with me. Seventh grade. I couldn't believe it. I don't blame you if *you* don't believe it. But it happened. I can't remember what we danced to, but the song I now associate with first-slow-dance-type vibes is for sure Boyz II Men's "End of the Road,"* a transcendently sappy pop-soul hyper-ballad that gathers just a breathtaking amount of momentum despite moving in slow motion. That's a little wonky, sorry. What I mean is that it's the ideal soundtrack to your brain exploding.

It's awkward in theory but just ungodly ecstatic in practice, the first time you slow-dance with somebody. The life-altering magnificent cringe of that moment, when you don't know what to do with any part of your body. Do you put your hands on their shoulders? At their waist? What is the appropriate distance between your bodies? (Refer to the R&B group Next's soft-core 1998 hit "Too Close" for more on the physical-distance topic, though maybe don't play that one for your mother.) Think back to how awkwardly you swayed, back and forth, in broken, hapless time to the music. Did you look them in the eye? Were you desperate not to look them

---

* Boyz II Men, if memory serves, are from Philadelphia, and were shepherded to glory by Bell Biv DeVoe's Michael Bivens, and blew up with their sneakily slow-jam-heavy 1991 debut *Cooleyhighharmony*. But "End of the Road," which first surfaced on the soundtrack to the rad 1992 Eddie Murphy romcom *Boomerang*, blew up to an absurd degree and spent 13 weeks at No. 1, kicking off their streak of breaking and then re-breaking chart records. Yeah, I'm almost positive they're from Philly.

in the eye? Was the room, was the gym spinning? Is this what romance is? Is this what true love is? Did your brain explode? Did your heart explode? How did any of us survive this? If you were lucky, you had Michael McCary to cling to, emotionally, while you clung physically to whoever was clinging to you.

Girl, you know I'm here for you

Michael McCary is the sonar-depth bass voice on the first six Boyz II Men records, and he often provides rumbling spoken-word song intros of the "Hey baby, I'm sorry, I never meant to hurt you" variety, as an invaluable listener-orienting device.* But his listener-soothing bridge on "End of the Road"—*You just don't understand how much I love you, do you?*—is his masterpiece, and further rolls the song up the mountaintop until we hit the ecstatic a cappella chorus at the end, and holy shit this awesome song just got awesomer, and there in the gym, the closer you get to the person you're clumsily slow-dancing with, the higher you are off the ground. The end of the road is the beginning, your final push into lovestruck adolescent orbit, into the exhilarating vacuum of space. And you'd float away forever if Michael McCary's gently booming voice wasn't so transcendently earthbound, and if he weren't physically holding on with one hand to just your one foot, because whatever happens with this person you're first-slow-dancing with, now you belong to *him*, and he belongs to you.

---

* My theory, in fact, is that Michael McCary should say a few words in the first 15 seconds of every song, released by anybody, forever. He can explain the song's concept. Provide context. Orient the listener. No more wondering what a song's about. *Girl, this song's about driving in a car with one headlight.* And so on. He should do this for all movies, too: *Girl, this movie's about a pet detective.*

* * *

NEVER HEARD THIS ONE on the radio, not even once:

Fuck and run
Fuck and run
Even when I was 17

It vexes me to admit to you how I first encountered Liz Phair's exalted 1993 debut album *Exile in Guyville*. It's not my finest hour. (I do *have* finest hours, by the way, but I prefer to keep those *private*.) So I'm in college, and I pull this CD from the stacks at my college-radio station, and I *scan the tracklist for the dirty songs*. That's my first encounter. Yikes. My understanding—gleaned, most likely, from *Rolling Stone* or *SPIN* or perhaps even *Magnet* magazine—is that Liz Phair* is *a dirty-talking lady*, and this interests me, intellectually, as an intellectual 19-year-old yutz.

I am also aware that Liz has formatted her debut album—among the most shocking, cataclysmic, inimitable, influential, and hard-to-live-up-to debut albums in pop-music history—as a track-by-track response to the 1972 Rolling Stones mega-classic *Exile on Main Street*, itself one of the most deified and bro'd-out rock 'n' roll records ever born. "I listened to it over and over again, and it became like my source of strength," Liz told the author and

---

* Born in New Haven, Connecticut; raised primarily in Winnetka, Illinois, the Chicago suburb best known as the setting for the 1986 cinematic masterwork *Ferris Bueller's Day Off*; educated at Oberlin University, a/k/a the least Ohioan physical location in Ohio; but based mostly in Chicago, home to a thriving but alarmingly bitchy indie-rock scene she's about to disrupt all to fuck, pardon my language.

filmmaker Jessica Hopper for a 2010 *Exile in Guyville* oral history in *SPIN*. "My involvement with *Exile* was like an imaginary friend; whatever Mick was saying, it was a conversation with him, or I was arguing with him, and it was kind of an amalgam of the men in my life. That was why I called it *Guyville*—friends, romantic interests, these teacher types—telling me what I needed to know, what was cool or what wasn't cool." She means Mick Jagger, not that you needed that mansplained to you.

> *Fuck and run*
> *Fuck and run*
> *Even when I was 12*

I do not play "Fuck and Run" on the air on my college radio station, because playing songs with 200-pound swears in 'em is against the rules, and I follow the rules, and anyway I'd rather play Soul Coughing or Cake or whatever, because I am an *intellectual*. But from this moment forward *Exile in Guyville* takes on this illicit, forbidden quality for me, and imagine my surprise when I do finally get around to listening to "Fuck and Run" and I realize it's a deceptively straightforward rock 'n' roll song that starts with the line "I woke up in your arms" but is actually about rejection, about mortification, about loneliness, about the fear that you'll be a yutz forever and you might be alone forever, too.

"Everybody thinks my song 'Fuck and Run' is about sex, and on one level it is," Liz writes in her lovely and defiantly non-linear 2019 memoir *Horror Stories*, right after telling a story about falling out with a dear college friend after he accidentally cracked her in the nose with a meat tenderizer. "But it's also about these moments when real connection and feeling is abandoned in favor of self-preservation. We come together and fly apart like colliding billiard balls because, for whatever reason, we sense annihilation."

Listen, this is uncouth, but I'd like to think she'd appreciate my being direct: "Fuck and Run" is way more about the running than the fucking. Yeah, I feel weird saying that; I feel weird reading about *Exile in Guyville* at all. Even Liz Phair's biggest fans have a tendency to write wildly out-of-pocket shit about Liz Phair; even glowing reviews of *Exile in Guyville* can be super-gnarly, dude. Summoned by her sneaky-deadpan voice—and the dense, nervous, blurry furtiveness of her guitar-playing, not to mention her blunt and exasperated and legit-genius lyricism—new Guyvilles sprout up around Liz Phair wherever she goes, and with every challenging but inevitably misunderstood new album she makes. (Her best song ever is "What Makes You Happy" off 1998's *Whitechocolatespaceegg*, FYI.) All these Guyvilles usually intend to praise her, but they also seek to control her, to define her, to opine on what she should do next to stay in our good graces.

Exile in Guyville, in short, becomes a sort of self-perpetuating Guyville generator, in part because it's a singularly fantastic, momentous, era- and genre-defining album, yes, but also because Liz Phair is, indeed, a dirty-talking lady, and society tends to respond very poorly to dirty-talking ladies. Did I just say *legit-genius lyricism*? Ugh. They're not always pleasant revelations, but "Fuck and Run" has proven very helpful to me in interrogating what I think I know and exasperatedly pointing me in the direction of all the shit I don't know. The other day my wife and I were watching that Netflix teen-Goth-murder-mystery show *Wednesday*, and at one point Wednesday's tailing the police chief, right, and she sneaks into his car, and he gets in and drives off, oblivious.

"That would never happen," my wife says. "He would notice. He would check the car before he drove off."

"Really?" I ask, wisely.

"Really," my wife says, exasperated. "Don't you check in the back of the car every time you get into it, before you drive off, just in case there's somebody hiding back there? I do that every time I get in the car. All women check, every time, just in case some creep is hiding back there. You don't do that?"

"Of course not," I reply, less wisely.

And my wife just gives me a look like, *Guyville*.

I successfully wooed my future wife in part with burned mix CDs, the noble descendants of all the dubbed cassette mixtapes I made for all the unfortunate ladies I haplessly wooed throughout high school and college. Songs that I put on cassette mixtapes for girls from roughly 1996 to 2001 include U2's "With or Without You," Des'ree's "Kissing You," Weezer's "Susanne," Built to Spill's "Reasons," Matthew Sweet's "Your Sweet Voice," Oasis' "Slide Away," A Tribe Called Quest's "Electric Relaxation" with the line about *your fat-ass thighs* faded way down because I didn't want to offend the girl, Metallica's "Nothing Else Matters," Beck's "Deborah," Susanna Hoffs's "Eternal Flame," the Spin Doctors' "How Could You Want Him (When You Know You Could Have Me)," Type O Negative's "Love You to Death," and most importantly, the Goo Goo Dolls' "Iris." "I just want you to know who I am. I just want you to know who I am. I just want you to know who I am."

Please don't make me prattle on about the lost art of physical cassette mixtapes that you painstakingly dub yourself, and then you scrawl out all the artists and song titles in your lousy childlike handwriting, and then you give the whole tape some cutesy pompous quasi-literary title like I AM NOT AFRAID OF STORMS, and then you slip it to Your Crush Who Sits in Front of You in AP Biology or Philosophy 101 or whatever and you just pray the tape conveys some semblance of an idea of what a sensitive and passionate and charismatic person you are. It's a beautiful thing. The first song on Side 2. Even burned mix CDs don't got the first song on Side 2. It's not the same thing.

I don't want to talk about it. Nor do I want to talk about the time I wrote out the lyrics to Sunny Day Real Estate's "In Circles"* and mailed them to a girl.

Meet me there
In the blue
Where words are not
Feeling remains

Oh, Jesus. That young lady did not deserve this. The song ends thus:

Oh I dream
To heal your wounds
But I bleed myself
I bleed myself

---

* Off their rad 1994 debut *Diary*, which topped *Rolling Stone*'s 2019 list of "The 40 Greatest Emo Albums of All Time"; as you might imagine, Sunny Day Real Estate didn't much enjoy being called an emo band, but that's a pretty emo state of affairs, isn't it?

Jesus, Rob. What a closing line, though, and what a startling distillation of the emo experience, the rock 'n' roll experience, the teenage experience: *I'm gonna save you, baby, right after you save me.* Sunny Day Real Estate were from Seattle and had a very Seattle-in-1994 vibe: raging guitars, startling dynamic shifts, an indifferent fashion sense, and a ferocious sort of vulnerability conveyed by frontman Jeremy Enigk's pinched and piercing voice. They pretty much never got played on alt-rock radio, but they still made total sense to an uncool meat-and-potatoes alt-rock kid such as myself who could recognize the classic formula: two guitars, bass, drums, and *impassioned wailing.* Comfort food. This music's not trying to sneak up on you or trick you; it's not a Trojan horse for something else. And it's not afraid of storms, either.

"*Sommmmmmetimes,*" Jeremy wails passionately on "Sometimes," *Diary*'s half-speed demolition derby of a closing track. "*Sommmmmmetimes.*" If you happened to be dialed into the precise emotional frequency here, there's something so dense and abstruse and fascinating about this band, because you so rarely understand the words Jeremy's singing, and you only fleetingly have any sense of what he *means*, and he absolutely never sounds like a lead singer conventionally tuneful and coherent enough to get played to death on the radio. Not even "Seven," *Diary*'s regular-speed demolition derby of an opening track, featuring another great Jeremy Enigk line: "December's tragic drive / When time is poetry." What a perfect emo line, and rock 'n' roll line, and teenage line—semi-tuneful and not entirely coherent and all the better for it. But sometimes you need maximum tunefulness and maximum coherence, and that's when you break the glass and pull the bright-red fire alarm with a cool silver streak down the middle.

I can't make you love me if you don't

No offense to Sunny Day Real Estate, U2, Metallica, or the Goo Goo Dolls, but Bonnie Raitt's "I Can't Make You Love Me" is on another level on every conceivable level, and I never put it on a mix-tape for a lady because (a) of course I could make anyone love me, and (b) this song possesses such a fearsome, lovelorn power that it would've somehow physically erased every other song on the tape.

Bonnie Raitt was born in Burbank, California, in 1949, and if you're like me, every time you even hear her name, you immediately picture her shrouded in this elegant, roaring campfire of deep red hair with a silver-white streak in the middle; she says that streak came in naturally when she was 24, and soon the silver expanded as the red faded, so she started dying her hair but preserving that little streak, because as she told *Parade* magazine once, "I've been told it means you've been kissed by an angel." That silver streak is a bit on the nose, as metaphors go, for a young instant-classic blues/rock/jazz/pop singer, for an old soul, for a masterful song interpreter somehow hitting a dazzling new peak at 42 years old and on her 11th album.* But she's got no time for ambiguity, for abstruseness, for fucking around.

And I will give up this fight

Even as an alt-rockin' chowderhead teenager who thought 42 was primo nursing-home age, I cowered ever-so-slightly in the

---

* "I Can't Make You Love Me" appears on 1991's *Luck of the Draw*, the deft follow-up to her blockbuster 1989 comeback album *Nick of Time* that won, like, 400 Grammys, though she often joked that she'd never been a big enough star to even qualify for a "comeback."

presence of "I Can't Make You Love Me," the monster piano-driven heartbreak ballad to end them all: I had my little crushes, and my little mixtapes to feebly woo all my little crushes, but subconsciously I recognized this song as *adult*, as *the Real Shit*, and more importantly I recognized myself as being *nowhere near adult enough to go near the Real Shit*. In college, during my regrettable Open-Mic Night Guy era, I'd sometimes play guitar or piano while my friend Carly sang—James Taylor, Sarah McLachlan, Ani DiFranco, that sorta thing—and part of me regrets that we never did "I Can't Make You Love Me," but the greater part of me knows that was the right call. You don't play this song at an open-mic night. You shouldn't even be allowed to *listen* to "I Can't Make You Love Me" until you've got a little silver-white in your hair. The angel will kiss your forehead when you're ready. Until then, maybe just stick with the Spin Doctors.

Misinterpret This, Pal:

And I come into you

Yes, Dave Matthews really sings that. Is there a French or perhaps German word for when you hear something so crude that your brain refuses to process how crude it was, and you just assume, as a defense mechanism, that what you just heard has some other, more benign and romantic and poetic meaning?

And I come into you

"I feel like it's an incredibly romantic song," the filmmaker Greta Gerwig explained at the 2017 Toronto Film Festival, after a screening of her truly splendid directorial debut *Lady Bird*, which does indeed lovingly needle-drop the Dave Matthews Band swoonfest "Crash into Me" twice. "And I always wanted to make out to that song, and I never did." To my mind that's the highest possible compliment you can pay a song, to imagine yourself smooching to it but to lament that you never have. That combination of desire and thwarted desire.

Tremble in awe before the towering and *perpetual* commercial success of Charlottesville, Virginia's own Dave Matthews Band, whose second major-label album, 1996's *Crash*, peaked at No. 2 and has since been followed by *seven straight No. 1 albums*, an active streak as of 2018, and *that's not the trembling-in-awe part*. In 2009, touring-industry bible *Pollstar* magazine declared DMB its Top Act of the Decade, which means they were the highest-grossing touring artist in North America from 2000 to 2009, racking up $429 million in ticket sales and, y'know, selling a few T-shirts, and all told pretty objectively reigning as the most successful '90s rock band of the 21st century.

Tremble-in-awe success on this scale immediately made DMB's fan base its own subculture, its own ecosystem, its own gleefully mocked stereotype. Frat houses. Backward baseball caps. Hacky-sacks. Cargo shorts. Trustafarians. Red Solo cups. That one shop on every college campus that sells bongs. That one irritating guy at every keg party who pulls out an acoustic guitar. Jimmy Buffett for poli-sci majors. You know the stereotype. It's a boring stereotype. A cliché ripe to be exploded. Not that Dave Matthews Band need defending. These fellas do not require *critical reevaluation* or *prestige redemption*; they didn't need *Lady Bird* half as much as *Lady Bird* needed them.

What I know is that in the mid-'90s, if you were sitting in somebody's dorm room and paging through his or her CD booklet—one of those giant zip-up Case Logic deals with sleeves for four CDs per page—you were pretty much guaranteed to stumble across *Crash*, and probably also DMB's 1994 monster breakout *Under the Table and Dreaming*, and maybe even their pre-fame 1993 indie release *Remember Two Things*. What I also know is that back then, paging through somebody's CD book was the single most intimate activity you could engage in with another human being. It was like drinking beer out of someone else's mouth. It was, like, 75 percent of the way to just making out with them. You might as well make out with them at that point. *No modern equivalent.*

What I know is that "Crash into Me" sounds like two teenagers in a closet trying to climb one another. What I know is that I'll never forget the first time I heard "Crash into Me," and relax, I wasn't in a closet. I'm 18 years old, I'm in high school, I'm sitting in a car with a couple girls and at least one other guy, but relax: There is nothing amorous transpiring between anybody in the car (to my knowledge). We're just driving, probably either to or from a Denny's, or perhaps driving from one Denny's to another Denny's. And one of the girls goes, *You gotta listen to this song. I love this song.* And she puts on "Crash into Me." And four or five teenagers just sit, in a moving car, in deep contemplation, in *silence*, for five minutes and 16 seconds.

This sounds mundane, I realize, and sure, I'd love to tell you that the first time I heard "Crash into Me," I was climbing Mount Kilimanjaro or something. But I hope you understand that this moment felt, to me, at the time, just as momentous. Four or five teenagers in a car keeping their mouths shut for an entire song is, to my mind, an accomplishment on par with climbing Mount Kilimanjaro. Just the focus, the *reverence* in that car. To really *listen* to a song, to listen *hard*, and to know that everyone around you is listening hard, too—that's its own kind of intimacy. That's the highest respect a teenager can pay. To pay that respect together, in an enclosed space—that's 80 percent of the way to making out with someone. I'll never forget it, even if I wish I could forget 80 percent of the lyrics.

While we're sitting around contemplating teenage horndog mundanity-as-sublimity, let me sing you the ballad of Dysentery Gary.

That's not his name. I picked that name at random. So I'm 14 or so, and I'm on the bus home from junior high, and this buddy of mine—code-named Dysentery Gary, and historically a bit of a ladies' man—is sitting in a bus seat by himself, silent, looking forlorn, looking outright distraught. He's not crying, but the vibe is bad. So we get off the bus and I go to Gary's house, up to his bedroom, and Gary explains to me that he's sad because his girlfriend dumped him. But now he gets angry, as he's telling me why he's sad, because his girlfriend broke up with him because he was immature. She called him immature. Gary cannot believe that she called him immature. And Gary gets so irate that he goes to his dresser and pulls out a pair of underwear—*clean* underwear, tighty-whiteys—and puts the underwear on his head and starts dancing angrily around the room shouting, "I'm immature! I'm immature! I'm immature!"

And here was a vital life lesson: Chicks aren't into immature

guys. Did I, personally, at 14, utilize this information? Fuck no.*
But I think of that day every time I revisit Blink-182's "What's
My Age Again?" which appears on their 1999 album *Enema of the
State* and made me laugh out loud the first time I heard Blink-182
singer-guitarist Mark Hoppus sing this:

We started making out
And she took off my pants

It's the infantile shock of that line; it's the more sophisticated
shock of the lack of a rhyme in that line. Blink-182 are pop-punk
brats from the suburbs of San Diego with zero anxiety about selling out and even less anxiety about naming their 1997 major-label
debut album *Dude Ranch*. I would divide Blink-182's early songs
into roughly two categories: *Girls are a waste of time* versus *Girls have
decided I'm a waste of time*. And I would for sure put "What's My
Age Again?" in the latter category, hinging as it does on the lines,
"And that's about the time she walked away from me / Nobody
likes you when you're 23." Nobody much liked me at 19 when this
song came out, and anecdotally they liked me even less when *I*
turned 23. As a consequence, this is a tremendously sad song to me:
There is something akin to regret rattling in the bones of "What's
My Age Again?," even if it's a Sorry Not Sorry sort of regret.

---

* A partial list of fantasy sports team names I have used as a legal adult: The Dirty
Sanchez Posse, Wanton Pantslessness, Kicked in the Taco (Frank Black reference),
Moises Alou's Hands (Google it), Cervix-a-Lot (ugh), Maxi Priest Holmes (LOL),
Grab Some Saku Koivu (hockey), Them Heavy People (sophisticated Kate Bush reference), The Six-Foot Kayak (less sophisticated Souls of Mischief reference), Boda-
cious Tatís (even less sophisticated Fernando Tatís reference), and Le Pettitte Mort
(that one is *incredible*, and I'm not explaining it).

But let me also tell you about the funniest thing anyone's ever said to me. So a while back my wife and I are watching *Normal People*, the 2020 Hulu-via-BBC series based on the 2018 Sally Rooney novel about two young, sexy, depressed Irish people who have sex 10 percent of the time and sit around being depressed the other 90 percent of the time. And my wife's on her phone looking up if the sexy *Normal People* people have been in any other movies or TV shows, and she looks up the lead actor, Paul Mescal, and then she says, "He was in a sausage advert." And there's like a 10-second pause, and then my wife yells, at me, *"I'd like to see YOUR sausage advert."* And that's just one of the thousands of concrete lessons my wife's taught me: *If nobody loves you because you're too bawdy and immature, just find someone bawdier than you are.* Because *I'd like to see YOUR sausage advert* is the funniest thing anybody's ever said to me. Maybe you had to be there. But I'm sure glad you weren't.

MYTHS VS. MORTALS

SONGS DISCUSSED:

Nirvana, "Smells Like Teen Spirit"
The Notorious B.I.G., "Juicy"
Selena, "¿Qué Creías?"
Dr. Dre, "Nuthin' But a 'G' Thang"
Whitney Houston, "I Will Always Love You"
Britney Spears, "...Baby One More Time"
Aaliyah, "One in a Million"
Tupac, "California Love"
Geto Boys, "Mind Playing Tricks on Me"
Lauryn Hill, "Ex-Factor"
Shania Twain, "Man! I Feel Like a Woman"

H E WAS, AND WILL FOREVER BE, the loudest voice I'd ever heard. Fall 1991. I'm 13 years old and hanging out with my buddy Matt. We'd ride bikes. We'd watch dopey preteen Nickelodeon shows like *Hey Dude* and *Salute Your Shorts* and *Welcome Freshmen.* We'd eat icing sandwiches, which is where you spread a ton of cake icing between two graham crackers. We'd play vaguely goth video games on his computer. We'd discuss the junior high girls we had hopeless unrequited crushes on. We'd be dorks. Kids. Children. Innocents. Until that day. Until that voice. I'm sitting in Matt's computer chair in his bedroom, and he says, "Dude, you gotta hear this." I don't remember what he said. I added the *dude* because I'm 44 now, and that's how I imagine a 13-year-old in 1991 would talk. But no, dude, that's totally what he said: "Dude, you gotta hear this." And then Matt strolled over to his stereo, and slid in the CD, and cranked the volume all the way up, and spun around just so he could watch me hear it.

I cannot convey to you how loud—how comically, crushingly, terrifyingly loud—Nirvana's "Smells Like Teen Spirit" was the first time I heard it. You will assume I'm exaggerating for melodramatic effect, and you will be correct, but no, no, dude, seriously: I've gone to probably 1,000 concerts, and spent cumulative decades of my life with overburdened car stereos screaming into my ears and noise-canceling headphones screaming even more directly into my ears, but, no, dude, for sure, I am telling you that Kurt Cobain's voice will forever be the loudest, most terrifying noise I've ever heard in my life.

I am woefully unprepared for this. I have no emotional vocabulary to describe him, or his effect on me, or who I am now because of him. I have no context. I don't know where he's from—I think he's from Seattle. (No.) I don't know the words he's singing/screaming—a few months from now a likewise enraptured kid in my junior high lunchroom will insist that Kurt ends the song by screaming, "BLOODY NIGHT OUT / BLOODY NIGHT OUT / BLOODY NIGHT OUT," and I will believe this. (No.) I don't know how you make electric guitars sound like this: so gargantuan, so inhuman, so viciously alluring, so Def Leppard but also totally totally totally not Def Leppard. Is this punk rock? (No.) Is this the future? Is this my future? (Yes to both.) Will I even survive hearing this song, this first time, or will I die right here, in my buddy Matt's computer chair, as Matt sadistically grins down at me and Kurt's voice—"HELLO HELLO HELLO HOW LOW"—tears my head apart from the inside? Or will just the innocent, childlike part of me die?

Oh, come on now, Rob. *Robby*. Chill out. But I remember this. I do. My shock, my terror, my bewilderment, my incomprehension. My near-certainty that I'm gonna go deaf, and my total certainty that any second now Matt's mom is gonna bust down his bedroom door with a fire ax and scream at us to turn down that racket. The threat of Matt's mom is vital, here: We need an element of suspense, uncertainty, parental disapproval, generational transgression. Melodrama. Lean into the melodrama, Robby. Amazes me, the will of instinct. *Whump whump whump whump.* Over the terrifying colossal inhuman transgressive not-punk-rock racket we can hear the plummeting bodies of feathered '80s hair-metal gods who flew too close to the sun and still didn't burn but then Kurt Cobain,

209

Tortured Voice of a Generation, incinerated their wings with one contemptuous breath and sent them spiraling down to earth, their bodies now crashing with a sickening mangled thud onto Matt's roof. Winger (*whump*), Jackyl (*whump*), Poison (*whump*), Slaughter (*whump*). Bloody night out, bloody night out, bloody night out.

How long did I sit there, physically and psychologically obliterated by *Nevermind*, until Matt's mom scraped me out of Matt's computer chair? How far into the record did we get? We got to "In Bloom," certainly: the thrashing, gouging, exhilarating screeches of Kurt's guitar strings *in between the chords* of "In Bloom." Love it. I love it. C'mon, let us keep going. Let us get to "Breed." I love "Breed." "GET AWAY GET AWAY GET AWAY." The seething wounded animal velocity of "Breed." "I'M AFRAID I'M AFRAID I'M AFRAID." Oh, man. You *really* gotta let us get to "Territorial Pissings," though. My childlike terror peaks on "Territorial Pissings," with its sneering, atonal, Greatest Generation-incinerating intro—"COME ON PEOPLE NOW / SMILE ON YOUR BROTHER / EVERYBODY GET TOGETHER"—and Kurt's blood-soaked, bone-chilling, throat-shredding climactic screams of "GOTTA FIND A WAY / AHHHHHH / AHHHHHHHH."

I don't know how I even survived this. Maybe I didn't. Maybe I never left my buddy Matt's room, or even got up from his computer chair. Nor do I want to, really, because if I leave this room I get older—I get, like, older-than-Matt's-mom older—and so does Matt and so does everybody and so does Kurt until Kurt doesn't anymore. So we stayed in Matt's room, forever. We're still there. I'm typing this on Matt's computer. And so of course now we get all the way through *Nevermind*, all the way to the eerie, shattered hush of

"Something in the Way," the self-annihilating dirge ballad about how Kurt totally used to live under a bridge back in Seattle. (No, to both the bridge and Seattle.) And so then we listen to Nirvana's first album, *Bleach*, which features lots of Tortured Voice of a Generation screaming—"I'M ASHAMED / NO RECESS / DADDY'S LITTLE GIRL AIN'T A GIRL NO MORE"—but doesn't sound nearly as much like the whumped hair-metal guys splattered across Matt's roof so we don't like it as much but don't tell anybody.

And so then we listen to *Incesticide*, the B-sides collection with the gnarly cover that Nirvana put out after every dopey preteen in America bought *Nevermind*, and damn, not so much hair-metal action here, either, though once Matt and I get a little wiser and emotionally perceptive we can appreciate how the whole ballgame here—the whole Kurt Cobain generational arc—hinges on the Blitzkrieg Beatles Bop of "Sliver": the cuddly bassline, the soothing distortion bath of the chorus, the childlike innocence with which Kurt recounts being babysat by his grandparents and eating mashed potatoes and ice cream and riding his bike and watching TV and chanting a line I initially misheard as "NEVER TAKE ME HOME." That's the key to him, the key to everything, the way Kurt howls, "I WOKE UP IN MY MOTHER'S ARMS / AHHHHHHHHHH." Isn't that the missing piece, the great reveal? It must be. We figured him out. He really gets us, and now finally we really *get* him, the way our dopey parents* never will.

---

* One time I was watching MTV with my mom and the video for "Weird Al" Yankovic's "Teen Spirit" parody "Smells Like Nirvana" came on, and Al got to the line "It's hard to talk / *Glarbl gralph* / With all these marbles in my mouth" while spitting out marbles and my mom just about died laughing, and OK maybe I blushed, just a little, for just a second.

And then we listen to Nirvana's ultra-scabrous new album, *In Utero*, which Kurt keeps saying in interviews is The Real Him, the raw and uncompromising sound that's always been in his head, not that *Nevermind* bullshit, that sounds like Mötley Crüe to him now, that *embarrasses* him now, aren't we all embarrassed by it now? And so now we're embarrassed, just a little, by how much we love(d) *Nevermind*, and no no totally we totally love *In Utero* instead, which seems to consist entirely of the thrashing, gouging, exhilarating screeches in between the chords of "In Bloom," and there's tons of I No Longer Wish to Be the Tortured Voice of a Generation screaming—"HEYYYY GO AWAYYYY"—but we're into it, totally, no more Mötley Crüe cheeseball shit for us, no sir, and when he screams, "GO AWAYYYY," he doesn't mean us, no way, and also, oh, hell yeah, Nirvana did *MTV Unplugged*. Awesome. "Smells Like Teen Spirit" is gonna sound so rad on *Unplugged*.

But wait, what the hell, man, there's no "Smells Like Teen Spirit" on here. What the hell is even on here? Is this a joke? Are the Vaselines even a real band? And what's with all these Meat Puppets songs? You mean the guys we saw once opening for Stone Temple Pilots? And then we play the goddamn *Unplugged* CD already and it shuts us all the way up and our silence is the second-loudest sound we'll ever hear by the time we get to "Where Did You Sleep Last Night," and we'll totally find out who or what Leadbelly is later but for now shhhh we've gotten to the end of the song where Kurt shrieks, "I'LL SHIVERRRRR." Then there's a long pause. "THE WHOLE." He's, like, *whimpering* now, and then he takes a final, ragged, generation-defining breath. "NIGHT THROUGH." But stop.

We have to stop.

We have to stop at "THE WHOLE." He can't ever take the breath. If he takes the breath the song keeps going, and the song ends, and the CD ends, and we leave the room, and everyone keeps getting older all the time, and we're older now, too, and then suddenly we're on the school bus at the corner of East Union and North Harmony, right in front of our old junior high, when the radio tells us that he's gone. What do you mean he's already gone by the time the *Unplugged* CD comes out, before he shuts us all up, before he takes the breath, before he keeps going after he takes the breath? No. Fuck no. He never takes the breath, we never leave the room, nobody gets older, nobody dies.

He was never real to me. Not really. I thought too much of him to believe he was real: a "real person," a mere mortal, a vulnerable flawed melodramatic human, a scrawny kid with an aching stomach. Yes, he's a kid to me now: I'm, like, 17 years older now than he ever got. He's a myth to me, a deified abstraction, a creator and destroyer of worlds: He destroyed the '80s of my childhood and created the '90s of my adolescence. I am never, if you want the truth, a true Nirvana superfan, but I mourn him all the same, and worship him all the same, because my understanding is that everyone worships him, here in the '90s he created, here in the computer chair in the bedroom I'll never leave. Never take me home.

That's not the line. That's not what he says. I misheard so much of what he said and misinterpreted most of the rest. But I'll never truly believe that, and you can't make me, and I can't make myself.

ANOTHER WAY TO PUT it is that you're nobody till somebody kills you, but once you're painted into a mural, you become somebody else. Anyone can go right now to 1091 Bedford

213

Avenue in Bed-Stuy, Brooklyn, and gaze up at the astounding two-story "King of NY" mural of the Notorious B.I.G., his pursed-lips expression indomitable but serene, the crown on his head jaunty but secure. And from right on that spot, you can turn and gaze across Quincy Street to 1110 Bedford Avenue, modest site of the 1991 street-corner freestyle battle at which 17-year-old Christopher Wallace famously made his presence felt, bellowing, "Yes it's me / The B.I.G. / Competition ripper ever since 13" with the coolest, deepest, warmest, and most awe-inspiring voice anyone had ever heard. Like if the Grand Canyon were a person. Wait, no—keep it in the neighborhood. Like if Brooklyn, in all its glory and atrocity, could be distilled into one person.

But what happens to the person, when his city gets distilled into him? Miraculously, that rap battle was caught on 1991-ass video and lives forever on YouTube, and if you want the truth that's the second miracle, the first miracle being every last concussive syllable in the phrase "competition ripper ever since 13," that preposterous barrage of Zeus-sized thunderbolts flung by—yes, it's true, believe it—a mere mortal. And above and beyond the waves of punishing grief unleashed by Biggie's death—waves of grief that have never crested, never broken, no matter how many murals we paint in his honor—what a bizarre and awful slow-motion transformation, the way that practically unknown bellowing teenager on the sidewalk became that universally beloved but fundamentally unknowable god-king surveying his domain from the side of the building across the street.

My favorite thing about "Juicy"* is the way Biggie gets to devise

* From the Notorious B.I.G.'s gold-standard debut album, *Ready to Die*, released in—you know what, it was 1994, but generally let's ease up on the context for a

and burnish his own myth for a change, paint his own self-portrait masterpiece that captures his essence but keeps some of his secrets. "It was all a dream / I used to read *Word Up!* magazine." Fact check: true, and that's also very arguably the greatest opening line in rap history, because you can *feel* the hunger in his voice, and you can hear his awe, too, as it dawns on him that his hunger might actually be sated. This is the moment where Biggie *makes it*, the moment where he ascends the mountaintop and maybe climbs up onto the cross. But delightfully, on "Juicy,"* he also…makes a few tasteful revisions to his life story.

Biggie's beloved mother, Voletta Wallace, would like to clarify† that her son never had to eat sardines for dinner. His gloriously hissed delivery of the line "No heat, wonder why Christmas missed us" is a genuine thrill—"Chrisssss-masssss missssssed ussssss"—but Voletta would like to clarify that Christmas only missed him in the sense that he was raised a Jehovah's Witness and they technically didn't celebrate Christmas. "Thinkin' back on my one-room shack"—*he means his bedroom*. For the record, *everyone's bedroom is a one-room shack*. Finally, my personal favorite: "Super Nintendo,

---

while, because I'm guessing you don't need much orientation with most of these people and most of these songs, and if you do, take it from 13-year-old me: Total disorientation can be surprisingly awesome.

* I'm gonna struggle with this Avoiding Context business, because I'm worried Puff Daddy will get mad at me if I don't mention that this song is a jubilant flip of the funk/soul group Mtume's 1983 hit "Juicy Fruit," though *flip* ain't the word: In the grand Puffy tradition, the "Juicy" beat is more just "Juicy Fruit" jostled slightly. You can picture Puffy just hitting play on "Juicy Fruit," but, like, extravagantly.

† She makes these clarifications in Cheo Hodari Coker's 2003 biography *Unbelievable: The Life, Death, and Afterlife of the Notorious B.I.G.*; Justin Tinsley's 2022 book *It Was All a Dream: Biggie and the World That Made Him* is essential as well. (Context like this doesn't count.)

Sega Genesis / When I was dead broke, man, I couldn't picture this." Voletta would like to clarify that to keep her young son in their Brooklyn apartment and therefore off the street, she bought him the boombox he wanted (he wanted either the Sharp or the Sony), she bought him the Fat Boys and Run-DMC tapes he wanted, and she bought him the video games he wanted. In the pre-Nintendo '80s, most kids wanted either an Atari, an Intellivision, or a Coleco-Vision. But young Christopher had all three, because that, in Voletta's view, was what it took to keep him indoors, keep him near her, keep him safe.

The pain, and destitution, and conflict, and hardship, and desperation of Biggie's upbringing—the glory but also the atrocity of his beloved Brooklyn—is palpable throughout *Ready to Die*, on hard-nosed but startlingly vulnerable songs like "Things Done Changed" and "Everyday Struggle." But there's something so tremendously charming to me about Voletta Wallace's never-ending multimedia fact-checking of "Juicy." I am charmed, I suspect, as a defense mechanism, as a feeble attempt to ease the excruciating pain of watching as this woman has to speak about the son she lost in every biography, every documentary, every new elaborate and justifiably hagiographic tribute. It's so gracious of her that she's still helping us honor and *humanize* him. For all his richly deserved reputation as one of the greatest storytellers in rap history—think "I Got a Story to Tell," think "Me and My Bitch," think "Warning"—Biggie was never more compelling than when he was telling (and embellishing) his *own* story. And what keeps "Juicy" present-tense for me, and keeps Christopher Wallace present-tense for me, is that I still hear it as *their* story: her son's, and his mother's.

* * *

YOU CAN FIND MURALS dedicated to Tejano superstar Selena Quintanilla Pérez in Los Angeles, Fresno, San Diego, Chicago, Miami, Milwaukee, Dallas, Houston, San Antonio, Corpus Christi, El Paso, and Monterrey, Nuevo León, Mexico. You can spend the rest of your life luxuriating in the Selena Content Industrial Complex—the star-making 1997 J.Lo biopic, the 2020 Netflix series, myriad books for all ages, and, best of all IMHO, Maria Garcia's immersive and stupendous 2021 podcast *Anything for Selena*. But before any of that, it is very important to me that you watch this YouTube video from a Selena concert where she's just absolutely roasting this dude at home plate of a college baseball stadium in Midland, Texas, in 1994. Selena is roasting this dude simply by singing her boisterous 1992 ballad "¿Qué Creías?" not so much *to* him as *at* him, or really she's singing *through* him. You watch this dude *erode*. You watch him *evaporate*. This is both the best and worst moment of this guy's entire life, because the second-best moment of his life is gonna look so much worse by comparison.

"¿Qué Creías?" translates to "What Did You Think?" In the song, Selena informs a loser ex-lover that despite his resurgent desire for her, he will, in fact, remain her ex-lover, so beat it. She usually performs this one live by pulling a gentlemen volunteer from the crowd and making him stand there—with his arms at his sides, if the guy needs to be prompted to do that—whilst she obliterates him as a gracious stand-in for the dumbass gentleman who inspired the song. And so at this Midland gig, as she roars, "No quiero saber de ti / Así es que puedes irte" ("I don't wanna hear from you / So you can leave"), Selena winds up with her right arm and *throws the guy out of the game like a pissed-off umpire* to a huge burst of applause. Second only to the Erykah Badu wig-bounce of personal legend, Umpire Selena is the most incredible Emphatic Pop-Star Gesture I have ever witnessed live, and *I wasn't even there.*

Every Selena record, from her self-titled 1989 debut forward, is a negotiation between Selena the Established Tejano Star and Selena the Future Global Pop Star. When should she cross over? *How* should she cross over? She is singing in English on the sumptuous prom-theme title track to July 1995's *Dreaming of You*; the song finally landed her on the *Billboard* Hot 100 at No. 22, and the whole record was the first *Billboard* No. 1 album mostly sung in Spanish, but these accomplishments came months after Selena's death,* and from that day forward Selena the Person, as we'd ideally remember her, now exists partly in the shadow of Selena the Sainted and Extravagantly Mourned Tragic Figure.

That conundrum is what makes the minor-league-baseball "¿Qué Creías?" so important to me: She's fluid and casual and spontaneous but also so clearly in total *control*; she's 800 feet tall and also five-foot-five. I found that clip in a four-part video series called "Selena Funny-Slash-Diva Moments," and I'm just as hung up on a much smaller but just as delightful moment, also from Part 2. Selena is being interviewed by a nice, quiet, intimidated-looking lady, and as they're sitting next to each other, the massive pop star leans over and fixes the nervous interviewer lady's clip-on microphone. That's it. "Here, look up," Selena says as she futzes with the thing; the lady looks mortified and extra-nervous, but

---

* No context, forget it, too awful.

also tremendously charmed. The whole thing takes, like, six seconds. I can't explain why I keep rewatching it, other than to say it's just such a beautifully *human* interaction that undercuts the Selena Myth while also, of course, burnishing the Selena Myth. Stars are manifestly *not* just like us, and yet they totally are, and that maddening contradiction will taunt us forever, but we should never stop trying to unravel it, and that, I suppose—beyond the mourning, the celebrating, the deifying—is what all the murals are for.

T HIS TINY HUMAN GESTURE racket I got goin' doesn't just work for era-defining tragedies requiring decades of tender collective international mourning: It's also pretty awesome when I'm just too overwhelmed to talk about, oh, let's say Dr. Dre. Did you hear me wince, just now? I just winced, audibly.

Dr. Dre overwhelms me. Ordinarily, to really talk about Dr. Dre, I would have to talk about N.W.A., and Eazy-E, and Suge Knight, and Jimmy Iovine, and Rodney King, and Dee Barnes.* I'd have to talk about gangsta rap, and the L.A. riots, and the way MTV and CNN, respectively, conspired to flood—to *invade*—the American suburbs with the world-altering disharmony that fueled gangsta rap and the L.A. riots. I'd have to talk about Leon Haywood, and Parliament-Funkadelic, and the Moog synthesizer, and G-funk, and the Solid State Logic mixing board Dr. Dre once described as "the first love of my life." I'd have to talk about weed,

---

* Dr. Dre's brutal assault of the hip-hop journalist Dee Barnes in January 1991—he pled no contest to assault charges but avoided jail time, settled Barnes' civil suit out of court, and has apologized a few times, including in the luxe 2017 HBO documentary series *The Defiant Ones*—is his legacy every bit as much as any record he'll ever make, any musical genre he'll ever help invent, any superstar rapper he'll ever mentor, any company he'll ever sell. Okay, thanks, end of footnote.

219

or at least I have to talk about Snoop Doggy Dogg and Dr. Dre talking about weed. Along those lines, I'd also have to talk—this is optional, but not really—about "The $20 Sack Pyramid."

I find all of this to be quite stressful. The context avalanche. The context apocalypse. But oooh, wait, get a load of this: Watch in amazement as I slam the giant shiny red Tiny Human Gesture button, and I magically get to avoid all that, and instead suddenly we're *all* watching in amazement as Dr. Dre and his young, relatively unknown Long Beach costar Snoop Doggy Dogg lope serenely through "Nuthin' But a 'G' Thang"* and weave a gorgeous cosmic sonic tapestry out of the following:

It's like this and like that and like this and uh
It's like that and like this and like that and uh

All I want to know is how these two guys mix up these six words—*It's, like, this, and, that, uh*—and turn them into the most profound, the most triumphant, the most harmonious, the most staggeringly beautiful 10 seconds of recorded sound imaginable. Forgive me for ignoring all the context and simply reveling in the more perfect union formed by these two people, talking to each other and mirroring each other and enjoying one another's company with a chemistry so pure it's theology. Both these guys are all-timers, titans, high-comic figures, and obdurate antiheroes; Dre especially is one of the gnarlier How to Separate the Art from the

---

* Off 1992's genre- and culture-defining *The Chronic*, to provide context I suspect you don't require, and if you want the truth, as far as that record goes I still prefer "Let Me Ride," but this is one of those completely sincere opinions that is indistinguishable, alas, from an obnoxious troll opinion, and so mostly I keep it to myself.

Artist challenges in music history. My advice: Don't ever forget any of that, but that doesn't mean you have to think about it all the time, and sometimes the most honorable thing to do is just take those six words and run.

WHITNEY HOUSTON WILL NOT be diminished and reduced so easily, no matter how sad it makes you to think about her; Whitney Houston will pack a galaxy's worth of staggering beauty and ecstatic release into just *three* words, and she'll do it herself.

There's a boy

Aren't you in a better mood now? Like, right now? Like, a 600-percent better mood? Three words. A giddy ascending melody. That's all it takes. That's all she needs. Imagine what she could do for you if you gave her *five words*.

There's a boy
I know

And hey, look at that, now you're on the ceiling. Dancing on it, perhaps. Clinging to the chandelier, perhaps. Drinking champagne from the chandelier while dancing, perhaps. You wanna get truly rowdy, though? Give her *11 words*.

There's a boy
I know
He's the one I dream of

Oh, wow. This is bliss personified. This is the world looking at you through rose-colored glasses. This is the giant floppy bow in Whitney's hair in the "How Will I Know" video. This is Peak 1985, right up there with Queen at Live Aid or a packed theater watching *Back to the Future* on opening night. The music in this song is lovely. Shout-out music. But have you heard the *a cappella* version? It's *phenomenal*. All we'll ever need is Whitney Houston's voice. The rest is noise. The rest is noise pollution. What if we just *luxuriated* in this voice, to the exclusion of all else? What if we burrowed deep into those 11 spectacularly unadorned words and refused to ever leave?

And what if we did finally, grudgingly leave, but only to sprint ahead to 1992 so we could burrow deep into 11 more of Whitney Houston's spectacularly unadorned words, delivered with exquisite, quavering, chart-throttling regret this time?

If I
Should stay
I would only be in your way

"I Will Always Love You,"* which graces the zillion-selling soundtrack to the 1992 mega-melodrama *The Bodyguard*, is one of these '90s songs so ubiquitous, so humongous, so inescapable that I don't blame you one bit for trying to escape it now, because if you hear it again you won't be able to stop thinking about it, which means you won't be able to stop thinking about 1992, and everything that

---

* Written and originally recorded by Dolly Parton in 1973, while we're throwing around context you don't require, and you gotta love the delicacy of this breakup song and the particular diplomacy of these opening lines, where "If I should stay" means *I'm not staying* and "I would only be in your way" means *You're in my way*.

happened after 1992, and specifically everything that happened to her.* What amazes me though is that this song can still bear the weight, bear the myth, bear the heartbreaking tragedy of it all, with a resilience and a dignity and a slow-burn *vivacity* even most zillion-selling songs can't manage for this long, all thanks to Whitney's pure volcanic force, and the song's pristine controlled sense of mega-melodramatic escalation, and *especially the fuckin' key change.*

Whitney Houston is the Mozart, the Picasso, the Frida, the Aretha, the Alpha and Omega of key changes, and the "I Will Always Love You" key change is her masterpiece: It's like you've been shot out of a cannon directly into another cannon, and then you get shot out of that one. Whitney Houston *is* the key change, the exhilarating paradigm shift, the evolutionary leap forward. And when she hammers that climactic "AND IIIIIIIII"—to say nothing of that climactic "YOOUUUUUU"—with the strength of 10,000 conquering armies, she is ferociously present-tense forever, and she'll paint her own murals, thank you, and then demolish the buildings they're painted on.

What I'm saying is that sometimes you gotta let the singer be the singer and let the song be the song, and not hold its former culture-throttling ubiquity against it, nor hold its long-term unbearable biographical baggage against it. Empty your mind of all unpleasant and unnecessary context. Approximate, as best you can, the mentality of a disastrously naïve 13-year-old. Try it. Let's try it with something else.

Oh baby baby

---

* Nope. Not a word of Whitney Houston context either. It's too upsetting. That's why we started with the bliss personified of "How Will I Know": Go listen to the a cappella version again and forget everything you know about how this story ends.

Shit.

Oh baby baby

Shit, here comes Britney Spears. The final boss of unpleasant and unnecessary context, forever wielding the present tense[*] like a flamethrower. Is it really a good idea to reapproach Britney's culture-throttling 1998 debut single "...Baby One More Time" with total naïvete? (No.) Can we really make ourselves forget everything this song did to her, and did to many of our brains? (Also no.)

It's all there, all the chaos and catastrophe, right there in her hiccupped delivery of the words, "Oh baby baby." Every phase of the frantic and treacherous Teenage Pop Star experience. The gritty and humble origins. The meteoric rise. The jubilant, screaming fans. The sneering haters, some of whom are screaming *even louder*. The snide accusations of lip-syncing and other alleged inauthenticities. The backlash. The backlash to the backlash. The whiplash that comes with growing up in comically exaggerated fast-forward. The withering light and stultifying pitch-darkness of true superstardom. The innocence you lose when you insist you're not that innocent. You career through all of that—the rise and the fall and the rise and the fall—in three seconds. Three words, three seconds. Two of those words are *baby*. The most spectacular and iconic and morally fraught delivery of the word *baby* since Ronnie Spector.

---

[*] Please do not make me attempt to summarize even the last five years in the public Britney Spears experience. She is "free," now, and I'm not sure what makes me use scare quotes there, other than a broad sense that the public's ongoing fumbling attempts to reassess her, "redeem" her, and most importantly *apologize to her*—meaning apologize for her public treatment, from, oh, let's say 1998 to 2008 (for starters)—often only serves to build her a gilded cage of a different sort. Just leave her alone.

Shit. This song—written and coproduced by our old friend Max Martin, who understood the baffling provocation of having a 16-year-old girl sing the phrase, "Hit me baby, one more time" repeatedly, even if he insisted he was just doing the melodic math—is too much. She's too much. Britney's too-muchness works for her, spectacularly, if you manage to just focus on the song, focus on her triumphantly apocalyptic diction. Focus on the percussive mega-ton explosiveness of her syllables: "Oh baby baby / The reason AH breathe AH is you AH." Each syllable triggers an aftershock. Each syllable leaves a crater. Every breath is a bomb. Think about how well you know "...Baby One More Time" even if you don't like it, how ingrained this song is in your psyche even if you've never once listened to it by choice. Think about the *power* of that, the power that exerts on the world, and the power the world then tries to exert over the teenager with all that power. Or, even better: Stop thinking! No thinking! The whole point was not to think about any of it. Give us one more transcendent pop song to not think too hard about.

Love it baby

Shit, shit, shit.

Love it baby

Here comes Aaliyah. Or, *finally*, here comes Aaliyah with her sultry and insinuating 1996 marvel "One in a Million," finally made available, alongside the bulk of her tiny but invaluable catalog, for streaming and legit download *in 2021*, after years of chaos, catastrophe, confusion, and heartbreak. (The best song on the *One in a Million* album is called "Heartbroken," by the way—hear me now and believe me later.) The context here—from her early producer/songwriter/mentor R. Kelly's* repugnant and eventually annulled 1994 sham marriage to her when she was 15 to her shocking death, at 22, in a plane crash—is a constant threat to crush the music itself. Aaliyah's 1994 debut album *Age Ain't Nothing But a Number,* produced and mostly written by R. Kelly, is one of the most fundamentally cursed† documents in pop-music history; cruelly, for years, thanks to all that industry chaos, it was also the only Aaliyah album you could easily hear.

Love it baby

Aaliyah has a smokey, sinuous voice and a truly staggering charisma-to-force ratio: maximum charisma, minimum force. Her falsetto can float off into the stratosphere, and her lower register can drill down into the core of the earth without disturbing the ground beneath her feet. "One in a Million"—written by Missy Elliott and Timbaland—features one of the best '90s song openings in which nothing much happens, a subdued and self-contained Timbaland beat suffused in chirping crickets and in fact conjuring up a whole swamp, a whole ecosystem, a whole *planet.* The squiggles,

---

* Jim DeRogatis's book *Soulless: The Case Against R. Kelly* and dream hampton's Lifetime documentary series *Surviving R. Kelly,* both from 2019, are the definitive word on Kelly, who will almost certainly spend the rest of his life in federal prison on a seemingly endless array of charges ranging from child pornography to child sex trafficking.

† Kathy Iandoli, in her 2021 biography *Baby Girl: Better Known as Aaliyah,* writes that at the onset she considered keeping R. Kelly out of the story entirely, but she concluded that "disregarding R. Kelly's chapter in Aaliyah's life would be denying Aaliyah another title she so greatly deserved: 'survivor.'"

the airplane whooshes, the narcotized rhythm that staggers like a drum-and-bass track stuck in quicksand: A lesser singer would be overwhelmed, would be *engulfed* by all of this. A lesser singer would try to do too much with it and end up doing virtually nothing.

Aaliyah, by contrast, lets it all just wash over her. The harmonies—"Your love is one in a million / It goes on and on and on"—do the heavy lifting. An army of her. It's maximum swagger rendered in delirious slow-motion: It's maximalism disguised as minimalism, turning less into more, and more into *the most*. You could hear the future in this song in 1998, and it still offers up the best possible version of our future 25 years later.

AH, CRUD, I JUST thought of somebody else I really oughta talk about if I'm talking about Dr. Dre: Tupac. And as a defense mechanism I immediately seize upon the only posthumous Tupac content you'll ever need, which is the 2006 third-season *Chappelle's Show* sketch where Roots drummer and hip-hop renaissance man Questlove is DJing in the club, and he announces, "Here's a new Tupac song...rest in peace," but in the song it's obvious Tupac is still alive because he's commenting on current events and also antagonizing specific people dancing in the club. I don't mean to belabor this comedic premise, especially when the funniest moment comes when Tupac, voiced by Dave Chappelle himself, bellows, "What the fuck is that? / IT MIGHT BE DOO DOO." The key to a great Tupac impression is the vigor with which you attack those long vowels: "I'M NOT *ALIIIIIIIVE*." The silliness keeps the darkness at bay.

I take a perverse comfort in the fact that unless you grew up in very specific pockets of his New York City birthplace in the '70s, or you studied poetry and theater at the Baltimore School for the Arts in the mid-'80s, or you haunted the nascent rap scene in Marin City in Northern California in the late '80s, then the first time you heard Tupac Shakur's voice was probably on a Digital Underground song. Specifically "Same Song," from 1990. "Now I clown around when I hang around with the Underground," his verse begins, and what a joy, truly, that probably the first four words you ever heard him rap were, "Now I clown around," while he was surrounded by the masterful Bay Area goofballs who graced the world with "The Humpty Dance."

Cut to 1995, and Tupac's the polarizing megastar with the "Thug Life" tattoo who already seemingly hasn't clowned around in years, but his singular tenderness can always beat back the darkness, too, like on the lovingly ferocious "Dear Mama," where he sweetens his famous bark as he leans into the long vowels of "And even as a crack fiend, Mama / You always was a Black queen, Mama." The repetition of the word "Mama" is somehow especially tender* there, and the granular lyric analysis keeps the ever-darkening context at bay.

"This 'Thug Life' stuff, it was just ignorance," Tupac tells *Vibe* reporter Kevin Powell in his famed April 1995 prison interview† from New York's Clinton Correctional Facility, a/k/a Dannemora. "My intentions was always in the right place. I never killed anybody, I never raped anybody, I never committed no crimes that

---

* I have, quite frankly, zero interest in the Biggie and Tupac of it all, in part because all of that has been covered so skillfully and exhaustively by so many others, and in part because I find both rappers' respective fraught relationships with their mothers to be far more engrossing than their feud with each other.

† Following a November 1993 incident involving three other men and a 19-year-old girl in a New York City hotel room, Tupac was acquitted of sodomy and weapons charges but convicted of first-degree sexual abuse; he spent eight months in prison while also recovering from being shot five times in the lobby of NYC's Quad Studios in November 1994, a confusing incident that turbocharged his feud with Biggie (who denied any involvement), a feud that would only end with both rappers' deaths.

weren't honorable—that weren't to defend myself. So that's what I'm going to show them. I'm going to show people my true intentions, and my true heart. I'm going to show them the man that my mother raised. I'm going to make them all proud."

I'm getting bogged down in context and I hate it. I hate it so much. In October '95, fearsome Death Row Records co-owner Suge Knight posts Tupac's $1.4 million bond, signs him to the label, and flies him out to L.A., where Tupac heads straight to the studio to pound out his February 1996 double album *All Eyez on Me*, the last album released while he was alive, rapping with world-historical fury on alluringly vicious anthems like "Ambitionz Az a Ridah" and "Heartz of Men." All of that backstory, that setup, that swallowing darkness clashes so discordantly with the record's pop supernova "California Love," which becomes Tupac's sole No. 1 hit (technically a double-A-side deal with "How Do U Want It," his best song in my opinion, but never mind that now) and stands now as a bombastic, gigantic, all-universe anthem with very little relationship to anything going on with anyone around it.

This is emphatically not one of these deals where I argue that "California Love" is secretly a dour and tragic song—the whole point is that despite all the troubled circumstances of its creation, it isn't. "California Love" is a song of ecstasy and frivolity and victory and camaraderie—in part with robo-funk luminary Roger Troutman but primarily with our old friend Dr. Dre, who takes the first verse and produces the bejesus out of the whole thing even if he's got one foot out the door the whole time—even if all that lasts *only for the length of the song itself*, even if none of that ecstasy and frivolity and victory and camaraderie ever really existed. It is a gorgeous and permanent mirage, like California itself, like Love itself.

Rapper camaraderie—that tangible sense of distinct voices fusing and clashing and goading one another to dizzying new heights or deliriously grisly new lows—is such a vital, precious, mystical thing to me, even when it's temporary, even when it's illusory, even when I'm a cowed knucklehead teenager with no idea what those voices are really trying to tell me. Houston's Geto Boys—especially their most canonical lineup of Willie D, Bushwick Bill, and Scarface, going left to right on the cover of their 1991 classic *We Can't Be Stopped*, and no way am I getting bogged down in the horrific real-world context of that album cover—were so fuckin' *scary* to me in high school. So illicit, so far outside my coddled icing-sandwich frame of reference, and therefore so *cool*, a rap group as a supernatural horror movie as a constant censorship target that had received, by '91, a quite incendiary mixture of industry respect and disrespect.

But an attempted muzzle doubles as a bullhorn, and the *We Can't Be Stopped* masterpiece "Mind Playing Tricks on Me" obliterates all this adolescent cool-scary-cartoon shit in an electrifying instant: It's a shockingly gorgeous and harrowing song about mental illness, and isolation, and hallucinations, and fear, and guilt, and suicidal thoughts. In its jaw-dropping and bone-cracking totality, it's a reminder that "horrorcore," as garish and gory rap music of this sort is often described, isn't necessarily fueled by cinematic or fantastical horror. Real life is horrible enough. The jolt when Scarface raps, "*Bang* and get it over with," is shocking enough.

They were never real to me. Not really. I thought too much of them to believe they were real. But if you're an icing-sandwich-eating teenage knucklehead, then sometimes brutal context is necessary to snap you the fuck out of it. Scarface's 2015 autobiography *Diary of a Madman* starts with a suicide attempt when he's 13, and not his first attempt; he winds up in the mental-health wing at Houston International Hospital, and he leaves there, of course, but part of you never leaves there. And now, forever, anyone can hear it in his voice: where he's been, what he's seen, and what he's felt, no matter how cartoonish or outrageous or wildly offensive any one song might get. He writes about how people in the industry were so quick to condemn the Geto Boys, but not the environment that made the Geto Boys: "They always wanted to say that we were glorifying violence or the street life or drug dealing or sex or whatever it was. Anything that made them uncomfortable, we were 'glorifying' it. I never understood that. We weren't glorifying shit—it was just there. How do you glorify reality?"

'Cause no one's hurt me more than you
And no one ever will

How does Lauryn Hill convince all those "people in the industry"—how does she convince her millions of devoted and newly *expectant* fans, many of them knuckleheaded teenagers—that those lines from "Ex-Factor" could just as easily apply to *them*? I could be the billionth person to rhapsodize to you about the greatness of the Fugees,* and the genre-eradicating audacity of the New Jersey trio's 1996 blockbuster *The Score,* and the Voice of a Generation magnificence of Lauryn's Grammy-dominating 1998 solo debut *The Miseducation of Lauryn Hill,* but you don't really need to be told how great this song is, how great this record is,

---

* Speaking of rapper camaraderie and that tangible sense of distinct voices fusing and clashing and goading one another. For the record: Pras is hilarious, and Lauryn's the laughably obvious breakout star, but I will love Wyclef Jean's deft and silly 1997 solo album *Wyclef Jean Presents The Carnival* until the day I die.

how once-in-a-generation great *she* is, do ya? Could I convince you though to go back to "Ex-Factor"—a heartrending post-love song ("'Cause no one loves you more than me / And no one ever will") widely presumed to be about Wyclef, though she ain't gonna talk to you about it—and try hearing it anew as a song about the crushing expectations of the millions of people who bought and loved and swiftly canonized *The Miseducation of Lauryn Hill*, and then insisted that Lauryn Hill make another album just like it or just as good as it, and then another, and then another, and then another?

> *See I know what we've got to do*
> *You let go*
> *And I'll let go too*

What really fascinates me is the way Lauryn Hill helped define the '90s but then refused to let the '90s define her, or let *anyone* define her, including—especially—everyone who loved her. She refused the pedestal we tried to raise her up on, lest she be trapped forever up there; she refused to be painstakingly cast in marble or lovingly painted into our perpetual mural of All-Time Greats, lest she stay stuck forever the way we first imagined her. Lauryn Hill gave us one solo masterpiece, and then took a final, ragged, generation-defining breath that she has refused to ever exhale in our presence for our mere edification or entertainment.[*]

---

[*] All she'd give us, really, was a polarizing 2001 *Unplugged* record defined by its lengthy, casual, and yet calmly confrontational stage banter about how she's not really a performer anymore, she doesn't dress up for us anymore, she's not held hostage by her public persona anymore, she had to do some dying, etc., etc., etc. None of which is especially *fun* to hear, but she had to say it, and we had to hear it.

I believe I mentioned a while back that I've spent more time waiting for Erykah Badu to take the stage than any other musician in history *with the exception of Lauryn Hill*, and I mean that quite seriously; I mean it *mathematically.* I was there at the chaotic 2007 free outdoor show in Brooklyn where Lauryn didn't take the stage for hours, and when she finally did she bombarded us with near-heavy-metal versions of *Miseducation* songs that unnerved and pissed people off to the point where a bunch of teenage girls behind me starting singing the indelible chorus to "Doo Wop (That Thing)" mid-show, during some other song, almost like a protest. And I was there a couple years later at the Blue Note, a tiny jazz club in the West Village in Manhattan, when Lauryn didn't take the stage for hours, and by the time she did the two very genial and excited thirtysomething people sitting next to me—clearly super excited to see her, and clearly on a date—had long ago left in disgust because they were sick of waiting.

I believe Lauryn played "Ex-Factor" at both shows, neither version terribly faithful to the original, or more to the point, neither version was faithful to our romanticized image of her. She's a real person, a mere mortal, a vulnerable human, and she'll let go of us for good if we can't let go of who we want her to be.

Let's go, girls

At 18 years old, Eileen Regina Edwards—a native of Windsor, Canada, who'd already endured several lifetimes' worth of personal hardship and family strife—was living in Toronto, writing country songs, and desperately trying to Make It. Also, sometimes she'd go out with her friends to gay bars, load up on eyeliner, spike up her hair, dress to excess, and dance all night to Madonna's "Material Girl" and Prince's "When Doves Cry" and UB40's "Red, Red Wine." There's an argument to be made that this, right here, is the artist soon to be known as Shania Twain at her happiest— not as a famous person *singing* about dancing and clubbing, but as a not-at-all-famous-yet person who *actually gets to go dancing and clubbing*.

Shania's 1997 mega-anthem "Man! I Feel Like a Woman!"* exuberantly fuses the '80s of my childhood to the '90s of my adolescence, and masterfully celebrates the plain fact that many of us often wish we were someone else, or some other version of ourselves. But by the late '90s, who did Shania want to be? She writes, in her ultra-harrowing 2011 memoir *From This Moment On*, about being a superstar but wishing she'd get the flu just so she'd have to take the day off. She writes about standing in a luxe Las Vegas hotel suite with floor-to-ceiling windows, and fantasizing about getting a running start and crashing through one of those windows, not like a superhero, but like an ordinary human who desperately needs a break. So back we go, on "Man! I Feel Like a Woman!," to the gay clubs of Toronto. Not her, of course: She's too busy, too famous. She wants *us* to go, so that she can *live vicariously through us*.

So you, there, cavorting in the crowded bar, screaming along to this famous jubilant country-pop song, you may be, in this moment, imagining yourself as a super-famous pop star. You might

---

* From her ultra-blockbuster 1997 album *Come on Over*, produced by former Def Leppard cohort and her future ex-husband Mutt Lange, though honestly I'd rather talk about Shania's mastery of song-title punctuation, from "Whatever You Do! Don't!" to "Don't Be Stupid (You Know I Love You)" to "I'm Not in the Mood (To Say No!)," which delightfully combines her mastery of both parentheses and exclamation points.

be fantasizing about being Shania Twain. But believe it or not, in this moment, while she's actually singing the song and really being the super-famous pop star, Shania Twain might very well be fantasizing about being *you*. A normal, frivolous, average-sexy person having fun, with no suffocating pop-star responsibilities whatsoever, whooping it up in a crowded bar where no one notices her. She's just a real person, and so real that nobody notices her or demands that she be someone else. With the lights out, it's less dangerous, and for a change, why don't we all entertain ourselves?

BIG FEELINGS

SONGS DISCUSSED:

Tom Petty, "It's Good to Be King"

Janet Jackson, "Together Again"

Black Box, "Everybody Everybody"

Mariah Carey, "All I Want for Christmas Is You"

The Verve, "Bitter Sweet Symphony"

Gin Blossoms, "Hey Jealousy"

Counting Crows, "A Long December"

Mary J. Blige, "Real Love"

Bone Thugs-N-Harmony, "Tha Crossroads"

Lisa Loeb, "Stay (I Missed You)"

S O THE NURSE HANDS ME MY SON. My newborn, first-born son, born, like, 90 seconds ago. The doctors are tending to my wife, and I am standing there in a hospital room—trembling, quite a bit—and holding a baby. Holding my son. I am a father now. And you can spend your whole life imagining this moment, and you can spend the long months of your wife's pregnancy in a laughably inept scramble to prepare for this moment, and you can spend the hours and hours and hours of your wife's quite difficult labor praying for this moment, but you have no idea how, exactly, you will feel, or what, exactly, you will do, when this moment arrives. Or at least I didn't. All the people who tell you When Your Kids Are Born It Changes Your Life and Things Will Never Be the Same, that's all true, but quite vague and not terribly helpful in terms of, uh, prep.

So the nurse hands me my son. I am holding my newborn, first-born son. I am appallingly unprepared. I have no idea what to do. And so, with no premeditation whatsoever, I do the first thing that pops into my head. I sing my son a Tom Petty song.

Goodnight baby, sleep tight my love
May God watch over you from above

"Alright for Now," from Tom Petty's 1989 album *Full Moon Fever*. I picture my newborn son Shazamming this song, Shazamming me as I sing to him, his little baby hand holding up his phone to my mouth, like, *Who is this trembling guy, and more importantly, what's that song he's singing? Is this Tom Petty? I gotta look this up.*

I'm not even a Tom Petty fan like that, in this moment. No offense. It would not have occurred to me, 90 seconds earlier, to do this, to sing this song to my son, to sing any Tom Petty song, to sing any song by anybody. But my thought process, as best I can reconstruct it, is *Oooh, crying baby. Soothe crying baby.* And it pops into my head and out of my mouth. Did "Alright for Now" soothe my trembling newborn son? Maybe. Did it soothe me? Hell no. But I was beyond grateful for this song, which I do think was equal to the gravity of this moment, and did convey some sense of my Life-Changing awe in the presence of my son, and conveyed some sense of my perpetual unease, as well. Because I always liked the *for now* part of "Alright for Now." I think the peace, the safety, the comfort, the *alrightness* Tom describes so tenderly in this song is all the more precious for the acknowledgement that it's temporary.

I am operating under the assumption that you do not require a lengthy, laborious Tom Petty primer. Born in Gainesville, Florida, in 1950. Radicalized by Elvis, re-radicalized by the Beatles, pledges his soul to rock 'n' roll, co-founds the band Mudcrutch, which heads out to L.A. and gets a record deal and flames out and reassembles as Tom Petty and the Heartbreakers, whose first album, self-titled, comes out in 1976 and ends with, geez, "American Girl." The band's third album, 1979's *Damn the Torpedoes*, makes Tom a true superstar; his eighth album and first official solo endeavor, 1989's *Full Moon Fever*, makes him a true superstar to me. (The Heartbreakers are a truly fantastic band who hang around with Tom Petty all the time; it's just that on Tom Petty solo albums, he doesn't have to listen to their opinions.) *Full Moon Fever* came out when I was 12 years old and Tom was 38 years old, and as a 12-year-old, I thought 38-year-old Tom Petty was a charming, wizened, impossibly old Rad Old Man. A grandfatherly paragon of classic-rock excellence and graceful decrepitude. He was our link with history. He was holding court from a wheelchair on an ice floe drifting off toward the horizon.

What made Tom Petty so rad to me by 1989? MTV. The super-jaunty hats in the dusty, post-apocalyptic video for 1982's "You Got Lucky." The impressively macabre "cutting up Alice from *Alice in Wonderland* like she's a cake" video for 1985's "Don't Come Around Here No More." The also-macabre "twirling around with Kim Basinger's lifeless body" video for 1993's "Mary Jane's Last Dance." MTV in the '80s and early '90s arbitrarily had this revitalizing effect on a handful of lucky '70s rock stars who were willing to embrace the Music Video Revolution and risk looking ridiculous and/or criminally lecherous. Aerosmith, for example, arguably peaked in 1993 with their fabled trio of videos—for "Cryin," "Amazing," and "Crazy," in my personal order of preference—starring future *Clueless* starlet Alicia Silverstone. But by 1994, Tom Petty stands apart, somehow, in his ability to convey youthful vivacity to each new generation, a spry and laconic classic-rock guy who doesn't feel past tense. (Yes, he's in the Traveling Wilburys with Bob Dylan and George Harrison and Roy Orbison and Jeff Lynne, but he's the *youngest* Traveling Wilbury, and that feels important.) Plus he's got so many hit songs that you don't ever need to buy a Tom Petty album to qualify as a Tom Petty expert. His music is invisible and ubiquitous and free and necessary to sustain human life on Earth, like oxygen, or lust.

Wildflowers—Tom Petty's second solo album, produced by our old friend Rick Rubin and broadly regarded now as one of the best things Tom ever did—came out in 1994, and I was immediately struck by the slow, elegiac, hypnotically chill "It's Good to Be King," with its lovely child's-first-piano-lesson piano riff and its startling quality-over-quantity guitar solo reminiscent of the Beatles' "Let It Be." (My favorite Beatles song, which these days makes me cry whenever I hear it, because that's the kind of guy I am now.) And then there's the plainspoken wistfulness in Tom's voice as he sings, "Can I help it if I / Still dream time to time?" with the full weight of what he wishes he didn't know now that he didn't know then.[*]

But even as a teenager some other, intangible element of "It's Good to Be King" called to me, but from a great distance. I knew I liked it—I knew I probably loved it—but I didn't know *why* yet. I didn't know what it was trying to tell me, and I had this subconscious sense that I wasn't *ready* for what it was trying to tell me.

And then I figured it out.

So the nurse hands me my daughter. My newborn daughter. This is Halloween 2020, our third (and last!) kid. We'd like to think we know the drill at this point, but for my wife this is another quite difficult labor. And everybody turns out alright in the end, but there's a substantial emergency when my daughter is born, and the nurse hands me my newborn daughter in an operating room crammed with about 20 doctors who proceed to tend to my wife quite vigorously for the next hour or so. I am holding my daughter; we are sitting in a chair next to my wife's head, with the rest of her body obscured by screens and curtains and so forth, and we are watching the doctors operate on my wife.

I recall basically nothing about what I thought, or did, while

---

[*] "Wish I didn't know now what I didn't know then" is from Bob Seger's wistful 1980 jam "Against the Wind." My dad loves that line, and I love that my dad loves it.

this transpired. There's a good chance I sung "Alright for Now" to my daughter as well, but it's a blank. Which was my brain, I suppose, running in Safe Mode, as we watched all this happen, leaving me unable, for my own protection, to musically orchestrate this situation in my own head, as is my wont.* Everybody turned out alright. Tom Petty might as well have written "You Got Lucky" about how lucky I was to find my wife. But I try to picture my headspace now in that operating room. I'm ecstatic to be holding my daughter; I am terrified about what's happening to my wife; I am swaddled in a chaotic-monologue-free blankness I can't access now. I can't tell you what it feels like, or more importantly, what it *sounds* like. But I suspect it sounds like the delicate and devastating piano riff at the end of "It's Good to Be King," an exquisite loop buttressed by gentle strings, a wistful reverie that has always made me shut up and gaze out my car window and just *think real hard* even if I wasn't in a car, if you get my drift.

As a teenager, I think "It's Good to Be King" was an Instant Nostalgia deal, redolent with the sort of ultra-melancholy I've always been drawn to: the fields of gold, the glory days, I'm older now but still runnin' against the wind, that's just the way it is, some things will never change. But as a super-emo 45-year-old, now the "It's Good to Be King" piano riff is just running in a loop in my head forever, usually so softly I can't even hear it, but if you strip everything else away, like in that operating room, that's what's left.

---

* The doctors did have the radio playing, just plain old pop radio, and at one point Third Eye Blind's "Jumper" came on, mid-operation, and like a tenth of a percent of my brain was still able to go *Oh, Jesus, not now, Third Eye Blind, ain't I got enough to contend with.*

It's the sound of all the bad things I worry about, and it's there to soothe me when something bad is actually happening.

Excuse me if I
Have this place in my mind
Where I go time to time

That's the other line from "It's Good to Be King" that flattens me, because it so eerily *describes* me. My spaciness, my daydreaming, my awkwardness, my forgetfulness, my ADHD so ingrained that my parents had to remind me, in my early forties, that I *had* ADHD. My inclination toward super-emo nostalgia even as a teenager, my nostalgia-in-advance, my florid romanticism, my overpowering musical obsession that fuels all of this and is fueled by it in turn, and above all my suspicion that I've passed a great deal of this onto my kids: All of that is here, in these lines. Now I watch my 10-year-old first-born son bouncing around the living room to the loud, fast, shrill, grating, flabbergasting, and impressively parent-antagonizing music from a video game he likes called *Friday Night Funkin'*. (Don't get involved if you're not involved.) And he's bounding from wall to wall with some grand imaginative tableau in his head that I'll never have any access to, and as I stand there gritting my teeth at this music's baffling shrillness, it dawns on me what he's doing (he's doing what I do) and who he is (he's my son).

My younger son, meanwhile, plays a lot of piano, and as an 8-year-old he's already *composing*, even if he's got his own mystifying notation system and he doesn't name his songs, he numbers them. But also sometimes he just *freestyles*, if that's the word, looking away from the piano, his eyes drifting up toward the ceiling as if he's picking each individual note out of the air, or maybe he's visiting the place in his mind where he goes time to time. Like anything great about my kids, I just assume he got that from his mother. I don't know where either of my boys go and I never will. But I know why they go there.

AND THEN ONE AFTERNOON I'm bumbling around the house with my wife and vibing obliviously, as I do, to Janet Jackson's dense and sumptuous 1997 album *The Velvet Rope*, and the effervescent pop-house anthem "Together Again" comes on and I vibe obliviously *harder*, if that's possible, and at some point I look over and finally notice that my wife is crying, and I go *Ahh-hhhh* and snap out of it. And she starts telling me about this college friend of hers who just collapsed and died one day their senior year, and when my wife and all her friends got the news they piled into a car and raced to the hospital, but of course the girl was already gone, and nobody could believe it, and then sometime later my wife's at a party with all this girl's friends, and "Together Again" comes on, and suddenly all this girl's closest friends are dancing and singing along and waving around these colorful boas and crying, and my wife's crying telling me this, and now I'm crying, and "Together Again" is still playing in our house, and that's how I found out "Together Again" is Janet Jackson's best song.

Janet, too, I have always revered as this towering, colossal *presence*, a laughably huge and huge-laughed Olympian pop star whose giant hit songs seemed to somehow tower above everyone else's giant hit songs. (These days I cry every time I hear "When I Think of You," also.) She's a majestic 2-year-old's birthday party of a person, a foundational element to human life, like oxygen or lust. But it took me quite a while to fully wrap my head around *The Velvet Rope*, her deepest, darkest, most vulnerable, most traumatized, most confrontational, and most cathartic album, and quite possibly her best album as well, once you wrap your head around it. By 1997 Janet had 10 billion hit songs and an unprecedented $80 million record contract, but she was also quite depressed, and dealing with self-esteem and body-image issues stretching back to her childhood, and processing a past abusive relationship, and navigating the pitfalls of being born into a famous musical family, and suffering through the slow deterioration of her relationship with husband and frequent collaborator René Elizondo Jr. *The Velvet Rope*, at first blush, is a confounding but beguiling jumble of confessional super-heaviness and hard-R-rated blindfolds-and-piercings mischief, the achingly sincere rubbing up against the disarmingly prurient, or maybe it's the disarmingly sincere rubbing up against the achingly prurient.

"Together Again," at first blush, feels like an uncomplicated respite from all the prurience and super-heaviness, all sweetness and light and tears-of-joy-on-the-dance-floor ecstasy. Janet does not have a bazooka voice in the Aretha Franklin/Whitney Houston vein, but her slow caress of the descending melody as she sings, "There are times when I feel your love around me, baby" is as sublime and cathartic as it gets. She doesn't oversell the drama, which of course only deepens it.

And then you get to the line, "Sometimes hear you whisperin', 'No more pain'" and ah, God, it turns out those aren't dance-floor tears of joy. "I dedicate the song 'Together Again' to the friends I've lost to AIDS," Janet writes in the *Velvet Rope* liner notes. "Dominic, George, Derrick, Bobby, Dominic, Victor, José...I miss you and we will be together again. This was written for you."

Ah, God. "I decided I wanted to do a song about my friends," Janet once explained to MTV's John Norris. "I wanted to do something uplifting, rejoiceful, that would reflect their personalities. I do believe that it doesn't just end here. There's a—we go into another life, and I will see them again." This song is Janet Jackson being the change she wants to see in the world, or I guess the change she wants to see in the afterlife. "Together Again" is a lot. It's an effervescent delivery system for a lot. It's feather-light and unfathomably heavy. It's her best song. It waited, patiently, until I was ready to hear what it had to tell me. And I am eternally grateful to my wife for finally forcibly wrapping my head around it.

The truth is I spent my bumbling late-'80s/early-'90s adolescence in thrall to MTV, in thrall to Janet, in thrall to the fizzy and stormy dance-pop universe Janet represented, in thrall to the much less consequential bumbling-adolescent sadness that turn-of-the-decade dance-pop somehow conjured up in me. There's me grappling with Deee-Lite's gloriously frivolous 1967-via-1990 hippie-house smash "Groove Is in the Heart," a delightful song that made me sad on account of the groove that I did not, in junior high at least, feel in my heart. There's me gazing out my car window and *thinking real hard* as the car radio serves up Enigma's almighty 1990 jam "Sadeness (Part I)," a baffling and irresistible German breakbeat-and-Gregorian-chant situation that hit the Top 5 in America outta nowhere, and a delightful song that made me (understandably, I guess) sad. There's me vibing obliviously to Technotronic's "Pump Up the Jam" and the giant sentient T-shirt cannon that is C+C Music Factory's "Gonna Make You Sweat

(Everybody Dance Now),"* two relentlessly upbeat and delightful songs that, on account of the fact that inevitably I was neither
sweating nor dancing nor pumping up the jam, made me sad.

But the mother of them all, if we're talking Songs About Dancing That Make Me Sad Because I'm Not Dancing, is "Everybody
Everybody," the 1990 bummer-joybomb from the Italian house
group Black Box. Hand me one of my high school yearbooks
and/or ply me with 1.5 alcoholic beverages and I'll warp myself
back to my teenage bedroom with my Michael Jordan poster, and
my handheld liquid-motion bubble toy that you could flip over for
a vague sense of stress relief, and my '90s-core see-thru touch-tone
phone that never rang because the girls I never danced with never
called me, and my childhood boombox tuned to my local pop station's Saturday-night dance party and oh, Christ, they're playing
"Everybody Everybody," a song with an indelible ascending chorus
of "Everybody everybody / Everybody everybody" that only serves
to remind me that everybody's out dancing at a Saturday-night
dance party, everybody but me.

I'm fine now, thanks. As a nominally less maudlin rock-critic-ass
adult, I detect an aura of indignance shimmering beneath the glorious communal euphoria of "Everybody Everybody," on account
of the fact that Martha Wash, the song's San Francisco-born and
gospel-fueled powerhouse lead vocalist, was not initially credited

---

* A 1990 jock-jam super smash masterminded by Robert Clivillés and David Cole,
who met at the storied NYC dance club Better Days; I should also mention that once
I was at an Oakland A's game, and we were losing to the New York Yankees because
their star pitcher CC Sabathia was unhittable, and my buddy Tommy yelled out,
"YOUR MUSIC FACTORY SUCKS!" and everyone laughed.

as such, nor is she the fashion model awkwardly lip-syncing in the "Everybody Everybody" video and awkwardly crouching on the cover of Black Box's 1990 album *Dreamland*. Incredibly, Martha also sang powerhouse lead vocals on C+C Music Factory's "Gonna Make You Sweat (Everybody Dance Now)" but initially got no credit and didn't make the video and didn't grace the cover of the group's 1990 hit album *Gonna Make You Sweat*, replaced once again by someone deemed more video- and album-cover-friendly.*

Wash successfully sued both Black Box and C+C Music Factory, and got her belated credit and her richly deserved royalties, but in 2014 *Rolling Stone* still described her in a headline, with deep admiration, as "The Most Famous Unknown Singer of the '90s." By then she was getting her magazine profile, getting her spot in the hit 2013 backup-singer documentary *20 Feet From Stardom*, and getting the lion's share of the credit for "Gonna Make You Sweat" and particularly "Everybody Everybody" as they kept popping up on Best Songs of the '90s lists and whatnot. Is that better, for Martha, long-term, then getting to be MTV-star famous at the time? You'd have to ask her, though maybe don't. Suffice it to say that if hearing "Everybody Everybody" still makes her a little bit sad, she's got a way better reason than I ever did.

THE PROFOUND LONELINESS EMANATING from "Everybody Everybody" tipped me off to the plain fact that

---

* Incredibly, the same thing happened to Missy Elliott when she cowrote, coproduced, and guest-starred on child actress Raven-Symoné's 1993 debut single "That's What Little Girls Are Made Of," except that ain't Missy lip-syncing her rap verse in the video, and let me assure you that this poor video lady looks ridiculous trying to pretend that she's the one rapping a Missy Elliott verse.

even the most jovial and rapturous pop songs can conceal—or not really even *attempt* to conceal—vast oceans of dejection and isolation and sublime misery. Even the greatest (and most rapturous) Christmas song of my lifetime and possibly anyone else's lifetime; even, yes, Mariah Carey's unstoppable "All I Want for Christmas Is You," which came out in 1994 and was the No. 1 song in America for most of December 2022* and still sounds classic, sounds timeless, sounds like it was playing in the manger when Baby Jesus was born.

And it's an incredibly sad song. I'm not trying to ruin it for you; I'm trying to heighten and *deepen* it. The question you gotta ask yourself is, *Who is the "you" in "All I Want for Christmas Is You"?* The answer, I fear, as Mariah Carey tells her story now, is that there was no *you*. There was nobody. She had nobody, really. This song is a fantasy. This song is aspirational. This song is a reminder that pop music—and maybe especially Christmas-themed pop music—can be as transportive, can provide as much desperately needed escapism for the singer (and songwriter) as it does for the listener.

Mariah Carey was born in Huntington, New York, and *does* have a five-octave bazooka voice in the Aretha Franklin/Whitney Houston vein, thank you very much. I think of her as the Eddie Van Halen of '90s pop vocalists: astounding technical ability but bent to the service of equally astounding *songs*. Pop songs. Eddie had finger-tapping and *shredding*; Mariah has the impossibly high

---

* Now that streaming numbers drive the pop charts, "All I Want for Christmas Is You" will likely camp out at No. 1 every December for the rest of any of our lives, making it pretty objectively the most vital and present-tense and inescapable song released in the '90s. The second-best Christmas song of my lifetime is either Wham's "Last Christmas," Run-DMC's "Christmas in Hollis," or the Waitresses' "Christmas Wrapping" (you know it).

whistle register and of course has melisma, smoothly transforming one-syllable words into 35-syllable words. Over her first several blockbuster albums, you can hear Mariah honing her craft but in a way that feels effortless, and natural, and graspable. Each one of those 35 syllables tells a story. Each syllable is *necessary*.

Mariah's 2020 memoir *The Meaning of Mariah Carey*—cowritten with author, editor, and stylist Michaela Angela Davis—is *bleak*, man. It is *Dickensian*. It's like if Oliver Twist had a five-octave range. Her childhood is rife with poverty, family discord, neglect, racism, and abuse that sometimes turned physical. But she transcends, and emerges in 1990 as a generational pop star, and in 1993 marries her label boss, music-biz mogul Tommy Mottola, and the happy couple settle into a deluxe mansion/panopticon in upstate New York that Mariah nicknames Sing Sing, as in the prison, because by her account Tommy won't let her go anywhere or do anything. There's a very silly and also profoundly sad scene in the book where Mariah's in her fancy home studio recording with the rapper Da Brat, and they concoct this elaborate *Ocean's Eleven*-type scheme to sneak out, jump into one of Mariah's own cars, and go get fries at Burger King, and come right back. That's it. It's framed as an unimaginable act of rebellion, just as many of Mariah's biggest early hits are now framed as super-cheery and carefree glimpses into an alternate universe the real Mariah Carey could only dream of inhabiting. "I created the fun and free girl in my videos so that I could watch a version of myself be alive, live vicariously through her," she writes. "The girl I pretended to be, the girl I wished was me."

In other words, that's not really her in her early videos *even though it's really her*. Keep this in mind the next time you stumble across the "All I Want for Christmas Is You" video, in which Mariah seems awfully fun and free, and Tommy Mottola cameos as Santa Claus. *That* Santa ain't real, kids; Mariah and Tommy got divorced in 1998. Just block him out. Just focus on her. My favorite bonkers vocal run on this song comes on the bridge, when she thunders *Santa won't you bring me the one I really need* like a tinsel machine gun. Christmas songs broadly fall into two categories: They are either Describing Holiday Revelry That Is Currently Happening, or they are Actively Yearning for Holiday Revelry That Might Not Happen at All. The miracle here is that Mariah yearned so vividly and exuberantly that the revelry felt real, and over the course of a quarter-century eventually *became* real, an annual blockbuster to which everybody is invited.

SOMETIMES A MAMMOTH, RAPTUROUS pop song doesn't even try to conceal the ocean of sublime misery roiling underneath; sometimes that song is literally called "Bitter Sweet Symphony." The first thing you oughta know about Richard Ashcroft, the glum philosopher-poet frontman for English rock band* the Verve, is that you can *hear* this dude's cheekbones. Three words outta this guy's mouth and you just think, *Wow, he's got incredible cheekbones.* Just, *whoop*—just the perfect rock-star face. The smoldering, pointy glower of geometrically precise rock stardom incarnate.

The second thing you need to know about Richard is that Oasis wrote a whole sublimely downcast song about him, 1995's "Cast No Shadow," composed with uncommon empathy by Noel Gallagher

---

* Specifically Wigan, England, home to both the world's largest baked-bean factory and the corporate headquarters for Uncle Joe's Mint Balls (it's a candy).

and sung with uncommon tenderness by Liam Gallagher. It's a heartfelt ode to a lonely and noble soul "bound with all the weight of all the words he tried to say" who meets a grim end: "As they took his soul they stole his pride." The tension running beneath all this disarming loveliness was that Richard might never write a tune better than the one somebody else wrote about him.

And then Richard Ashcroft wrote his own colossal hit, even if it cost him, well, not his soul and his pride, necessarily, but certainly all of his royalties. The convoluted arc of the four-bar sample that powers "Bitter Sweet Symphony"*—basically, the Staple Singers did a definitive version of Gospel standard "This May Be the Last Time," which the Rolling Stones seized upon for their early 1965 hit "The Last Time," which Stones producer/manager Andrew Oldham himself covered in 1966 as part of the Andrew Oldham Orchestra album *The Rolling Stones Songbook*, which is where Richard got the loop—is, uh, convoluted. The point is that thanks to notoriously merciless Beatles/Stones super-manager Allen Klein, the Verve had to give Mick Jagger and Keith Richards all the credit for the whole song, not to mention all the money,† and this tragic music-biz farce is now an essential component of the song itself: "Bitter Sweet Symphony" is a song about what happened to the guy who wrote the song after he wrote the song. The song is about the guy losing the song even as he's singing it, and specifically as

---

* From 1997's *Urban Hymns*, a truly great record ("The Rolling People," my friends) from—and don't let Richard's cheekbones distract you from this—a truly great and cohesive band (atmospheric guitar god Nick McCabe, my friends).

† In 2019, Richard Ashcroft tweeted that Mick and Keith had graciously reversed course: "They are happy for the writing credit to exclude their names and all their royalties derived from the song will now pass to me." Better 22 years late than never.

he's singing, "Try to make ends meet / You're a slave to the money / Then you die."

That is for sure a shit sandwich,* but there are, of course, far greater surprise-hit-song tragedies, and not all of them so clearly labeled. "Hey Jealousy," for example, doesn't raise any red flags, as a song title, or as a just-scruffy-enough exemplar of bummer '90s power pop, or as a fount of brutally lovely dirtbag-sweetie lines like "If you don't expect too much from me / You might not be let down." The idea of smuggling really sad lyrics into a bright and catchy pop song did not originate with "Hey Jealousy," or with the '90s, or with rock 'n' roll, really. But the Gin Blossoms were better than pretty much anybody at that old magic trick back in 1992, and that worked out great for everybody except the guy who actually wrote the song.

The Gin Blossoms formed in late-'80s Tempe, Arizona: a bunch of random dudes from a bunch of other random bands who joined forces and aspired to the hallowed jangly-guitar lineage that stretches from the Byrds to Big Star to R.E.M. Millions of bands have aspired to the lineage, obviously, but only one of them became the de facto house band at a Tempe hot wings joint called Long Wong's. Regional fame ensues. The Gin Blossoms release their debut album, *Dusted*, in 1989, recorded locally, released locally, a pretty big deal locally. But only that, at first, and at first maybe that might've been enough. Maybe just track 9 would've been enough. The song's called "Hey Jealousy," and it was written by a guy named Doug Hopkins.

---

* The question of why I talk like this is likely too complicated to address in a footnote, but just be aware that I'm aware that I'm a 45-year-old guy who still uses the word "rad" a lot.

In retrospect Doug Hopkins was the Pete Best of the Gin Blossoms, though when he was actually in the Gin Blossoms, he was arguably the Paul McCartney of the Gin Blossoms, or the John Lennon, or both. People say that he could've been what Noel Gallagher was to Oasis, actually: the cranky mastermind, the genius songwriter, the conscience. Doug didn't sing much, but it was his voice, his *angst*, and in the early '90s especially, your angst was the most sacred and powerful and monetizable thing you owned.

You ever wonder about the "Hey Jealousy" line that goes "You can trust me not to think"? Doug Hopkins's original line was "You can trust me not to drink," which, unfortunately, is way better. So the Gin Blossoms sign with a major label and eventually find themselves in Memphis, Tennessee, recording at Ardent Studios, fabled birthplace of all three albums from power pop gods Big Star. This is the band's big break, and Doug is struggling, in this famous studio, beneath the weight of these great expectations, and all the drinking he's doing to manage these expectations. He plays guitar all over the record the Gin Blossoms would release in 1992 and call *New Miserable Experience*, but he meant to re-record, to *improve* a lot of those parts, but he just couldn't, and his bandmates kicked him out before they'd even finished the record, though it's possible that the label made them do it.

So Hopkins gets the boot, and *New Miserable Experience* comes out, and initially, it bricks. The revamped Gin Blossoms tour relentlessly in the shitty van on the album cover, but it's going nowhere, and the whole thing looks like an abject failure until one of these vague record-label stories where the suits decided to give "Hey Jealousy" *one more push*. They'd shot a video for $5,000, and then another version for $10,000, but now they decide to drop

$40,000 on yet another video, and it's super boring: They're all just hanging out in somebody's house, frontman Robin Wilson sings to a fish in a fishbowl and also to a blender, I don't know, man. But it clicks. "Hey Jealousy" climbs the charts, and other jangly-bummer hits follow—"Found Out About You" is the one everyone loves, and "Pieces of the Night" is the one no one could ever love enough—and meanwhile Hopkins starts another band back in Tempe, and regional fame ensues, but the story goes that he quits that band, onstage, after botching a guitar solo, and afterward those guys won't take him back either. So instead he sits at home and watches his old band play his old song on Jay Leno's *Tonight Show*, and he's pissed, and he feels betrayed, and he wonders what his royalty cut might be.

Eventually Doug gets a Gold record for "Hey Jealousy," like the plaque you hang proudly on your wall, and he hangs it proudly on his wall, and then a few weeks later he smashes it, and sometime after that he buys a gun at a pawn shop, and he's found dead, of a gunshot wound, on Sunday, December 5, 1993. He was 32. *Variety* runs a small obituary noting that it was his sixth suicide attempt in 10 years, and quotes his sister, Sarah, as saying, "When I saw him Thursday, I knew I'd never see him again. I just said, 'Goodbye, Doug,' and my mother did the same."

Doug Hopkins does play the guitar solo on the famous version of "Hey Jealousy." It's projection—all of this is projection, always—but it's comforting to think you can still hear him there, and hear him the way he always wanted to be heard: the darkness but also the sweetness, the inner turmoil but also the greatness.

As unfathomably naive as this may sound, I have to say I'm extra shaken by the realization that writing a song as perfect as "Hey

255

Jealousy" does not solve every problem you've ever had, forever. "When everybody loves you / You can never be lonely," wails Counting Crows frontman Adam Duritz on "Mr. Jones," the first breakout hit from the San Francisco roots-rock band's unexpectedly massive 1993 debut album *August and Everything After*, and even at the time I knew he was being bitterly ironic—I'm not, like, an idiot—but yeah, I totally thought that's what would happen if everyone loved you.

"Mr. Jones," as you may have observed, is just about as funky and as meta as debut rock 'n' roll singles can be, in that it's a warm and tuneful but tangibly uneasy song about wanting to be famous that made Adam Duritz famous, which in turn made him world-historically uneasy. That's rock 'n' roll for you. From the extra-yelpy "Round Here" to the extra-wistful "A Murder of One," *August and Everything After* feels like a complete thought, a fully populated universe. Is it populated by various amalgamations of Adam Duritz's ex-girlfriends? Probably. But he's always been an expert at selling his own drama in a way that made other people want to buy it. On his band's first two records, he introduced you to Maria, to Anna, to Margery, to Elisabeth. He took you to Omaha, to Baltimore, to Sullivan Street, and climactically, to Hillside Manor sometime after 2 a.m. There's a narcissism to it, to songwriting this specific and self-centered. But what is charisma, really, if not the ability to convince other people that your narcissism is fascinating and relatable?

August and Everything After was yet another of these records with gigantic radio singles so ubiquitous I didn't have to buy it,*

---

* I do remember eavesdropping as two high school classmates named Scott praised this record to the skies, rhapsodizing to one another about how beautiful and poetic and profound it was, and so now I just assume that anyone named Scott automatically loves Counting Crows.

which makes it even weirder that I totally flipped for the next Counting Crows record, 1996's *Recovering the Satellites*, which is very explicitly about Adam Duritz's struggles with mobbed-on-the-street-type fame, with intrusive media attention, with the relentless grind of touring. Not Enjoying Rock Stardom was practically an Olympic event throughout the '90s, but I found Adam Duritz's specific brand of Not Enjoying Rock Stardom to be the most engrossing, the most—oh, dear—fascinating and relatable. It helps that once again, this album feels like a complete thought, a complete universe; it super fuckin' helps that the second-to-last song is "A Long December."

The last-call piano melancholia is immaculate; the startling quality-over-quantity guitar solo is immaculate; the accordion is immaculate; every last self-pitying word out of Duritz's mouth is immaculate. But it comes down to one line for me: "And all at once you look across a crowded room / To see the way that light attaches to a girl." How did the guy who strung those words together not have it made? What makes "A Long December" so devastating for me is the horrifying realization that someone could write a sad song this fantastic and reap the spoils of doing so but *still* not be happy. This is an alienating sorrow so suffocating that writing a perfect song about it can't get you out of it. Where do you even go from there?

I used to have this idea that my life would culminate with me creating one perfect thing that would justify all of it, right? A song, a record, a novel, a screenplay, a viral short story, a Smashed McDouble-caliber Tweet—I don't know. The fantasy changes. The goalposts move. But "A Long December," when the winter light hits it just right—when the song hits *me* just right—feels like the

257

platonic ideal of that endpoint, that artistic and professional peak of my whole existence. Make something this pure and this beloved, and you'll be as happy as you can be.

And you know what? I *still* have that idea, and I still refuse to believe Adam Duritz meant all that happy-as-you-can-be talk in "Mr. Jones" ironically. "There's a way in which I resent the songs, or how, for all those years, it didn't matter what happened in my life because I wrote songs," Duritz told the *Onion A/V Club* back in 2012. "That isn't a good replacement for life. That's just a way of describing life. So, I guess a part of me now resents my own habit of substituting songs for people, songs for relationships, songs for whatever. You can't wait too much longer to get your shit together, because you only have so many years to live."

Don't listen to him. You can totally write a song—or a novel, or a podcast, or whatever—perfect enough to wipe away all of that. I don't know if I'd even recognize myself if I ever stopped believing that. There is a "Bitter Sweet Symphony" lurking inside all of us. Take that any way you like.

THEN THERE ARE BELOVED artists whose explicit purview is Big Feelings, whose songs, while not a *replacement* for life per se, are expertly designed as a *blueprint* for life, and who sing stuff they thought about themselves to encourage their millions of subjects to think stuff about their own selves for the express purpose of giving those subjects guidance, giving them solace, giving them *hope*. Yes, millions of *subjects*, not millions of fans, because this is what we talk about when we talk about Mary J. Blige: We frame her as royalty ("The Queen of Hip-Hop Soul"); we frame her as a messiah-prophet ("You know, I heard the pain of a generation," raved one of the many guys[*] credited with discovering her in the 2021 documentary *Mary J. Blige's My Life*) we frame her as a galactically scaled new marketing slogan ("Ghetto Fabulous"). This is an awful lot of psychic and spiritual and societal and commercial weight to dump on a simple and deceptively breezy song called "Real Love," but the song can bear it, and so, quite famously, can the singer.

Mary J. Blige was born in the Bronx in 1971; she grew up singing in church in Savannah, Georgia, before her family moved to Yonkers, specifically the Schlobohm housing projects, which she'd later describe, in that documentary, as "a prison within a prison within a prison." Setting aside the lurid details known and unknown, when worshipful fellow singers describe the pain in Mary's voice, it's the pain of a generation, absolutely, but on "Real Love," the bouncy breakthrough hit on her 1992 debut album *What's the 411?*, it's also undeniably *her* pain and hers alone, and ah, Christ, no, wait, I swear I'm not back to doing the thing where I insist that a buoyant and happy song is secretly a crushingly sad song.

No. "Real Love" is pure sunlight to me: I love how nimble her voice is, the skipping-stone deftness of her syllables, the way the bass kicks in right when her voice does, the way the jaunty piano and stuttering drums demonstrate what real love would sound and *feel* like. All I'm saying is that a huge part of what makes this song so buoyant and carefree is how much weight Mary packs into the

---

[*] This'd be Jeff Reed, an Uptown Records artist working at the GM plant in Tarrytown, New York, with Mary's mother's boyfriend, who passes Jeff a tape of 17-year-old Mary singing Anita Baker's "Caught Up in the Rapture" in one of those make-your-own-record booths at the Galleria Mall in Westchester. If you have that tape, please send me that tape.

opening line "We are lovers through and through / And we made it through the storm." That's not "Mr. Jones"-style bitter irony, either: She just knows another storm is coming, and another, and another.

Her best album is 1994's *My Life*, by the way: That's the one that ends with the tentatively bumptious "Be Happy," as in "All I really want is to be happy." Here in 2023, it's wise to be skeptical of anyone throwing around terms like *self-help* or *self-care* or *self-love*: These are cynical marketing categories and cloying Instagram captions now, and the words SCAM LIKELY should start flashing in giant neon letters in the sky whenever anybody starts talking to you like this. But from "Real Love" forward, Mary J. Blige made the notion of self-love feel logical, and true, and real, and *attainable*.

Then there are the beloved songs about the worst Big Feeling of them all. Pete Rock and C.L. Smooth's "They Reminisce Over You (T.R.O.Y.)." Boyz II Men's "It's So Hard to Say Goodbye to Yesterday." Master P's "I Miss My Homies." Men at Large's "So Alone" (trust me). And also, sure, yes, absolutely: Puff Daddy's "I'll Be Missing You." But the collective, overwhelming, purifying grief radiating from Bone Thugs-N-Harmony's 1995 monolith "Tha Crossroads"—dedicated, in its chart-topping remix form, to the Cleveland rap crew's late mentor, Eazy-E—is something else, something immortal.

The Bone Thugs experience, lightning-fast and impossibly melodious, is a singular marvel* no matter what they're speed-rapping about, but "Tha Crossroads" transcends time and space and planes of existence. It's a song about mourning the dead until you join

---

* "We sit down and get high as fuck," Layzie Bone told *The Source* in 1994 when asked about the group's creative process, "And we damn near become the same motherfucker."

them, but you're not alone when you die, nor are you alone when you mourn the dead, because death is inevitable, and grief, too, but that means everyone shares in it. Everyone bears the weight. These guys are the best-case scenario for who you could get to reminisce over you, and the most important line in this song's chorus, sung slowly and tenderly and repeatedly so you don't miss it, is "So you won't be lonely."

Another line that slaps me upside the head every time: Wish Bone's "I miss my Uncle Charles, y'all." Uncle Charles was Wish Bone's mother's brother, and he took young Wish Bone to his first concert: Prince at Cleveland's Front Row Theater. And now, thanks to the fact that "I miss my Uncle Charles, y'all" is a fantastic line/melody/earworm, Uncle Charles has inspired his own bootleg merch. T-shirts. Notebooks. YouTube explainers. A *Key and Peele* shout-out. Memes. He's a pop-culture character now. Millions of people have sung-rapped about missing Uncle Charles, who they almost certainly never met. And that's a tricky but beautiful thing. When your grief is this infectious, this joyous, this *anthemic*, now it belongs to everybody, and belongs even to the people who aren't grieving. But then again, everyone is grieving somebody, and if you aren't, then one day you will. I don't mean to bum you out. I just want you to know that when it happens, you've got options when it comes to what to do, where to go, who to lean on.

But as for the soundtrack, you don't always get to decide.

So my senior year of high school, four kids died in a car accident—two girls from my school (including a close friend of mine) and two boys from the next town over. I remember somebody calling me with the news; I remember calling other people to give them the news. And it was awful, and devastating, and an utterly foreign experience for me: I believe that's the one and only time I've been a pallbearer for someone younger than me, which by default makes it the worst day of my life so far.

So I go to the wake—I think possibly the joint wake for both girls—and it's held in the packed basement of the funeral home, and I walk in—I *descend*—and it's, you know, this 360-degree panorama of sobbing teenagers, and my close friend's younger sister is there, deep in unimaginable mourning, surrounded by sobbing teenagers desperate to console her, and still to this day any '90s alt-rock song with the word *sister* in it anywhere is quite destabilizing to me. But for now, yeah, I'm at this grueling wake, and I, too, am a sobbing teenager, and also Lisa Loeb's "Stay (I Missed You)" is playing on a loop because that was my friend's favorite song.

Now, first of all, I very much doubt this song was *playing on a loop the whole time*, right? That sounds quite melodramatic. That's a sobbing teenager's embellishment, I suspect. I wonder even if it was the basement of the funeral home: That feels melodramatic, too. *I descend.* I don't know. A joint wake, a *dual* wake? I don't know. They played "Stay (I Missed You)"* at least once, and okay, maybe two or three times. *The whole time*, the whole night? I don't think so. But you'd think playing it once is enough, right, to bind this song to this singularly terrible moment in my head forever. Certainly, until the end of time, whenever I hear Lisa Loeb's voice in any context, I will now picture my friend, alive, alone, happy, oblivious, traipsing

---

* Lisa Loeb: born in Maryland, raised in Dallas, got a degree in comparative literature at Brown, and abruptly vaulted from the early-'90s NYC singer-songwriter scene to the top of the charts when "Stay (I Missed You)"—dope offbeat lyricism, great video, cool glasses—landed on the soundtrack to the 1994 romcom *Reality Bites*, in which Winona Ryder ended up with the wrong guy.

around her bedroom, listening to her favorite song. You'd think that, wouldn't you? You'd think I'd never want to hear this song again.

So why can I still listen to it? Logically, "Stay (I Missed You)" should be—I don't want to say *destroyed*, but yeah, it oughta be *inextricable* from this cavern of grief and despair, *synonymous*, in my head, with a funeral-home basement full of sobbing teenagers, myself included. But it's not. I can hear Lisa's crystalline coffee-shop opening riff, and listen to the whole thing, and think medium-hard about this song semi-professionally, and simply indulge in some good ol' wistful nostalgia, and not dwell on any of that terrible shit at all, and I'd like to know why.

My best guess is I've got some kind of subconscious internal defense mechanism; it's tempting to say that "Stay" is *masterfully written and durable enough to withstand all that emotional baggage* or whatever, but quite frankly I don't think the song or the songwriter has anything to do with it at this point. It's just that there's an individual personal threshold for melodramatic and tremendously painful memories triggered by old songs. It's not quite *denial*—it's not quite a *repressed* memory. But the Lisa Loeb song comes on and some deep, mysterious, clandestine sleeper cell in my brain that I'm truly grateful for activates and just whispers, *Don't.* And most of the time, I don't. I can listen to anything I want, all the time, until the day I die, because that's what I do and who I am. But I can only feel so much.

ACKNOWLEDGMENTS

I'M STRUGGLING WITH the *finality* of the whole book process, quite frankly. The ink-and-paper of it all. The idea that at some point I can't add to it anymore. As a guy who's done 100-plus episodes of a show with "60" in the title, I find this quite troubling, the letting go, the stopping. In lieu of any Grand Unified Conclusion, let me just stay that I mourn for the roughly 200 other artists/songs I meant to mention, if not pontificate upon at incredible length, and I will actively resist the urge to constantly rewrite this entire book in my head with those other 200-plus songs instead. This is my problem, not yours, obviously. Thank you for reading this (apparently permanent) iteration of my problem.

I owe so many people so much, so let us now apply this troubling intimidated-by-permanence issue to thanking as many of them as I can.

My wife Nicole is the funniest, smartest, most creative and exuberant person I know, and my favorite writer, too, and none of this happens without her, and that goes for both the book and [*gestures broadly*] all the rest of this. Thank you, baby. I love you. Here, I made you a mixtape.

Max and Griffin are really upset that I haven't interviewed them on the show yet; Mirabel is really upset that we won't let her hold the whole bag of Cheetos. All three of them are constantly barraged by annoying, archaic music played by their father at all hours. I'm sorry. Thank you. I love you. You make me laugh every day; you make me proud all the time.

Justin Sayles has been my editor, producer, sounding board, life coach, and oracle for the lifespan of the show, and he has read more words by me (~600,000 and counting) than anybody should have to read by anybody else. Thank you. God bless you. I'm sorry about the 10K-words-per-episode era. Sincere thanks/apologies as well to Jonathan Kermah, the Rick Rubin of podcasts, and his noble predecessors Devon Renaldo and Isaac Lee.

Thanks to everyone at *The Ringer*, especially Sean Fennessey (his idea), Bill Simmons (his empire), and Amanda Dobbins (her patience/wisdom). My apologies to all my coworkers who have endured myriad Slack dad jokes and poor Photoshops; it's an honor to work with such creative and exuberant and remarkably *chill* people. Thanks as well to all my long-suffering coworkers at *The Other Paper* (RIP), the *East Bay Express* (RIP as part of a polarizing national chain), the *Village Voice* (RIP), Rhapsody (RIP), *SPIN* (RIP in print), and *Deadspin* (RIP in original spirit).

Thanks to everyone at Twelve Books, especially Sean Desmond for the jovial guidance and support and enthusiasm (and for editing ~100,000 words of me, which is plenty). Thanks also to Jim Datz for the visual splendor and Megan Perritt-Jacobson for helping me look (slightly more) media-savvy. I have dreamed of having

ACKNOWLEDGMENTS

a literary agent for like 20 years, and Ethan Bassoff is the platonic ideal; thank you, good sir, for your guidance and insight. Tara Jacoby's illustrations are my favorite part of this whole thing, so thank you, Tara, for being, indeed, the best part of this.

I'm eternally grateful to all the wise and hilarious and tremendously patient guests who've come on the show to set me straight, including Leslie Gray Streeter, who has done so like 400 times. Many thanks as well to Yasi Salek, the Anthony Kiedis, John Frusciante, and Flea of podcasts.

Much love to Garrett Kamps, Tommy Craggs, and Nate Cavalieri, the very personification of California (the good parts) to me. Let us Brodeo soon. Please be well, Garrett (and Danielle). Much love and respect to Mike Majba, my attorney, my reliable source of unamusement and (delightful) contempt. Thank you for reading multiple drafts of that whole-ass novel. Much love and continual defamation to Jerry and Steve Trepkowsi, Brian Chapman, Mark Dotson, and the various doctors who tended to us post-cabin. Thanks to Cool Uncle Nick and the whole Skladany crew; thanks to Cool Uncle Roger and the whole Harvilla crew. Thanks as well to Jessica Hopper (her idea originally), Jon Caramanica, Puja Patel, Geoff Redick, Dan Parker, Dan Eaton, Andy and Amber Ankowski and their delightful children, and Mary Jo and Jim Ankowski for all the love and support.

Thank you to Ryan Harvilla for 40 years now (!!) of musical counsel, video-game expertise, truly extraordinary kindness, and your companionship at like 1,000 concerts where we ideally stand way in the back so we don't block anybody else's view. Thanks also for the mushrooms. Much love to Beth and Baby Jack.

One summer in my teenage years, I spent a week at a literary workshop at Bowling Green University, and my parents both drove me there and back and sat through an hours-long climactic student reading in which I recited a poem about dreaming about being a bean in a bowl of chili. They did not have to do that. I majored in magazine journalism in 1996; they did not have to let me do that. I spent 80 percent of my childhood and adolescence listening to loud and tremendously uncouth music; you get the point. Their love and support have meant the world to me; they showed me how to be a good husband/father/person and are still patiently helping me stumble toward the standard they set. Thank you, Mom and Dad. I love you. I don't recall referring to that U2 show from junior high as "The Bomb," but of course I will take my mother's word for it.

Finally, eternal thanks to anyone who either read any of this or listened to any episode of the show, or both: Thank you for your emails, your DMs, your kind words, your own stories, your wild and possibly drunken theories, and your many excellent song suggestions. I will do that Tragically Hip deep dive soon, I promise. All of this has been the thrill and the honor of my career. Thank you.

ABOUT THE AUTHOR

ROB HARVILLA is the host of the podcast *60 Songs That Explain the '90s* and a senior staff writer at *The Ringer*; he's been a professional rock critic for 20-plus years with stops at *SPIN*, *Deadspin*, the *Village Voice*, and various other alt-weeklies that usually no longer exist. (Not his fault.) He lives with his family in Columbus, Ohio, by choice.